Protecting Love

by
Jenae Macias

I0571893

Auteur: Jenae Macias
Coverdesign: JCM Consulting
ISBN: 978-1-7378281-3-6
© Jenae Macias

Chapter 1

Delilah Reyes couldn't distinguish any individual sounds, as she watched the noon sun bounce off the glass raining down on top of her. Each piece creating an individual kaleidoscope of colors amongst the chaos of the seemingly endless sound of gun fire. Warm liquid ran down her right arm, she knew that she should be alarmed by it, but all she could think of was to get to Bobby.

She had just finished buckling her five-year old son into his car seat, turned to speak with her ex-husband Nate, when the silence of the col-de-sac seemed to explode in an instant. Her instincts had taken over, telling her to get as low as possible. Delilah could thank her rough upbringing for her preparedness, but nothing could truly prepare someone for the icy fear that gripped the heart of a mother who could not reach her son. As the continual shots rang in the air, she knew that if she got up, she was as good as dead.

The second the eerie hush fell over the neighborhood, replacing the chaotic roar, Delilah was on her feet and rushing to the back seat of her sedan. Bobby's screams piercing her heart, stealing the breath from her lungs.

God, he has to be alright! Please, lord, not my baby!

Delilah flung herself to the door, registering that it was still intact and without gun holes.

That is a good sign.

She tried uselessly to comfort the worry that was threatening to paralyze her.

"Mommy!" No sound had ever sounded sweeter. It brought the air back into her aching lungs and cleared the terror filled cloud that had deluded her mind. She grabbed for the handle of the car door; it was slippery with blood. Delilah froze in place, why would there be blood on the car? She felt the throbbing in her arm at the same time that she realized that the blood was hers. "Mommy!" Bobby second scream forced her to ignore the pain, using her other arm she finally succeeded in gripping the slick handle and yanking the door open.

Relief hit her like a tidal wave, sweeping away the fear that her son had been hurt. Bobby sat in his car seat, buckled in, tears streaming down his freckled face. His doe brown eyes were the roundest she had ever seen them, as he stared at her, with his small arms reaching out. Besides being scared to death, her son was fine.

She quickly undid the buckle on his seat, which was the only thing holding him back from leaping into her arms. The pain that shot through her arm was hard to ignore, but the wholeness she felt at having her son safe in her arms was a powerful pain suppressant. "Shhhh, baby, it's okay. Mommy is here, sweetheart. You're okay." Delilah cooed to her son in her most soothing voice. Wanting desperately to take away his terror and comfort him.

The blood in her veins turned to ice, threatening to freeze her heart dead in her chest, as she saw a car turning around in the col-de-sac. Nate's house was three houses down a rather long col-de-sac. It registered to her as soon as she saw the metallic blue car coming down the street, that whoever had shot at them, would have to turn around.

That is just the fear talking. I am seeing danger where there is none.

—

Delilah tried to reassure herself that it was her hyped-up imagination that was terror stricken and working over-time, but it was not exactly the type of car that soccer moms drove around. It was some sort of classic lowered to the ground, the glare from the sun bouncing off from the chrome that seemed to be everywhere on the car. She didn't want to assume, but she knew a gang bangers car when she saw one. The two Hispanic men, in the front of the car, also seemed to fit the bill. The older looking one, pointed at something on the lawn. She was terrified that at any moment he would look at them next.

Shit! I need to get Bobby out of here before they see us.

Even if the car wasn't the one that had shot at them, she decided to err on the side of trying to stay alive. As she grabbed Bobby out of the car and ran for all that she was worth into the front door of Nate's house. She sent up a silent thanks, that he had left it open when they had done their weekly exchange of their son.

A shot was fired, sending wooden splinters from the offended door frame, just above her head. Delilah dove onto the floor, trying to fall so that she would absorb most of the impact with her own body, protecting Bobby's more fragile frame.

She lay cradling her son when another shot rang out. The glass that rained down from the shattered window, was the only way she knew where the bullet had hit.

Delilah felt like the torrent of bullets would never end, she wrapped her body around her sons and prayed for it to be over.

The sharp sweet sound of a police siren pierced the air. She had not allowed herself to cry up to this point, but she could no longer hold the tears back. The screech of tires burning up the road, was another indication that the shooters car was gone. Delilah released some of the pressure that she been holding Bobby with. Her fear had turned her embrace into a vice grip, that she hoped hadn't hurt him.

"Help is here sweet boy. It's over." Delilah stroked her son's dark brown hair.

He looked like a mini version of his father, besides the freckles that were splattered on his soft cheeks, those were from her.

Oh, God! Where was Nate?!

She racked her brain to try and remember the moment the shooting had started. Nate had been standing between them and the front door. Delilah had asked him to wait a minute, she wanted to ask him if they could switch weekends. The following weekend was Mother's Day, but it was his scheduled weekend to have Bobby. Usually, Nate was a good sport about working with her on special occasions, but she wanted to ask him and not just assume that he would be fine with it.

Delilah thought she could remember him hitting the ground, similar to how she had, but she wasn't sure.

During her race to the house, her mind had been too focused on getting to safety to look around her. She shifted to a sitting position, just as an officer, entered the broken door with his gun drawn.

"Ma'am, I'm officer Porter. Are you hurt?" His voice sounded concerned and he looked at her with kind blue eyes.

"No, my son and I are fine. But my ex-husband, Nate, is he okay? He was outside too, when the shooting started." Delilah rambled on. She could hear how unsteady her words sounded.

"I'm sorry ma'am, but I don't think you're okay. Is that your blood, or the child's?" He approached them cautiously, like someone would creep up to a skittish animal. Afraid to startle it or cause it to bolt in fear.

What he was saying finally dawned on her, he was right she had been hurt. As if her acknowledging the wound on her arm was all it needed to remind her of its presence, the pain sharpened so badly it made her wince.

"Yes, that's right, I was shot, I think." She felt faint as she spoke about what happened out loud, almost like it wasn't real until it was voiced.

I have been shot. Someone shot at me, and Bobby, and Nate. Why?

She heard Officer Porter say something into his radio, but her mind was whirling with the unreal situation.

"Ma'am did you hear me?" Officer Porter asked her, appearing even more concerned than before.

"What?" She looked up at the officer, trying to focus. "No, I'm sorry, I didn't." Delilah was known as a virtual chatter box, apparently trauma put a lid on her verbal outpouring.

"I said that the ambulance is here. The paramedics are going to help you up and get you on the stretcher." She looked around the room at the group of people, how had so many people walked in without her noticing?

"Bobby, we have to get up sweetheart." His head was tucked into the space between her arm and her body, she didn't have to see his face to know that his thumb was in his mouth. They had worked over a year to get him to stop sucking his thumb, but right now she couldn't blame her son.

He looked up at her with his doe eyes filled with uncertainty. She could see that he was fighting back a fresh batch of tears, thumb still in his mouth, he shook his head in agreement.

She tried to stand while still holding her precious son, something that usually wouldn't tax her in the least, but a wave of dizziness forced her to sit back down.

"Careful there," an EMT had come to stand beside her, the woman placed her hand under Delilah's arm. "Let me help you up." Without waiting for her to agree, the EMT started to help lift her to her feet. She was forced to leave Bobby on the floor, he quickly got to his feet and wrapped his arms around her leg.

"Bobby, my name is Officer Porter, your mommy needs to go with the EMT. Do you want to come with me, while they make sure she is okay?" Despite the officer's attempt at trying to get Bobby to let go of her leg; he did not move an inch.

Her instinct was to keep Bobby with her, but she knew that she needed medical help, as she swayed trying to stay standing.

"Sweetheart, I'm not going anywhere, but I need them to look at my arm. Can you be my brave little man and go with Officer Porter, just for now?" It tore at her heart to see the fear that was so apparent on his little face. She swelled with pride as he bravely undid his death grip on her and put his small hand into the officer's much larger one.

"Come on champ, they are going to take your mom to the hospital, but you can ride along with me." Bobby's eyes widened as tears spilled down his cheeks, the idea of them separating wasn't any more pleasant to her.

"Bobby, you get to ride in a real-life police car, wait until you tell Dylan." Dylan was Bobby's best friend, and conveniently the son of her own best friend, Sarah Moore. "Maybe you will even get to play with the siren." At the mention of being in charge of the loud noise making vehicle, her son's face lit up a fraction.

The officer gave her a grateful smile as he walked out to his car holding hands with Bobby. She needed minimal help getting on the stretcher, not being able to put any weight on her right arm at all. Once she was strapped in place, they started moving her out of the ruined front door.

The horror of what happened was visible on the façade of Nate's beautiful Tudor house, it was pocked with bullet holes. It was a miracle that they had survived, now that Bobby was safe and she was getting help, her thoughts flew to Nate. The officer had not answered her earlier, she needed to know he was okay. That he could take care of Bobby, while she was at the hospital.

She looked up at the woman that was wheeling her to the ambulance, "My ex-husband, is he hurt?"

Delilah watched the pretty blond woman's face contort slightly with pity and sadness. "I'm sorry, there was nothing that we could do to save him."

"Nate is dead?" The words rang falsely in her ears, it was not possible. "No, he can't be."

The woman was saying something, but Delilah didn't hear her. Her world started to spin out of control, Nate was gone. Oh, God, Bobby! How would she tell him that his father was dead? It was more than her body could handle, between the blood loss and the trauma of the shooting, she felt her mind drift into blackness. She welcomed the reprieve from reality, as she slipped into unconsciousness.

Chapter 2

"This way, sir."

Seriously? A British butler, were the clients also British?

Sebastian Rockmiller could hardly believe his eyes as he walked down the marble ensconced hallway of the mansion. He had worked for some truly loaded people before, but these people might top the list. Though there was that Count with his villa in Tuscany, that had been pretty impressive. That had probably been his easiest job since starting his private security company. The Count's threats were all in his mind, so the job had required no risk of life and beautiful views to boot.

His client liaison Candy Wilson had informed him that in the case of this client there had already been a drive by shooting. So, he knew this one would be dangerous, which suited him just fine. Seb was no stranger to dangerous situation.

The almost comically stiff butler stopped in front of an open door, apparently, he would go no further. Seb shook his head at the ridiculous formality that some people felt was necessary in life.

Seb walked into a formal sitting room, there were fresh flowers on several side tables. The walls were covered in stripes of several different varieties of beige. The floor yet a different shade of beige, topped off with three antique couches that he could only assume represented the only other variation of beige. If not for the burst of color from the floral arrangements, the room would be the visual equivalent of a yawn.

"Mr. Rockmiller, please feel free to sit down. Mr. and Mrs. Hawthorne will be right with you." Came the British voice once again.

Looking at the antique couches Seb couldn't help but cringe.

How much coin is it going to set me back, if I break one of these fragile looking things?

Seb was not a huge man, but at 6'2' and his affinity for taking any stress out at the gym, well he knew that his presence was hard to miss. With a silent prayer, Seb sat on the surprisingly soft couch, it held.

He managed to wipe the relief from his face before the couple that matched this house walked through the door.

Mr. Hawthorne was not a tall man, maybe 5'8" at the most, he had a ring of white hair that started just above his ears and wrapped around his head. The man had a stony face with a square jaw, his brown eyes seemed to be looking over Seb with extreme attention to detail. His wife was obviously distraught, around her piercing green eyes, the skin was puffy and red. Seb saw a slight shake in her hands, as they introduced themselves. Whether it stemmed from something medical or emotional, he didn't know. But he leaned toward the latter based on the fact that her son had just been killed.

"Thank you for coming so quickly, Mr. Rockmiller." Mr. Hawthorne had a strong dry baritone. *Not British then.*

"Of course, with these types of situations there is rarely time to waste." Seb tried to give them the reassurance that he had handled this type of thing before and that he took it very seriously. When in truth this was brand new for him, he was used to protecting rich women in danger of their own making. Maybe the occasional man that made a deal with the wrong type of scumbag and needed someone to watch his back for a while afterward. But that was not what the Hawthorne's had in mind.

"I must admit. I don't quite understand why we had to meet before you could begin protecting Bobby." Mr. Hawthorne's voice was laced with barely controlled impatience.

"It will not take long to go through the preliminaries, I promise." Seb could tell already that working with the couple would be tedious. "In my experience it helps to hear the situation from someone other than the victim, who is usually not up to recounting the story after a trauma."

"No offense implied, but what exactly is your experience?" It was the first thing that Mrs. Hawthorne had said, her words wavered with emotion.

He hated it when people did that, hired him, and then decided he needed to defend his capabilities to them. Seb felt it showed little to no forethought on the parts of his clients.

"No offense ma'am, but you decided to hire my company and asked for me specifically. These do not seem like the actions of someone that is unsure of what they are getting." Seb tried to curb the anger that was boiling under the surface of his skin. "So, if you don't mind, I would rather be spending this time discussing your grandson and what you know. Instead of discussing my illustrious career."

As he spoke, he watched the Hawthornes closely to make sure that he wasn't crossing over a line that he couldn't come back from. Even though his company was doing well, it could not afford bad word of mouth from people this powerful. His partner Cody West would be royally pissed at him if he lost this client due to his temper. To his relief, the only reaction to his words that he saw, were Mr. Hawthorne raising his eyebrows and Mrs. Hawthorne looking down at her still shaking hands.

"Fair enough Mr. Rockwell. Unfortunately, we know precious little of our son's tragedy. His ex-wife was there, along with our grandson Bobby, when our son Nathaniel was gunned down in front of his home. From what the police have told us, it is a miracle that Bobby survived the ordeal." Mr. Hawthorne stated the facts in a pragmatic way. Seb had to give it to him, if he was hurting, he was hiding it well.

"Tell me about the break-up of the marriage." Seb told them more than asked.

"For heaven's sake why?" Mrs. Hawthorne's outraged question sent off alarm bells in Seb's head, he had obviously touched on something she doesn't want to talk about.

"Miriam, please, we are wasting time. If Mr. Rockmiller needs to know then we will tell him." She looked back down at her hands, but not before Seb saw a tear streak down her cheek. "Nathaniel met Delilah when he was in college, she would not have been our first choice, or even our tenth choice for that matter. But maybe that is part of the reason he married her, to rebel against his strict up-bringing. We will never really know, because at the time he swore that he loved her. After they graduated, they moved to the Vallejo area. My son worked with at risk children, he was an excellent attorney, he could have had a very lucrative career."

13

"When did they get a divorce?" Seb knew that was the part that they were holding back on.

Mr. Hawthorne sighed deeply. "It was four years ago, right after Bobby turned one. I might as well tell you because I have no doubt Delilah will throw Nathaniel under the bus as soon as possible. Nathaniel strayed from their marriage, while she was pregnant with Bobby, I don't know any of the details."

Holy shit! What a scumbag! To cheat on your wife while she is pregnant with your child takes a certain level of low life, as far as Seb was concerned. He hoped that his disgust with their son didn't show on his face, he relied on his training to hide his emotions.

"She was not a wife to him. He would complain to me about her constantly." Mrs. Hawthorne vehemently defended her son.

"Okay, so it is safe to say the divorce was messy?" Seb was trying to determine if the ex-wife would be receptive to having her ex-in-laws help to protect her son. If she won't be it will make his job considerably harder.

"No, not at all, actually. Delilah left him and she has never asked for anything. As far as we know they have, excuse me, had an exceptionally good co-parenting relationship. My son had seemed happy the last couple of years, maybe a little overtaxed this last couple of months, but other than that, happy." Mr. Hawthorne explained.

"Why was he stressed out the last couple of months?" Seb hated that he had to pull information out of some people, he much preferred working with people who were open books.

"He wouldn't or couldn't talk about it in any kind of detail. All I know is that he was defending someone in a big case, he was unusually frazzled about the possible outcome. Like I said earlier he was excellent at his job, he usually had things well at hand." Mr. Hawthorne was finally showing signs that this conversation was wearing thin with him. Seb couldn't blame him; he had just lost his son after all.

"Just so I am clear, we are being hired to secure the safety of only your grandson. Or are we to protect this Delilah woman as well?" Seb felt like he knew the answer before they spoke, but he had to make sure.

To his surprise it was Mrs. Hawthorne who answered his question. "We are in no way concerned about the well fare of Delilah Reyes. Your job is to protect Bobby, at all costs."

It was by far the most emotion that she had shown since Seb had arrived. Clearly, the woman disliked her ex-daughter in-law. It wasn't really his job to figure out why, but it did make him curious.

He spent the next fifteen minutes going over the details, of how often he would be checking in with them and for how long his services would be needed. As he expected the couple had no idea how long they would need him for, because they did not know what they were up against yet.

If it were just a random drive-by then his job would virtually be over before it even started, but from what they said regarding their son's behavior weeks before his death. Seb had a sinking feeling that there was more to this situation.

Seb pulled up to the apartment building. The address that the Hawthornes had given him was not in the worst part of town, but he wouldn't let his sister live there. He laughed at himself, as he let the thought of trying to stop his strong-willed sister from doing anything she set her mind to sink in. His sister Melanie was three years younger than his own 32, but she had a tendency to act like a mother hen with him. Which included rarely taking his advice because she always thought she knew better.

Walking up to the plain looking stucco covered three story building, he noticed that at the very least it was well maintained. It might not be fancy, but it wasn't falling down and dilapidated. He searched for any sort of security system that he might be able to hack into, which would make his job a little easier.

He sighed. *No such luck, I guess it is the old fashion way this time.*

Either that or he would hide a couple of his own, which was technically illegal, but only if he got caught. The priority was protecting his client, if he needed to skirt the edge of the law to do that, he would.

He was relieved to see that there was at least a buzzer system on the front door, it would hardly be a deterrent for anyone motivated to get inside the building. But he knew that sometimes in life threatening situations the difference between survival and death was a matter of seconds. Seb's years of service as an Army Ranger had taught him that lesson several times over.

Seb searched for Reyes on the box with the buzzers, after finding it he pressed firmly and waited for the reply.

"Yes?" Came a naturally sultry voice. Visions of what this woman would look like based on her voice raced through his head.

"Hello ma'am, my name is Seb Rockmiller, and I was hired by the Hawthornes. Can I meet with you?" Seb had little to no hope that this meeting would go smoothly. It was an unusual situation, his company had been hired to protect a child before, but it was usually by the parents. And Seb never took those cases, but this time he was asked for specifically and it was too much money to pass up. So, here he was, attempting to protect a child with a possible unwilling parent in the picture. It was going to be a complete shit show.

"Okay." Her voice was reluctant, but at least she was willing to speak with him.

The apartment was on the second floor, which was decidedly better than it being on the first. He knew that he hadn't spoken with Ms. Reyes yet, but his mind was already on the job.

Standing in the doorway was a woman that matched the voice to a T, she was tall and shapely. Long dark curls framed her flawless face, striking grey eyes, were assessing him. He usually preferred blondes, but he had to admit this woman was a complete knock out.

"Come in, but please be quiet, the boys are napping." She motioned for him to come in with her hand, *boys? As in more than one?* He decided to side bar that question for now.

He strode into a living room that did not match the elegant woman. It looked like a crayon box had exploded, landing on the furniture in no particular order. The couch was an unpleasant orange color that was so ugly it almost physically hurt to look at. Even the walls were painted a bright yellow, while the rug that covered the floor was a swirl of purple and green. If he had to guess a general theme for the room, it would have to be circus vomit. The whole place made him want to cringe and have the owner's sanity tested.

He looked at the gorgeous woman that sat on a dark blue velvet chair that was across from the couch he sat on; *well, no one is perfect.* God had gifted this woman with a bombshell body and the decorating skills of a blind person.

"I know this may not be a welcome surprise, but the Hawthornes are very concerned about Bobby's safety. After the tragic death of his father. They have hired my company to make sure that during the investigation into the death of his father, Bobby is kept safe." Seb tried to ease into the idea that he was going to be hanging around whether she liked it or not.

The woman's face lit up, making her even more beautiful. "That is such a relief to hear, I have been worried sick. The last two days I have hardly been able to sleep, not to mention the nightmares that Bobby has been having. But now that you are here, maybe it will give us all a little piece of mind."

He was shocked at how open and welcoming she was to the idea of having a personal security person that was hired by people who clearly did not think much of her.

"It doesn't bother you that I was hired by the Hawthornes?" Seb knew that he should leave well enough alone, but he couldn't hold back his curiosity.

"I don't give a hoot who hired you." Her sincerity was evident, then she hesitated a bit. It was the first sign of reluctance he had seen on the woman. "We only have one problem that I can see."

Here it comes, I knew it couldn't be that easy.

"And what is that?" Seb asked, running possible scenarios through his mind of what her argument could be.

"We will need to convince Delilah." The words floored him, *if she isn't Delilah Reyes, then who the hell is this woman? And where is Delilah?*

Chapter 3

The last thing she needed, the absolute last freaking thing!

Delilah's hands shook with anger, as she rode in her brother's car. He had shocked her by showing up yesterday at the hospital, but she guessed she shouldn't have been. After their parents had died in a car crash, Max and Delilah were all the family that each other had. She could imagine that if someone called her and told her that something happened to Max, she would be there in a blink of an eye. But Max had a very secretive government job, she always joked with him that he was a spy. He would just roll his eyes and tell her that if he told her, he would have to kill her. Total spy thing to say!

"You need to calm down." Max looked at her, as he pulled into her apartment building.

"I don't need to do anything but get some security douchebag out of my apartment and away from my son." Delilah said. Wanting to cross her arms over her chest in defiance, but something told her that if she tried it with only one arm, it would look ridiculous. Her right arm was in a sling, the bullet had been a through and through. They told her at the hospital that she had been very lucky, the pain that radiated from her shoulder begged to differ.

"Nice language there, sis." Max rolled his eyes at her; he did that a lot.

"Oh, shut up, you know that you were the one born with the pretty manners. I was the one born with an affinity for blunt honesty and a colorful vocabulary, at least when I'm not around Bobby." She tried her best to control her wayward tongue, when in front of her impressionable child.

"It's good to know that even you have boundaries." Max grinned as he teased her.

"Come on, the sooner I pick this guy up and toss him out the better." She didn't wait for his reply as she hopped out of the car, the best she could with only one arm. Delilah was right-handed, so only having her left to do everything with was embarrassingly debilitating.

After fumbling with the keys, she heard her brother say something under his breath and grab for them and unlock the door. He entered first like he owned the place, which under normal circumstances would have peeved her off, but she was too distracted to really care.

"Hello, my name is Seb Rockmiller and I'm here..." She had to step around her tall brother to see the man connected to the rich raspy baritone.

"Oh, I know exactly why you are here. You are here because the Hawthornes think that there is no issue that you can't throw money at, and then watch the problem go away. If you think for even a split second that I am going to have some stranger hanging around my son, you are out of your mind." Delilah had only barely finished her tirade, when she let the appearance of the man standing in her living room really sink in.

He was as tall as her brother, but much wider, his shoulders were massive. Delilah was expecting anything besides the beautifully silver hair that was styled in a short military like haircut. But the most arresting part of the man was the intense emerald-green eyes that were drilling a hole into her. He wore grey cargo pants, and a black polo shirt that was tight enough to show off the contours of his sculpted chest. She tried to shake off the fact that the man was ridiculously good looking and remind herself that she wanted him gone, the sooner the better.

"Now is your chance sis, pick him up and throw him out." Max grinned down at her, amusement twinkling in his dark blue eyes, that were the same color as her own.

"Excuse me?" Mr. Rockmiller looked from her brother to her and back again, trying to figure out what Max was talking about.

"Shut up Max you're not helping." She glared at her brother for all that she was worth.

"Is he ever trying to be helpful?" Delilah turned her attention to the stunning woman that had just walked into the room. Her best friend and childhood confidant, Sarah Moore. She knew where all Delilah's skeletons were buried, and she trusted the gorgeous woman more than anyone else. Unfortunately, mixing Max and Sarah was similar to combining lighter fluid and a match, it had always been that way.

"I will have you know that I am very helpful when I want to be." Max stared at Sarah very intently while he spoke.

"I don't want to interrupt, whatever this is, but I do need to speak with you Ms. Reyes." Mr. Rockmiller's voice snapped her mind away from the tension between Max and Sarah and brought it back to her real problem.

22

Before she could reply, two balls of energy charged into the room at full speed. Her son hugged her legs with such force that it pushed her back against her brother. He instinctively grabbed her shoulders to stabilize her, making pain shoot in her arm as she released a hiss from her mouth.

"Sorry sis." Max sounded frustrated at himself, for not being more careful.

"Mommy, are you hurt bad?" Bobby leaned back enough to look at her with his deep brown eyes. Emotion threatened to overwhelm her as she hugged her son with her left arm, she had missed him so much.

"No, it is like a bad scratch. The doctor is making me where this thing just to make sure I don't use my arm until it heals. But it is nothing to worry about sweetheart." She felt her heart warm as she saw the relief in his little face.

"Bobby, Dylan, how would you two like to walk down to the park with Uncle Max and I?" Her brother shot Sarah a look that said he was not in agreement with her. She brushed him off, like she usually did.

"And mommy?" She watched as her son registered that there was a stranger in the room. "Who are you?"

"Bobby don't be rude." She ignored the snort that Max let out when she scolded her son's manners. "This gentleman is a friend of your grandmother and grandfather."

"Why does he have old man hair?" She felt heat rise to her cheeks, embarrassed by her son's borderline rude question.

"Bobby…" She started to correct him again, but Mr. Rockmiller cut her off.

"That's okay, he is right. I do have old man hair. You know that was actually my nickname in basic training. Everyone used to call me Old Man, because of my hair." As he spoke to Bobby, his face softened, and his green eyes seemed to light from within. Her words died in her throat, she was unable to do anything other than stare at the sexy man in her living room, who was being so kind to her son.

"Can I call you old man?" Bobby asked smiling.

"Sure." "Absolutely not." She and Mr. Rockmiller answered simultaneously.

He chuckled a little then amended his response. "Not if your mom says no, buddy."

"Okay, come on Bobby, your mommy has boring things to talk over with Mr. Rockmiller. Let's go play on the new play-set at the park." Sarah suggested, winning her another glare from Max.

The boys whooped with excitement, and she watched as Max's resolve melted away. When it came to his nephew, he was nothing but a huge softy.

"I don't know if going to the park without me is a good idea." She had not expected Mr. Rockmiller to speak up, but he did.

"I will watch out for him." Max spoke with an edge to his voice; one she had never heard from him before. The two men were locked in some sort of male appraisal ritual, after which they both nodded their heads as if something had been decided. *Men are idiots!*

The four of them walked out of the apartment, with Max toting one boy on each of his shoulders. She had to smile at the sight of the people she loved most in the world, going to enjoy the park. The smile faded quickly as she turned back to find Mr. Rockmiller staring at her, his gaze completely unreadable. All she wanted was to soak in a nice lavender scented bath and then collapse into bed, and now she had to deal with the Hawthorne's lap dog.

The woman that curled her small legs under her on the couch he had just vacated, fit this room perfectly. She was clad in tie-dye short overalls, underneath that she appeared almost naked, which had made his eyes bulge when he had first seen her. At least until he recognized that she in fact wore a pink tube top under the colorful clothing. It didn't do much to slow his initial reaction to the woman though, she had come through the door like a lit firecracker.

Her almost sapphire blue eyes were shining with anger as she stepped into him with both feet, speaking her mind with a soft feminine voice. To top it all off, she had a thick ponytail of dark red curls, several of which had worked their way out of the restraint and curled around her lightly freckled face. He probably wouldn't have had to work so hard to control his libido if it hadn't been for her mouth. She had a perfect full heart shaped mouth; it was the type of mouth that begged to be sampled. Which is what his body urged him to do when she first walked in.

"So, Mr. Rockmiller, what do I need to do to get you to leave?" Delilah's question pulled his attention back to the subject at hand and away from his lusty thoughts.

"Nothing at all." Seb could see that this was going to be a battle of wills.

25

Her perfectly shaped eyebrow arched. "Then you will just leave?"

"Absolutely not, I will protect your son. Just like I was hired to do, whether you like it or not." Seb had to work hard to keep his face a blank mask, the look on her face was adorably funny.

Good lord she is fired up!

"I realize that you are just trying to do your job Mr. Rockmiller...." He could tell she was trying to remain calm, and on the verge of failing.

"Please, call me Seb, we will be spending a lot of time together." Seb was not prepared for the furious blush that lit her cheeks, as her gem-colored eyes widened.

"You are mistaken, Mr...." He wanted to laugh at how impossibly stubborn she was being.

"Seb." He intervened, he heard her say what sounded like profanity under her breath.

"Like I was trying to say, your services are not needed here. Period, end of story." The fire in her eyes, daring him to argue. Seb loved a good fight.

"So, you were not in a drive-by shooting in which your ex-husband died? One in which you and your son were lucky to survive?" Seb tried to remind her of the severity of her situation.

He saw her reluctance to answer his question, probably already guessing where he was going with it.

"You know damn well that I was." The fire inside this woman awoke something primal inside of Seb. She had enough fight in her for three women, twice her size. Delilah reminded him of a vicious Polly Pocket, and he would be damned if he did not find it sexy as hell.

"Okay, so please explain to me, why you do not need protection for your son?" Seb drove his point home.

"Because whether the shooting was a freak happening or they were after Nate, either way they were not after my son or myself. So, there is no reason for us to have protection. This is all just the Hawthornes trying to obtain some control over Bobby now that Nate is dead." The fire within her faded, replaced with a sorrowful look, that made him want to hold her and give her comfort.

He shook his head to clear his thoughts, he did not hug clients! And he would do well to remind his male instincts that this woman was nothing more than a client. Period!

"That may be the Hawthornes intention." Seb sucked in his breath as her big blue eyes shot up, looking at him, her eyes filled with the raw emotion that only loss can bring. *She must have really loved her ex-husband.* He forced himself to continue. "But it is not mine. My only intention is to make sure what happened to your ex-husband does not happen to your son."

A picture of the small boy forced its way into Seb's mind, the big doe brown eyes staring up at him. When he first saw her son Bobby, he was transported back in time, to a place he tried not to think of. To a different little boy with almost identical brown eyes, a boy that he had failed. He had failed to protect him from the violent world that surrounded him. Seb swallowed back the emotions that were building in his throat, knowing that it would soon cause his stomach to ache. It didn't matter, the pain was a reminder, a reminder of what happened when you let your guard down and let yourself care.

"Are you alright, Mr. Roc…. Seb?" Delilah was seated on the couch by him, he had no idea how she had gotten there, but he tried not to appear surprised. What would she think, if she knew he had gotten lost in memories and not even noticed her movement? Would she ever trust that he could take care of her son?

"Yes, I'm fine." Seb tried to sound as nonchalant as possible.

"You didn't look fine. You went white as a sheet. It looked like you saw a ghost." Delilah's voice was soft and soothing, it was a struggle to remain professional.

"Don't try to change the subject, we were discussing your situation." Seb was satisfied when he saw the flame reignite inside her eyes.

Good stay mad at me, do not care about me!

She surprised him by rising from the couch and walking to the front door. He tried not to watch as her shapely bottom trounced across the room, but he failed miserably. Seb was caught in the rhythm of her sway as she turned to confront him. He almost wanted this job to be done before it started, between the woman and the son, this would an assignment that threatened all of his weaknesses.

"Our discussion is done; you are leaving, and I am going to try and pick up the pieces of my life." Delilah opened the door as she spoke, sending him a message that he was no longer welcome in her apartment.

He knew that he would make no more head way today, but if she thought he was giving up, she was crazier than her living room indicated she was.

"I will leave," Seb waited until he saw relief wash over her frustrated features. "For now, but let me ask you this first. Did you see who killed your ex-husband? The car, license, make, model, any detail that could be used to identify the shooters?"

She refused to meet his eyes, and her silence told him that the answer to at least one of his questions was yes. Which meant that this woman and her son, were still in danger and in need of protection.

"That is what I thought. I will be back first thing in the morning to begin my protection detail. In the meantime, I suggest you think about whether maintaining your privacy and refusing help from the Hawthornes, is worth your son's life." He walked out of the door, feeling like a piece of shit for being so harsh with Delilah. Seb tried to tell himself that he had no choice, he had to convince her that she needed him.

Chapter 4

Delilah slumped against the door that she had slammed behind the infuriating man that had left so calmly. His parting words stabbed her as sharply as knives. She had not let herself admit how much trouble she was possibly in. The idea that her son might still be in danger, it terrified her.

She knew that she had not seen the men's faces clearly, or the license number, but she had seen the car and it had been rather unique. She didn't think that there were many metallic-blue vintage El Caminos, with black racing stripes down the center, driving around town. She had told the cops all that she saw but had fooled herself into believing that she hadn't seen enough to put them in danger. Obviously, Seb disagreed with her, and his words sank like stones in her belly.

If he was right, then they were still in danger and in need of help, but she didn't trust her ex-in-laws. She knew that they had fought with Nate, urging him to try and get full custody of Bobby. Delilah had always been grateful to Nate for refusing their pleas. If he had sided with them and forced the issue, she might have lost her son. They had so much money compared to her meager counselor's paycheck. Between her wages and Nate's help she got by, but the Hawthornes could provide a whole different world for Bobby. Private schools, country clubs, not to mention the fact that their house is a full out mansion.

Her instincts told her that the Hawthornes, well most specifically Miriam Hawthorne, would love any excuse to take her son from her. The woman had hated her since Nate had brought her home their junior year of college. Delilah had not known to hold back her amazement at their immense wealth, she had oohed and awed at it. Which had made Miriam paint her as a low-class gold digger, she had never even given Delilah a chance.

Now here she was, possibly in need of help that only money could buy, but without the resources to purchase it on her own. The police hadn't offered her any sort of protection. They hadn't even ruled out the shooting being completely coincidental.

Delilah knew that Nate had been very strained lately, he had told her that the case he had landed was not an easy one. When Nate said that it usually meant that he knew his client was guilty as sin and he hated to defend them, but he was too good of a lawyer to not do his job. It had always been the part of his job that had made her blood run cold, when he got a criminal off, who should be in jail. The night after a case like that Nate would lose himself in alcohol, and she would try to stay clear of him.

She started sliding forward, it took her a moment to realize someone was trying to get into the apartment. Fear gripped her heart like a vice, her gaze raked over her apartment for anything that could be used as a weapon.

Shit! Why do all of my possessions look disappointingly non-lethal?

"Are you standing in front of the door, Pippy? Max's use of her childhood nickname melted her fear away. Replaced by the usual anger she felt when he called her Pippy. Her mother dressed her up as Pippy Longstockings one Halloween, and boom, she was as good as branded for life.

She stepped back to allow them to enter the apartment, a scalding comment on the tip of her tongue, when she noticed that it was only her brother and Bobby standing in the doorway. Bobby raced past her, on his way to his room.

"Where did Sarah go? What did you do?" Delilah knew how vicious the two of them could become when dealing with each other and she had no doubt that Max had hurt Sarah somehow.

Her jaw almost fell open in surprise as she saw Max's cheeks turn a light pink, *what in the world!?* She had never seen her brother blush; this couldn't be good.

"She just had to go home, said something about making dinner for Dylan. Told me to tell you that she had to work tomorrow, but she would call you in the morning to check in." Something about the way he spoke, made him sound guilty as sin, but guilty of what?

"If you won't tell me, you know that Sarah will." Delilah eyed Max intently looking for any clues.

"Just drop it, please." Max saying please was almost more shocking than the blush, her brother was so used to giving orders, everything that came out of his mouth generally sounded like a command. The pleading in his voice added to the blush, made her feel like maybe she didn't want to know. Lord knew she had enough going on right now, without dealing with the tension between her brother and Sarah. They were both adults and they would have to figure their own stuff out for now.

"Whatever, I have too much on my mind right now, but we will have a serious talk if I find out you hurt her. Understood?" He flopped down on her sofa and grunted his agreement, satisfied that that was the closest thing to a response she would get, she decided to move on to more important matters. "Are you staying for dinner, because I am starving."

Max chuckled at her as Bobby trotted back into the room and decided at that moment to launch himself onto his Uncle's tummy, knocking the wind out of his lungs. After a short bout of tickling, which sent Bobby running for the restroom, her brother replied.

"Yes, I am staying the night tonight actually, now that I see that you chased off G.I. Joe. Unless of course he is coming back?" Max eyed her skeptically.

"No, he is not coming back." Delilah wanted her brother to think that she had won the battle of wills against Seb.

"Delilah, tell me you are going to accept his help." Max's voice had a note of pleading to it, she would have to mark this day on her calendar. First a blush and now pleading twice, she checked her feet for chills, just in case hell had indeed frozen over.

"I can't tell you that bro, I don't want some stranger hanging around here. Plus, I have you. Strong government spy guy, who would mess with us with you around?" Delilah was only half kidding. She would love it if her brother would hang out for a while. Just until her nerves settled.

He looked at her with a grieved expression. "I'm sorry sis, but it was a struggle to come here for the past two days. To put it mildly, my boss wants to kick my ass for leaving."

"Oh God Max, you aren't going to be fired because of this, are you?" She was stricken with guilt at the thought.

The laugh that burst from her brother elevated her worry.

"Don't worry, do you think they would let go of their number one government spy guy?" His dark blue eyes were alit with humor, it almost made her forget about her own problems, until he opened his big mouth again. "So, you understand why you should take the protection that is being offered to you, right?"

Delilah could see an endless conversation in their future, where her brother insisted, and she refused. She sighed, preparing all the reasoning points that she could think of. Loading each one like a preverbal bullet into the chamber, readying herself for the fight.

Before she had time to shoot off her first verbal bullet, Delilah was on her back and dazed by the heavy weight of her brother's body lying on top of hers. Sharp pain radiating from her arm and the now familiar pop of gun fire, brought reality up to speed.

Bobby, where is Bobby?

All she could think about was her son, and his safety, the screech of rubber burning up the road seemed to surround them.

Again, how is this happening again?

"Stay down, I'm going to check on Bobby." Steal had more give to it than her brother's voice, it was not a request, it was a command. One that she had no problem following, the person she trusted most in the world was her brother. So, if she couldn't run to her son, she felt secure with Max going, he would keep Bobby safe.

Delilah lay on the floor until her brother returned to the room cradling her son in his arms. When Bobby saw her, he immediately reached out for her. She got up to embrace her frightened child. His crocodile tears were wetting her shoulder and running down her arm, he was getting so big that holding him with one arm was taxing. But she didn't care, right now she needed this as much as he did.

"I'm going to take you and Bobby to a hotel for tonight. Pack up a bag for each of you, while I go out and see if everything is clear." Max did not wait for an argument, stalking out the door cautiously with his gun drawn.

She wasted no time getting to work at her task, since she only had one arm, packing was impossible while still holding her son.

"Okay sweetheart, we are going to go on an adventure, and we need to pack all our favorite things." She attempted to sound upbeat, but to her own ears her voice sounded dreadfully hollow.

"Like Bilbo, mommy?" His sweet innocence at referencing The Hobbit, which was their current bedtime story, tore her apart. He shouldn't have to deal with this sort of thing, this is not their life. She had to force herself not to think back to her own violence ridden childhood, she had sworn to herself that her son would never have to feel the terror that she had.

Feeling like a complete failure, she made herself plaster on a fake smile and respond to her son. "Exactly, and we have no idea how long we will be gone. So, we need to pack everything that we will need. Do you think you can grab all your favorite toys and throw them into your dinosaur tote?"

His brave face looked up at her, tear tracks still visible on his rounded cheeks. "Yes mommy, make sure you pack all of your favorite things too."

"You are my favorite thing." The smile that her comment brought to his face, warmed her heart. "I don't think that you would fit in my bag though, I guess we could try." She started to walk to her room, he started to wiggle in her arms, trying to get down.

Delilah set her son down, loving to watch him laugh. "Mommy, you are so silly."

"I know. Now, let's go pack up." She led her son in the direction of their rooms, trying like the devil to hide how shaky and scared she felt.

He had been caught with his pants down, literally.

Since leaving Delilah's apartment he had only stopped his surveillance once, to run to the gas station to use the restroom. The rest of the time he had been camped out in his car, watching, because even though Delilah had not agreed to it, he was already on the job. The Hawthornes were not paying for their grandson to be protected only if their daughter-in-law agreed. *It would just be so much easier if she would*, if she didn't it would mean a lot of time spent in his car.

At the sound of the first gunshot, Seb was zipping up his pants. Adrenaline raced in his veins as he sprinted from the gas station to the apartment building. He was fast, he had always been the fastest one in his Battalion, but he missed the car as it peeled out of the parking lot. All he caught was the make and model of the car, it was too dark to even make out the exact color, let alone any sort of plate number. He cursed himself as he arrived at the apartment, looking at the message painted on the side of what he assumed was Delilah's car, he should have been here.

Keep Your Bitch Mouth Shut!

The message spray painted across her car in blue, was clear as a bell. Someone who was not messing around thought that Delilah knew something, which put both her and her son in imminent danger.

Seb was checking out the car for bullet holes when the corner of his peripheral started to move. He moved on pure instincts and training, crouching behind the vehicle, placing something solid between himself and the unknown person. Not knowing if they had spotted him yet, he kept low and tried to plan out a way to get from the parking lot to more of a vantage point, without losing all cover completely.

Man, this shit is so much easier when you have cover fire.

He remembered with a grin the feeling of yelling out "Cover me while I move!" Then essentially placing your safety in the hands of men you trust like brothers. There was no other feeling on the planet that he had ever experienced that had come close to matching it. Putting your life in someone else's hands, was like a free fall of trust. But instead of just falling if you were wrong, you would die. Seb pulled his attention from reminiscing on his days as a Ranger, to watch the person that was walking by the house. The person started to come towards him and the car.

The man became clearer and clearer the closer he came to the vandalized auto, Seb let out the breath that he had been holding, as he recognized Max. Seb was happy to see Max's slightly startled face upon seeing Seb pop up from behind the car.

"Holy hell, where have you been?" Max voice betrayed his surprise at seeing Seb.

"I have been here the whole time." Seb met the man's eyes, under the parking light, he could make out the worry in his eyes.

"Then you saw the shooters and whoever wrote this." It was more of a statement than a question, but knowing it to be false, Seb had to correct Delilah's brother.

"Actually no." He waited a moment to gage Max's reaction, his face had become a stone slab. Apparently, he was done showing Seb any emotions. *Oh yeah, this guy is some sort of government lackey.* It had been a feeling that Seb got from him almost instantly, he had no way of knowing for sure, but he would bet his Camaro on it. "I was answering nature's call, at the gas station. As soon as I heard the shots, I high tailed it back over here. Saw the car speeding away but didn't get anything that's useful."

"While you were busy at the local AM/PM, my sister and nephew could be dead. Is that how you do your job, poorly?" Cold anger emanated from Delilah's brother; he couldn't blame the guy. If someone were shooting at Melanie, he would be furious, but he couldn't let the man question his ability.

"I would have been able to use the restroom inside, if your sister hadn't of kicked me out." Seb pointed out the obvious.

The bravado that had masked Max's emotion seemed to melt away, the man sighed in frustration as he ran his hand through hair that was surprisingly brown compared to his sister's red.

"You're right." His admission surprised Seb, "Well, I will be damned if she will turn your help away again. Not after this. I think my sister is in serious trouble, and she needs your protection."

"I agree with you, but I have to tell you. I was only hired to protect Bobby, not your sister. The Hawthornes were very clear on that. I'm not saying that I will not do everything in my power to make sure they are both safe. But if the situation turns dire, and I have to choose who to protect, my choice will be clear. Just so you understand." Seb hated to sound so cold, to man that was clearly worried for his family member's lives, but he needed to make sure that Max understood his priorities.

"Both Delilah and I would not have it any other way." Max nodded to him, before turning and heading to his sister's apartment. He looked back at Seb, who hadn't budged an inch. "Are you coming?"

"I promised her I wouldn't be back until Morning." Seb admitted.

———

39

Max chuckled lightly, "Yeah well, this time you're coming as my guest."

Something told Seb that returning to the apartment at her brother's request was not going to make Delilah any happier to see him.

Chapter 5

He checked his rearview mirror constantly, even though the classic El Camino he had seen racing from Delilah's building was not a car that most people would use to tail someone. It was not exactly a vehicle that screamed ambiguity, then again neither was his own midnight black Camaro. It was his one indulgence, when he had retired from the Rangers. His childhood dream car, Seb decided that after surviving three tours in Iraq, he deserved a little "Congratulations your alive!" gift. There were definitely days in that sandy hell hole that he had come close to never getting to realize his dream. It wasn't a place he would let himself recall, at least not while sober.

Two very unhappy eyes glared at him from the back seat, she had been switching between comforting her son with silly jokes and staring at him like he had kidnapped them.

Like he had planned any of this! He was supposed to provide security detail for a small child at that child's place of residence, on the off chance that anything happened to risk that child's life. Not listening to some government spook tell him about going to a hotel that he trusted, while toting the child and his beautifully furious mother. Which is what she had looked like as she railed against Max and himself, earlier in her apartment. Her passionate fight had lit up her face and her eyes, causing them to lighten slightly and shine like gems. Seb had felt his gaze slip several times, mesmerized by her luscious mouth. Wondering what it would be like to grab her off her feet and sample that argumentative mouth with his own.

Seb cleared the un-business-like thoughts from his head. He was supposed to protect her son, not spend time fantasizing about kissing her.

They had been driving on Highway 12 for almost thirty minutes, with Max sitting in the passenger's seat giving him very vague directions. Seb was familiar enough with California to know that Max was leading them in the direction of Napa. It was a good choice for something a little more tucked away than the busier Vallejo.

Seb had grown up in North California, despite popular belief that did not mean San Francisco, which is where people not from California seemed to think the State ended. Essentially dismissing the existence of 300 miles' worth of beautiful land that actually constituted Northern California. He was raised in the small town of Weaverville, nestled in the mountains, his mother and grandma provided a warm loving home for him and his sister. Unless you counted the fact that his father had run out on his mother shortly after his sister's birth, his childhood had been ideal.

He had only ventured down to the Napa Valley a handful of times, but it was enough to recall the winding roads and rolling hills. Seb was not a huge wine drinker, but he had brought a girlfriend down here once or twice. They had even tried that grape stomping thing once. If he hadn't liked wine before, the idea that people's feet had been wading in your beverage was enough to put him off the vino for good.

Max told him to turn down a small road that the casual driver would have completely missed, unless they knew to look for it. Seb was even more impressed with Delilah's brother, when a group of log cabins came into view. There were several cars parked in the circular driveway, but it was clear by the number of buildings that the place was not at full capacity. This would do very nicely to keep Delilah and Bobby out of harm's way, at least for the time being.

Seb got out of the car, and pushed down the driver's seat, so that his passengers could get out. The classic muscle car was not exactly built to tow around a family. They had left Delilah's bullet ridden car at her apartment building, Max had told him that most of the holes had come from the drive-by. Which made sense because Seb had only heard two shots during this evening's warning, and it had very clearly been a warning. At least if you asked him, and he had a feeling Max would agree with him.

Delilah and Bobby got out of the car and wasted no time catching up with Max, who was walking toward the office building. Seb rounded the car and grabbed his own bag from the floor of the passenger seat, he was not prepared for the scent of sweet honey that assailed him.

Great, how long is my car going to smell like that feisty little woman?

Even though he told himself that he did not like the idea of his car smelling like a beautiful woman, he filled his lungs with a deep breath before shutting the door.

I guess there are worse things that it could smell like.

He was smiling as he retrieved Delilah and Bobby's bags, then walked to catch up with the trio standing at the reception desk.

As soon as Seb walked into the building, he was met with a little delighted squeal that pierced his ears. The unpleasant sound had come from a woman not much bigger in size than Delilah, she was staring at him with light brown eyes. He quickly evaluated her, putting her age somewhere around 24, she had shoulder length blond hair and was wearing shirt that fit her like second skin. Seb really hoped that the woman would not have to bend down to get anything, because he didn't think that Bobby was ready to see his first breast.

"Maxie, you told me the room was for your sister. You didn't even mention this silver fox." Seb cringed, it was not the first time someone had made the comment about his hair, but he did not care for it at all.

"The fox is here to watch over her, you understand?" Seb felt like Max was putting a lot of trust in this woman, he didn't like it.

A flash of seriousness briefly swept into the woman's eyes, *maybe she was more than she seemed?* "Gotcha, so the usual cabin is all ready to go. You know the rules. Any damage you do, is Uncle Sam's job to fix, not little ole me." She winked at Max, as she dropped the key into his hand.

Seb wondered if Max would spill the details about this place to him, because it was for sure not your run of mill kind of place. Knowing a place like this could prove particularly useful in his line of work, but he had the feeling that it might be strictly government access. They trekked further up the hill, deeper into the woods and further from the other cabins. He let out a small whistle of appreciation as the homey log cabin came into view. It was easily twice the size of the ones that they had first seen. Unlike the ones lower down, Seb could see little red lights that were strategically placed around the perimeter of the building. They would save Seb the work of putting up cameras himself.

———

"Oh wow, this place is cool." Seb couldn't help but agree with Bobby's evaluation of the interior of the cabin. The place was cozy feeling, from the entrance you could see the kitchen, a small dining area and a living room with a big stone fireplace. Everywhere you looked was rich lacquered wood, not necessarily his own taste but he had to admit it had charm. There was a staircase that Seb assumed led to the bedrooms.

"Glad you like it, sport. How does your mom feel about it?" Max looked at his sister, obviously hoping for her approval.

"It is very nice Max." Her brother's face softened at her appraisal. "How many bedrooms are there?"

"Two." Max looked straight at Seb when he said the next part. "So, I guess foxy is on the couch."

Oh great! How long is he going to hold on to that one?

"That is fine with me." Both Max and Delilah looked at him with surprise lighting there very similar blue eyes. "Is there any food in this place, because I am starving?"

"Oh yeah man, this place is stocked." Max's smile at the prospect of eating was contagious.

"I'm hungry too." Bobby looked from Max to Seb, sharing in their eagerness to eat.

"Men! In the middle of turmoil all you can think about is food." Delilah sighed.

"That is not true, we can think of other things too." Seb had not meant to say the words out loud, but he couldn't control himself from raking his eyes appreciatively over Delilah's curvy little body, if only for an instant.

45

"Not if you want to keep your foxy head on your foxy shoulders you don't!" Seb could practically see the anger seeping from Max's pours, he knew that he should back off. But if Max thought that puffing up his chest and getting angry was the way to get Seb to back down, he didn't know a damn thing about him.

"Don't you think it's about time we let go of the animal-based nicknames? You do know foxes are liable to bite when provoked, right?" Seb kept his voice calm but stared into Max's eyes with cold determination.

He had to give Max credit, he had watched lesser men cower time and time again under his threatening gaze, but Max did not waiver one inch. Not for the first time Seb wondered what exactly Max did for Uncle Sam.

"If you two are done measuring your you know what's my son is hungry." Delilah stood looking from one man to the other, a look of disgust on her face. "So, I guess that I will make us something to eat."

"We will cook. You only have use of one of your arms." Two sets of dark blue eyes challenged his statement. "Plus, I'm sure the doctor told you to take it easy." He knew that he had scored a direct hit when he watched them both waver. "Good, let's get cooking, Maxie."

Seb ignored the growl like sound that emanated from Delilah's brother as he followed him to the kitchen. He was starting to think that this would be a fun assignment, he liked picking fights with Max and he liked looking at Delilah. Even though it would make it a little harder to concentrate on his job, it would also make his job much more enjoyable.

She groaned as she sat back in her chair, rubbing her stomach in a very un-lady like manner. Dinner had been amazing, which had made it all the more frustrating as she struggled to eat with her non-dominate hand. She was pretty sure that she had gotten the same amount of food in her mouth, that had also wound up on her overalls. Despite the setback she could almost purr with satisfaction, after two days of hospital food, the spaghetti they had made was close to heaven.

"Now all you need to do is one of your customary table clearing burps." Max looked at her with a smile, that she would have liked to knock off his face..

"I have no idea what you are talking about." She lied; she didn't need G.I. Joe to know all the ways she fell short of being a lady.

"You have been over there moaning more than a bear after hibernation, and you ate enough for three people your size." She could tell that Max was holding back his laughter, as she could feel blood rush to her cheeks.

Did I really eat that much? Oh lord, did I actually moan?

"Mommy can burp really loud. Mommy show Rock how good you can burp." Her humiliation was cut short by Seb's reaction to her son's request.

His face turned white as a sheet, and he whipped his head toward Bobby so quickly she feared it might fall off.

"What did you call me?" His voice came out low and hollow sounding, its emptiness gave her the chills.

47

It must have affected Bobby the same way because she watched as his lower lip began to tremble. Delilah thought that he would be too frightened to answer, but before she could intervene, he squared his tiny shoulders and responded.

"Mommy said not to call you old man, and you don't like it when Uncle Max calls you foxy." She could tell he was trying to keep his voice steady. "I saw your name on your army bag, it was too long, but I read the first part. I want my own nickname for you."

She watched as Seb seemed to soften faster than butter in the summer sun, after hearing her son's explanation. Delilah had let out the breath she had been holding, caught between protecting her son and wanting to let him fight his own battles.

"I would prefer that you call me Seb." The emotion that raged in Seb's dark green eyes, there was a raw pain that she saw guarded in his look. The counselor in her wanted to help him, to get him to open up. Knowing that the only way to get over pain was to go through it, but she had to remind herself that this man was not one of the children that needed her help. He was an unnecessary nuisance sent by her ex-in-laws to "protect" her son. From the moment she had found out about him, she couldn't help but feel that the Hawthornes were up to something. She just didn't know what.

"Okay." Her son looked down at his plate, and pushed the last remaining noodle around, she could see he was fighting back tears.

Delilah shook her head. *The things we do for love.* With that thought she let out a truly horrendously loud belch, causing her son and brother to burst out in uncontrollable laughter, while the gorgeous man that was sitting across from her just stared at her in shock.

That should make my brother happy, now there is no way Seb will every think of me as a woman again.

Oh well, she didn't want him thinking of her in a romantic way anyway. She had spent her whole married life, pretending she was something that she wasn't. Tagging along to all of Nate's fancy parties and social obligations. Delilah tried to remember a single time she had burped in front of her ex-husband, and she could not. That is why she was so content living with just her and Bobby, they knew and loved each other unconditionally.

"Mommy you are the best." Bobby got up from the table and wrapped his tiny arms around her right side. She tried to hide the pain it caused her; she would endure anything to feel love from her son.

"Careful sport, remember your mom is hurt." Max's comment made Bobby spring back from her, she shot him a glare.

"I forgot." She could see tears threaten to well back up in her son's eyes, he had been through so much these past three days. It broke her heart to see her usually happy go lucky boy, so emotional.

"You know what?" She asked running her hand through her son's chestnut colored hair.

"What?" His voice came out impossibly small and innocent sounding.

"I think that your hug actually made my arm feel better." He looked up at her with his huge brown eyes filled with unshed tears.

"Really?" Bobby asked her with hope in his eyes.

"Yep, the doctor told me to get as many hugs as possible." She barely had time to prepare her body for the impact before her son threw himself at her once again. There was no way to hide the pain that it caused her, but she shot a silencing look at both the men sitting at the table. Daring them to make a comment. To her relief they both remained silent.

"How does a nice warm bubble bath sound?" Her brother's suggestion was a good one, it was well past Bobby's bedtime, and a bath would help mellow him out. "How about I give you a bath and put you to bed, so we can let mommy relax after all those healing hugs."

She didn't miss the sarcasm in her brother's tone, but luckily Bobby did.

Bobby quickly agreed to his uncle's plan, she kissed him goodnight and pretended to be disgusted as her brother planted a wet sloppy kiss on her forehead.

Them leaving left her seated at the table alone with the gorgeous man that seemed to be evaluating her with every glance. There was a sinking feeling in her stomach, that told her whatever chart he was measuring her by, she was coming up short. She knew that she shouldn't care, but she did. Delilah tried to tell herself it was because she wanted the spy that the Hawthornes sent to have nothing bad to say about her, but she knew it was more than that.

She shook her head at her own idiocy, as she started to clear the table.

"I thought you were supposed to rest." Seb's voice breaking the silence, sent shivers down her body, shivers that she was determined to ignore.

"I am hardly an invalid. The least I can do is help clear the table." She tried to remain determined despite the emerald eyes that followed her every move.

"Fine, but I'm doing the dishes." Since she had to admit that she had no idea how she would do the dishes with one hand, she decided not to argue.

Delilah had waited tables to put herself through college, Berkeley wasn't the most expensive school in the world, but it had been more than her parents could afford. So, besides grants and loans, she had to work to support her daily living expenses.

She watched as Seb's eyes grew larger and larger as she expertly stacked the dishes, balancing everything so that she could pick it up with one hand. Delilah saw the uncertainty that filled his gorgeous eyes, clearly not believing that she could hold it all in one hand. It egged her on to pile more than she had originally planned, she smiled at him triumphantly when she lifted to pile of dishes with her left hand.

Delilah just barely caught the smirk that curved the corner of his mouth, she felt ridiculously empowered by the fact that he had underestimated her. Even if it were at such a trivial task. She could almost feel him get up from the table to grab the few dishes she had not piled on and she had no doubt he planned to follow her into the kitchen.

Once in the kitchen she realized her mistake, while she could pile it with one hand and pick it up with hand, how in the world was she going to set it down with one hand? Delilah decided to try and slide the dishes onto the counter, if it had been a flat slab counter instead of a tiled one, it might have worked. But the minute the plate hit the dip in the grout between the tiles, the pile started to tilt. She let it drop onto the counter halfway, trying to wrap her hand around the back to keep it from falling onto the counter itself. She must have used more force than necessary because the pile started to lean precariously towards her.

She cursed as she was unable to keep the glasses on top from cascading to the floor, cursing her need to show off, and the fact that she wasn't wearing her sandals. Delilah stood there, frozen in place, surrounded by shattered glass.

It was too much for her, after the past three days of keeping everything together, controlling her emotions for everyone around her. Delilah let the warm tears fall upon her cheeks, as she looked around her, at the mess she had made. Feeling like the fragments of broken glass too closely resembled what her life had become. The reality that she was now the sole parent to her young child, and she was hiding in a cabin with a perfect stranger. Like a coward she had yet to tell Bobby about his father, she had no idea how to tell him. And there was no one that she could turn to for advice.

How has this become my life?

Chapter 6

It took an instant for the sound of breaking glass in the direction of the kitchen to register to Seb, he knew immediately that the little show off had had an accident. He remained perfectly calm, and was ready to gloat about being right, until he walked into the kitchen.

There she stood in the middle of the room, her good hand pressed against her belly, while glistening tears streamed down her face. Seb saw that she was bare footed and the reality that she could be hurt, was like a punch to the gut. He ate up the space between them, in two strides. Wearing his boots, he crunched the glass without a second thought. Careful not to touch her hurt arm, he grabbed her tiny waste, ignored the heat the touch created. Her hand came off her stomach in surprise, she placed it on his forearm, as he set her on the counter. Seb had to clear his mind, just like while in combat. If you didn't learn how to focus on the situation only, you could end up a dead man. So, Seb erased anything other than her from his thoughts.

"Are you hurt?" He was God smacked when he looked into her cobalt eyes, the pain and sadness that he saw, made him want to take her and hold her. To comfort her and protect her.

"I don't think so." Her sniffled response did nothing to reassure him of her well-being.

Seb stepped back from her, to grab her feet and check for any damage. He knew that it was dumb, but she had the most beautiful feet he had ever seen. Not that he spent a lot of time looking at women's feet. No, he could be accused of being a leg man, or a boob man, but not a foot guy. Her feet were small and delicate, like the rest of her. He ran his fingers against the sole of her foot, trying to convince himself he was feeling for glass, but knowing damn well that he was indulging himself.

Her sharp intake of breath pulled him from his self-indulgence. "Did somewhere I touch hurt?" As he searched her face, he no longer saw pain there, it had been replaced by a look that distinctly resembled need.

Delilah's face colored, as she shook her head. "No, I'm fine really."

Seb was unwilling or unable to let go of her shapely leg, as he spoke to her. Alternately running his hand over each foot, now only pretending to check for cuts. "But you were crying, I thought you were hurt."

Her eyes turned almost to indigo, as he watched her need bloom into full blown passion. Not relenting with his touching, his body was responding to her reaction. Urging him to run his hand up her leg, to feel how soft the rest of her was.

"It was dumb." Her voice took on a breathy quality; he was amazed that such a simple touch could be giving her so much pleasure. Seb let his mind wonder for a moment, a woman this responsive to his touch, he wanted to see how she would respond if he touched her elsewhere.

"In my experience, when a strong woman cries, it is rarely for a dumb reason." Seb knew that he shouldn't, but he was no longer in complete control of his body, as he started to slide his hand slowly up the velvety leg. Her eyes widened and her pouty mouth opened slightly. It took all of his will power not to claim that mouth with his own.

"It...was...the glass." Her eyes fluttered shut as he could see the flame of desire rage inside of her, Seb's body screamed for him to continue. He wanted to watch her lose all control, he wanted to lose all control while buried deep inside of her. The severity of his own reaction to her, was disarming.

"You cried because of the glass?" He continued to inch both hands up her silky legs, pausing only to knead the soft skin gently. She shook her head no, it was such a small gesture, that if he hadn't been watching her so intently, he would have missed it. Delilah bit down on her lush lower lip, as his hands had ventured all the way to her thighs, almost to the seam of her overalls.

He needed to stop; he knew that his mind was trying to yell that at him. Seb's propriety had almost won the battle when she reached out to him. Lightly touching the stubble on his face, all of his nerves seemed to stand on end, each one screaming out their need for her touch. Delilah's fingers slid to his mouth, she traced his lips, he almost groaned out loud. Seb had never known a touch like this. He swallowed hard drawing her attention to his throat, and his Adam's apple. By the time she got to running her fire making fingers along his collar bone, he was completely unraveled. Seb was mere seconds from grabbing her and crushing her body against his. The fire that was lit inside him, demanded a release, the heat that was coming from the two of them, threatened to burn the house to the ground.

"What in the hell, is going on here?!" A very male and very unwelcomed voice punctured the cloud of passion that had been all consuming. "Get your hands off of my sister!"

Sanity returned to Seb, clearly too late to avoid a confrontation with Max, but it returned. He felt ashamed of himself, he withdrew his hands from Delilah, they betrayed him by still tingling. His body did not agree with him giving up on his desire.

"She broke a glass. I was checking to see if she cut her feet." Seb was impressed with himself, his voice sounded calm and normal. Not betraying the desire that still raged inside of him, when he looked at the little red-headed vixen sitting on the counter.

"I could have sworn that you were nowhere near her feet." He met the man's gaze directly, knowing that his body and most likely his eyes would give away what his voice had not.

"You're right, I was way out of line. Trust me, it will not happen again." Seb knew that he had no reason to believe him, hell he wasn't sure that he believed himself. Now that he had touched her, he knew that it would be a distracting battle not to touch her again, and distractions got people killed.

"Will you two calm down, nothing happened. I was foolish and broke a glass, then Seb came and put me on the counter. It was most likely my crying. Some men respond badly to seeing a woman cry, obviously Seb is one of them." It was analytical and highly plausible, but Seb knew that it was a load of crap. His body hadn't responded to her because she had been crying, he had responded to the woman herself.

"Fine, I will let it go for now, but only because we have more important things to discuss." Seb couldn't help but feel relieved that they no longer had to discuss his out-of-control passion.

"Like what?" Delilah looked like a tiny, gorgeous warrior, as she squared her shoulders, winced from the pain, and challenged her brother. The fierceness behind her actions, impressed him and turned him on. He cursed himself, for finding this woman so fascinating and attractive.

They were both staring at each other, ignoring his presence, which was probably for the best.

"Like the fact that while I was kissing Bobby goodnight, he asked when he would get to see his daddy." The anger in Max's eyes faded to reveal the pain and sympathy. "Pippy, why haven't you told him yet?"

Feeling completely out of place in the middle of this conversation, Seb searched for an out. "I need to do a quick perimeter check, unless you need my help with cleaning up." He prayed they didn't, because the mood in the kitchen had shifted, telling him this was a very private matter.

"No, you have helped enough." Max was clearly not done talking to him about touching his sister, he knew that was to be expected. "It would be best if you got back to your job, which is protecting my nephew and I will take care of my sister."

Seb only nodded his head, before walking out of the kitchen, not even pausing to grab his jacket as he strode out of the house. The cool air that had come with the sun vanishing from the sky, did nothing to tame his libido. He still wanted to run back into the house, pick up Delilah and shield her. Keep her safe from the physical pain of the glass and from the emotional pain that he saw in her eyes after hearing her brother's question.

Seb ran his hands through his hair, furious with himself for losing control.

He decided that a long walk, around the land that surrounded the house would do him good. He needed to become familiar with where they were positioned, relative to the road and the other buildings. It was time he started readying himself to do his job. A small boy's life was in his hands, and this time he wouldn't let the boy down.

Not like I did last time.

Chapter 7

Her brother had given her a reprieve from conversation, only long enough to do the dishes and clean up the glass. Max had deposited her on the sofa, swearing to her that they were going to have a serious conversation, when he was done. Delilah remembered listening to the sounds of glass being swept and then the water running, but the rest was a complete blur.

She squinted her eyes against the bright morning sun, streaming through the window, snuggling deeper into the covers that cocooned her. Delilah had not slept well at the hospital, she never slept well when she was away from Bobby. She supposed that she must have fallen asleep on the couch, she smiled as she pictured the look of irritation that must have been on Max's face. While knowing that the "talk" that he wanted to have with her could not be postponed indefinitely, she was still satisfied that she had managed to avoid it last night.

Looking at her watch told her that it was 8:30, worry shot through faster than a bullet. Bobby was a very early riser, she never slept past seven when he was with her. She bolted from bed, only to realize that someone had removed her overalls last night, leaving her in only her tube top and panties. She groaned because whether her brother or Seb had done it, either way it left her feeling embarrassed and vulnerable. Her brother hadn't seen her in her underwear since she was a child, sure she wore a bikini when they went swimming, but this felt more revealing somehow. Something told her it had to have been Max, because if it had been Seb, she would have known it. After last night she was quite sure her body would react to his touch even if she were unconscious.

She didn't have time to dwell on the unbridled passion that stormed inside of her last night, she threw on a pair of her shorts and raced down the hall. The only other bedroom was remarkably similar to her own. Consisting of a queen-sized bed, two nightstands and a dresser, all decorated in warm colors to match the wood that lined the walls. Last night while the men had made dinner, she had helped Bobby unpack his belongings, in the hopes that it would make him feel more comfortable.

Delilah's tension eased a bit, when she saw a pair of discarded argyle socks at the foot of the bed. Only her brother wore sock that horrendous looking. He must have slept with Bobby last night. She should have offered her bed to him. But she knew that her son would not have passed up on an opportunity to camp out with his beloved uncle, even for her. It stood to reason that wherever Bobby was, he was safe with his uncle. After everything that they had been through, she knew that her nagging concern would not be quieted until she saw him though.

The smell of pancakes wafted to her nose right before she heard her son's laughter, mixed with a deep throaty chuckle that sent her pulse racing.

"Mommy." Her son jumped up from the table and wrapped his arms around her, she bent down to give him a good morning kiss. She stood up with an unexpected syrup lip stick, as she licked the sugary liquid from her lips, she was not surprised when her stomach rumbled.

"Morning." It was the same passion deepened voice that had asked her questions last night, while he ran his hands over her. "Are you hungry?"

She saw him frozen in place, standing in the kitchen, staring at her. His eyes turning the same dark shade of juniper green they had last night, the look he was giving her made her wonder if his question was truly about food. It made her ask herself if she wished it was about more than food.

"You are, right mommy?" She tore her gaze away from Seb's, concentrating on her son's question.

"Who wouldn't be hungry, it smells delicious in here." She forced herself to look only at Bobby, even though she could feel Seb's gaze on her.

"It's yummy, Seb is a good cooker." Bobby's eyes shined as he looked at Seb, it looked like her son might be nursing a case of hero worship.

"Thank you, Bobby. Your brother already ate, he said something about making some private phone calls. So, he went for a walk. Sit down and I will bring you a plate, you want coffee?" His tone was lighter, more casual than his greeting had been.

"Yes please, but I can get it." She protested.

His response was sharp. "No. You sit down, I was just bringing in my own, it's no problem to bring yours' also." He tried to soften his abrupt answer with an explanation, but she had felt the refusal like a slap to the face.

She tried not to take the fact that he did not want her in the kitchen personally.

He is here to do a job, not fool around with me!

Delilah surprised herself by admitting that she didn't trust herself to be in a small space with the gorgeous man and not engage in intimate fantasies, at least in her mind.

As he set the steaming plate of fluffy pancakes in front of her. They looked perfectly golden-brown, with a pad of butter trailing a path down the side of the stack. He had put a swirl of syrup on the top. She wasted no time grabbing her fork and cutting off a good-sized bite. They tasted like the exact right balance between sugary and salty. Delilah couldn't hold back a small groan of appreciation, closing her eyes to savor the taste.

"These are the best pancakes I have ever had." She said when she finally opened her eyes.

He was staring into his coffee cup, so intently, that she wondered if there was something more interesting than coffee in there. "Thanks." Was the only response that she received; he didn't even look up to say it.

"Yeah mom, I told you they were amazing." Bobby beamed at Seb again, she was grateful when he looked up from his cup to smile at her son.

Though the smile somewhat softened his stony face, she could see it didn't reach his eyes. She took a moment while he was looking at Bobby to study the lines of his face. Seb was a very handsome man, he had strong high cheekbones. His eyes were a little rounder than almond shaped, his eyebrows were almost black, she wondered if his hair had been the same color at one point. Delilah had found his almost silver hair off putting at first, thinking it made him look older than he most likely was. Now all she could think about is whether it felt as soft as it looked. His nose wasn't completely straight, there was a slight bump, where she assumed it had been broken at least once. The lips that she could remember feeling with her fingers, were full for a man's. His face was perfectly imperfect, and she was lost in looking at him.

The rumble in her stomach saved her moments before Seb turned his gaze back to her, or else she would have been caught exploring the contours of his face.

The last thing that she wanted was for this man to think that she was attracted to him, she could just imagine him reporting back to the Hawthornes. Telling them that she was some sort of wild woman, when the reality could not be more different. She could count on one hand how many dates she had been on since her divorce. Delilah didn't really see the point in dating, she didn't want anything serious, she couldn't have anything serious. She had already proven once, beyond a shadow of a doubt that she was no good at marriage.

Most people would assume because Nate cheated on her that he was the reason that the marriage failed, but she knew the truth. Nate cheated on her because she had failed the marriage. She had abandoned him both emotionally and physically before he had strayed from their marriage. It was painful to admit, even to herself, but it was the truth.

Seb's phone lit up on the table, he casually scrolled with his finger, and then clicked it off. She hated it when people looked at their phones while eating. It was so rude.

Max walked through the door; she could tell by the dark rims around his eyes that he hadn't slept well. She tried to hide her smile, knowing that her son was a kicker and a complete bed hog. Delilah was on the verge of laughter picturing her brother being woken up by a kick to the thigh, when she met his gaze, his eyes were filled with worry.

She got up from the table, knowing that whatever had her brother so worried, most likely involved her situation. Delilah froze on the spot when she saw the worry turn to anger, not understanding its source until he looked down at her clothes and then back up at her. Giving her his customary "Really?" look.

"What?" Delilah looked at him unflinching.

"You couldn't wear clothes this morning?" Max's voice was edged in frustrated anger.

"Mommy is wearing clothes, Uncle Max." Bobby jumped to defend her, she smiled down at her little knight in shining armor.

"Not as much as she should be." Max looked down at the back of Seb's head, obviously indicating that he found her attire inappropriate around the virtual stranger.

She lifted her arm that lay immobile in the sling, paying the price for her action with a healthy dose of pain. "You try and dress yourself with this thing on, besides, I'm more covered up than if we were all swimming."

"I will help you get dressed, but what are you going to do when I'm gone." Max issued the challenge, truthfully one that she was not ready for. She had no idea how she was going to get dressed or clean herself or do any of it.

"I can help mommy." Bobby suggested his face lighting up with the prospect of being helpful. "Or we can call daddy, he loves mommy, he will help."

The innocent suggestion stole her ability to draw in air from her body, she brought her hand to her mouth, to try and stifle the emotion she felt. She and Nate had always worked hard to make sure that Bobby knew that even though they were divorced they still cared about each other. They both agreed that they made better friends than they had ever made husband and wife. But to hear her son state how much Nate cared for her, it felt like her heart was being ripped from her chest.

"Sport, why don't you take your plate in the kitchen and wash up for me and then mommy and I need to have a talk with you." Max tried to keep his voice light, but she could hear the dread under the surface.

"Am I in trouble?" Bobby's doe eyes went quickly from her to Max, trying to figure out the adults and their emotions.

"No, honey, you're not in trouble. But Uncle Max is right, we do need to talk to you." She gave him a reassuring smile that did not match the emotions raging inside of her.

"I think that I will leave you three alone for this, it seems like a family matter." Only when Seb spoke did it register that she was standing inches from him. He was still seated at the table, with her standing this closely she could practically feel the heat coming from his body.

"I need to talk to you too foxy." She could see his jaw clench, it was clean shaven this morning, her fingers itched to reach out and feel the smooth looking skin. "I walk in the house, and you aren't even a little alarmed. How in the hell can I trust you with my family?"

As Seb jaw seemed to relax, a wicked looking smile formed on his face. For whatever reason she knew that he had her brother well at hand. She had to hold back her own smile at the idea that Seb was baiting her brother.

65

Seb stood from the chair, thankfully on the side opposite from her, or else they would have been sandwiched together in the tight spot. He looked at her brother with a stone-cold calmness, that she found impressive.

"I knew it was you and might I say that spitting on people's lawns is a nasty habit." Max eyes widened, she had rarely ever seen her brother surprised, it was a novelty.

"How in the he…...?" Before finishing his sentence, the reason seemed to dawn on him. "The cameras?"

Seb's only response was to nod his head, to her he looked a little bored with the whole conversation.

"Those are government encoded cameras, may I ask how you managed to get access to the feed?" Max voice sounded as cold as ice.

"No, you may not." The finality in Seb's statement was impressive, she had never seen someone handle her brother so cleanly. Despite her own emotions, she was enjoying someone getting the better of her overconfident brother.

"All done." Bobby's broke through the tension that had been building between the two men.

"Okay, Sport, why don't we all go in the living room." Max waited for them all to start moving, Seb didn't budge from his spot. "You too, Foxy."

She looked back to see the uncertainty flash in Seb's eyes. "I don't think that's a good idea." He said.

Her brother lowered his voice, but Delilah could still hear what he was saying.

———

66

"We are about to explain an extremely complicated situation to my very small nephew. When I tell him that he and his mother are in danger, and that I cannot stay, I need him to know that he has someone here to protect him. Am I mistaken, or isn't that your job?" Max's tone invited no argument, without a word Seb followed them into the living room.

I do not get paid enough for this.

He hated himself for the callous thought, but he was trying desperately to separate himself from the emotional scene in front of him. Delilah red faced with tears continually streaming down her beautiful face, both arms wrapped around her sobbing child. Max on the other side of Bobby rubbing his back, trying his best to comfort the little boy.

Seb sat quietly in the chair opposite the couch, feeling like he was intruding on a very private moment. His training taught him to stay as still as a statue even in the most uncomfortable situations. Sure, most of that training was more geared towards painful situations, but this one was bordering on becoming so awkward it was painful.

Bobby lifted his face from his mother's bosom, Seb refused to be the Creighton that focused on the wet spot that was noticeable on the pink tube top. Just like how his loss of appetite this morning had nothing to do with his mouth going dry when Delilah walked into the dining room half naked. He really needed her to wear more than the clothing equivalent of a bikini. Between her tiny shorts and the tightly stretched piece of cotton that barely cupped underneath her clearly bra-less breasts. He agreed with her brother that it would do his sanity a world of good, if she covered up a little more.

———

67

To Seb's surprise the little boy looked straight at him, his deep brown eyes, threatened to take Seb back in time. To a time and place that Seb kept deeply buried.

His tiny voice was different than the one from the past that haunted Seb's night terrors. The difference helped him keep his mind focused on the present.

"Is Seb my new daddy?" The question was the last thing he expected the child to say, it knocked the air from his lungs, like a physical punch.

"No, sweetheart. Seb is here to protect us…. I mean you from the bad men that hurt your daddy." If Delilah was fazed by her son's question, she did not show it.

He wished she hadn't specified that he was here only to protect Bobby, he knew it was the truth, but he didn't have to like it.

"Only me?" Bobby looked at his mom, trying to understand. Then he turned his chocolate brown eyes to Seb once more, the pleading look in his eyes, made Seb's defensive walls feel like they were crumbling. "Can you protect mommy, from the bad men too?"

"No, he can't.", "Yes.", Delilah and Seb had spoken simultaneously.

Not for the first time, two pairs of midnight blue eyes looked at him with surprise and disbelief.

Bobby looked relieved, choosing to believe Seb's answer over his mother's.

He had no idea why he had said it, but as he looked at her delicate face, framed in dark rust-colored curls. Her eyes staring at him, with what looked like a million questions in their blue depths. Something about her made his protective instinct kick into overdrive, he knew that if something happened, he would not be able to choose between the two of them.

"I can pay you." Delilah looked at him, a sad desperation in her eyes, that he would do anything to see go away.

"We don't need to discuss that right now." Seb knew he wouldn't take her money or put his protection of her down on paper. It was something that he felt like he needed to do for himself, Seb was unwilling to delve into the reason behind the need.

"But we will be talking about it soon." Max was looking at him with a look of clear suspicion.

He nodded at Delilah's brother, knowing that he would have the same reaction to any man that looked at Melanie the way he knew he looked at Delilah. Seb couldn't deny that he was drawn to her, and he wouldn't apologize for it either. Nor would he let it affect the job he was here to do; he had protected many women that would turn men's heads right off their necks. But it had never changed Seb's ability to do his job, neither would Delilah.

Chapter 8

After the most awkward, gut wrenching conversation in the history of conversations, Delilah had decided to take her emotionally exhausted son up to his room and lay down with him. Leaving Seb with one angry and mistrusting brother staring at him, as if he was something to be scraped off the sole of his shoe.

"Do you care to explain, why you are suddenly so eager to protect my sister. When only last night you were the one to assure me that you are only here for Bobby's sake." Max looked at him with open hostility.

"No, I don't." Seb always found that the easiest way to hide information is to limit how much information you put out. In other words, if you don't want someone to know something, don't say anything and Seb definitely didn't want to explain his interest in Delilah to her brother.

Hell, I can't even explain it to myself!

"Well, that isn't going to work for me. I can't stick around. I am in the middle of something that cannot be put off any longer. Even though it drives me crazy, I don't have any choice but to trust you with the two people that I care about more than I care about myself." Max paused and buried both his hands in his brown hair, that was so much different than his sister's auburn curls. "Bottom line time. Will you protect my sister and my nephew?"

"Yes." Seb answered without hesitation.

Max nodded his head, then asked the question that Seb was dreading.

"Will you keep your hands off of my sister?" Max looked him directly in the eye, if he thought that would unnerve Seb, he had no idea who he was dealing with.

"Yes." He kept his face a blank slate, willing himself to hide the small doubt that lingered inside. While Max still looked like he didn't fully trust Seb, the man nodded his head in acceptance. "So, what did you find out, because the look on your face when you approached the house, well, let's just say you didn't look happy."

Max let out a slow breath, "I called in a couple of favors, but the local detectives that are working Nate's death, are keeping it pretty tight lipped so far. All I know is that they did call in a couple of guys from the gang unit. Which I guess, by the caliber of Nate's cliental and by the car that my sister described, the fact that this is all gang related was pretty obvious. I don't know. It is the most frustrating thing that I have ever done, to have to walk away from this, and somehow concentrate on my work. I just want to take Delilah and Bobby and go hide away somewhere safe."

Seb's heart went out to the guy. If it was Melanie, he didn't know if anything would be important enough to keep him from being there. Especially not work, but those are some of the perks of being self-employed. He knew from experience that Uncle Sam was way less understanding when it came to familial responsibility.

"Speaking of safety level, can you tell me exactly where we are? How long we can stay here? And who is paying for this cabin in the woods?" Seb did not have high hopes that all of his questions would be answered, but a guy could try right?

"You drove here, so trying to hide any sort of location from you would be asinine. This is a place that I use sometimes for work, and as far as your concerned I'm paying for it. Wait, unless you can bill the Hawthornes for it? No, never mind, I don't want them knowing where Delilah is." Seb interrupted Max, his interest peaked.

"What do you have against the Hawthornes?" Seb's curiosity got the best of him. They didn't strike him as the most lovable people on the planet, but they didn't seem like complete monsters.

"All I can tell you is why I personally can't stand them. Ever since my sister started dating their precious son, they have made it no secret that they thought she was not good enough for him. Then after the divorce they harped on Nate to get full custody. Saying that he couldn't trust a woman that couldn't even take care of her husband to care for a child." Max let his dislike for the Hawthornes free his tongue, probably more so than he had planned.

"Understood, now as far as the safety of this place?" Seb asked.

"It's safe, you know about the cameras. As far as the reception desk is concerned, well, let's just say, as far as they are concerned this cabin doesn't exist. You're as safe as I can make you, for now." Max looked down at his watch and cursed. "I have to go. Will you tell Delilah that I said goodbye?"

"Sure." Seb was relieved that mister watch dog was not going to be peering over his shoulder constantly. He had a job to do, and he didn't need a babysitter.

He followed Max out to the front door, the fresh smell of the outdoors surrounded him, reminding him of home. Growing up in the mountains of Northern California, woodsy scents always calmed his nerves.

"Remember what I said Foxy." Max threw the comment over his shoulder as he headed down the unmarked path to the cars. Seb knew he didn't have car, but he was sure that the spook had made other arrangements.

"Yeah, I remember. Look, don't touch." Seb smiled, intentionally trying to ruffle the spook's feathers.

He was not surprised as Max spun around. "Don't even look!"

All Seb could do was laugh at the impossibility of the idea of being stuck within four walls with a woman that looked like Delilah and not even looking. Not to mention the fact that he had already broken that rule several times, already this morning. No, Seb was not in the business of making promises that he couldn't keep. So, instead of answering Max's ridiculous command, he decided to go back in the house. He could hear Max shout something else as he walked through the door of the cabin, but he couldn't bring himself to really care what it was.

Seb looked at the dishes that still held the remains from breakfast. Between the two conversations he had just had, his appetite was dead, he could only assume that Delilah's was as well. He started clearing the table and once that was done started on the small pile of dishes. It was hard for him to understand when people left messes lying around. Maybe it was the strict Army discipline in him, but when Seb saw something that needed doing, he just did it.

He could hear her soft footfalls before he saw her enter the kitchen area. Seb mentally prepared himself to see her, standing in the same room with him, wearing basically nothing.

Hot on the heels of hearing her, he could smell her, she smelt like a meadow full of the sweetest flower. For the life of him he couldn't place what exact floral scent wafted off of her. She must have taken a shower, part of his mind let himself imagine turning around and her standing there in a towel. Needing his help, or even better, just needing him. His chastised himself thoroughly for lusting after a client.

"Is there any coffee left?" Delilah voice sent his pulse racing.

"Yeah, I put it in the carafe. It should still be hot." Seb continued to do the dishes, not ready to turn and face her.

"Oh, good." He heard her walk over to the corner that held the coffee cups on a rack and both the coffee maker and carafe. Against his better judgment, he sneaked a peek at her, while she was busy pouring her coffee.

She wore a dress, if you could truly call it that. It had no sleeves, leaving her creamy white shoulders bare and it only came down to her mid-thigh. He thanked the lord that it was billowy and not skintight, because surely that would have been true torture. This outfit was only slightly better than this morning's ensemble had been. Delilah chose that moment to whip her head around, unfortunately catching Seb watching her. Was he losing his touch? Not that he made it a habit to check out women without them knowing, usually he made sure they knew. But usually, those women weren't his clients.

"I see you got dressed by yourself." Seb could hear the hitch in his throat, and he really hoped that she couldn't.

"Well, kind of." She leaned against the kitchen counter and sipped her coffee. "I managed to take the most aggravating bath, I'm right-handed so only using my left hand to wash and shave. Let's just say if there are cameras in the bathroom, someone got a good show today." Delilah stopped suddenly and turned the deepest shade of red, he had ever seen.

Understanding where her train of thought had probably gone, he did his best to reassure her. "They do not have cameras in the bathroom." At least they better not, the idea of someone invading her privacy, made anger boil beneath the surface of his skin.

Delilah flashed a relieved smile, "Good, that would have been embarrassing." She looked down at her coffee cup, running her finger along the rim of the cup, he found the motion mesmerizing. "Anyway, it has been over 48 hours since I was shot, so I could finally get the wound wet. Even though it did hurt like hell…. I mean heck."

75

He turned from the sink that was now empty, placing the last dish on the drying rack. Seb dried off his hands, experiencing an instant concern that urged him to see her wound for himself. Her midnight blue eyes widened as he approached her, he saw the red slit that he was sure at one point had been a hole. Relief shot through him, as he saw that it was nothing more than a flesh wound. But even seeing a small wound marring her beautiful skin made him work to control his anger.

"It looks good." Steeling himself for meeting her eyes, she was watching him, warily. "I'm surprised the doctor gave you a sling for that, it looks like the bullet barely made it into your arm."

Something he had said, lit a fire in her sapphire eyes, because she stared at him ready for battle. "I don't know if you have ever been shot, but it might not look like much, but it hurts like hell…. I mean heck."

Seb stood inches from her small body; he could almost feel her anger resonating off from her. "I didn't mean to offend you. I just don't understand why the doctor would give a sling to someone with such a minor wound, but it is none of my business." He was curious why she kept correcting her bad language too, did she think it would offend him? Seb couldn't help the smile that played on his lips, at the thought.

"The sling was only to prevent me from using it as much as possible." She looked sheepish now, the fight had drained out of her quickly. Leaving behind a beautifully vulnerable woman, the anger was easier for him to handle than the fragility. Delilah looked up at him, a small smile curving her pillow like lips. "Or maybe they just got tired of hearing me curse every time I moved my arm. I'm not exactly tough, when it comes to pain. I decided to leave it off after I took a bath, it was more trouble than it was worth. Now it is up to me to remember to use my arm as little as possible."

The sound of his laughter surprised even his own ears, but the combination of the look on her face and the confession, was too much. This sweet looking angelic woman, admitting that because she curses like a sailor, they had to give her a sling. It didn't take Delilah long to join him, with her own sweet melodic laughter. He had never heard her laugh before, so he was unprepared for the heat that it caused. Seb liked hearing her laugh, he probably liked it too much.

"So, should I expect to have to plug my innocent ears every time you mistakenly reach for something." Seb joked to get his own mind off from his body's reaction to her laughter.

She snorted, he raised his eyebrow, surprised at the sound that was so incongruent with her feminine appearance. "I don't think there is anything innocent about you."

She said it so matter-of-factly, but for some reason it made Seb want to reach out and show her just how right she was. No one had ever called Seb innocent before, and his thoughts about this woman, were anything but innocent.

Knowing that he needed to clear his mind of anything remotely sexual, Seb decided to switch gears. "Do you play cards?"

He had surprised her sufficiently, she scrunched up her brow and a slight frown formed on her kissable lips.

"Yes, why?" Delilah's face was alight with curiosity, he found it adorable.

Good lord is there anything that she can do, so that I don't find her distractingly gorgeous?!

"I assume that Bobby is sleeping, and it's a way to spend the time. These types of situations come with a lot of down time, while the cops figure out who is after you and your son. My job is protecting you, so I can't very well let you die of boredom." Seb regretted mentioning the danger she was in as soon as he saw the color drain slightly from her rosy cheeks.

Even though she worked quickly to cover up her momentary fear, it still tore at his heart.

"That sounds like a good idea." Her smile lit up her face, but Seb could sense that under the surface of it, it wasn't quite genuine.

He hated the idea that she had to fake a smile, especially around him. If he had it his way her smiles would all be caused by heart felt pleasure, but he had to remind himself once again that making her smile was not his job.

Delilah was losing, just like she had lost the two previous matches of Go Fish. Even though it had been Seb's idea to play cards, she quickly learned that all he knew were games more appropriate for a casino. So, they had finally settled on the childhood classic, Go Fish. She usually played this with her son, and on most occasions, she let him win. Being a naturally competitive person, the small act of kindness did not come easily to her. But her need to win came after her need to boast her son's self-esteem. Now that she was playing the game with a grown man, she had been ready to grind him into dust.

When he had won the first game, she had chalked it up to dumb luck. The second game had been a disaster. Every time she asked for a card, he never had it, then he would in turn always ask for the right card from her. It was infuriating, she wasn't a sore loser, but something seemed fishy to her.

"Do you have an eight?" Delilah stared into his twinkling green eyes, he had laugh lines that shot out from the corners of his eyes.

"Go Fish." Humor lit his face, causing a smile to tug at the corners of his mouth. She didn't understand what he found so darn funny.

She was trying to lose gracefully, not wanting to show him how ticked off it made her. Delilah leaned forward to pluck a card from the deck, she looked up as she did so, at the man seated across from her at the table. Aha! She looked down at her strapless dress that dipped precariously low every time she reached her a card. Seb was looking straight at the exposed skin, unaware that she was watching him.

"You little cheater!" At the same time as she spoke the accusation, she took the opportunity to set her cards down and pull her slipping dress up. He looked at her with mocked innocence, but he couldn't hide the wicked light that shone in his eyes.

"I don't know what you are talking about." He shrugged his shoulders and leaned back in his chair. Seb was the picture of a relaxed sexy man, that was completely at home in his body.

"The heck you don't." She stood up and placed her hand on her hip. "If you are so innocent show me your cards."

"No." Seb's eyes darkened as he refused.

"Fine I will look for myself." Delilah was fueled with self-righteous indignation, as she rounded the table.

He held his cards tightly to his chest, watching her. When she reached for them, he held them further out to his left side. She didn't think, too wrapped up in proving that she was indeed correct. Delilah reached across his body with her left hand, essentially draping herself over him. His enter body tensed, her thighs were leaning against his. She could feel him shift slightly in his chair, almost making her slip.

"Delilah." His voice had an edge to it, that she had never heard before. Causing warning bells to go off in her mind, screaming at her that what she was doing was highly improper. She looked at him over her left shoulder, big mistake. His dark jade eyes were alight with a desire that she could feel burning into her skin. The intensity of his gaze threatened to buckle her knees. Every cell in her body urged her to press herself up against this beautiful man, wanting there to be no space between the two of them.

That is crazy, she tried to override the siren's voice that was singing in her ears. She barely knew this man. She wasn't about to sit in the lap of a man she barely knew. Delilah knew that she wouldn't, but there was no denying to herself that she wanted to.

"Delilah, if you stay this close to me, I am going to break my word and I don't ever break my word." The need in his voice was clearly evident, she felt a renewed rush of desire, that this man wanted her just as much as she wanted him. It took her a moment for his words to sink in.

Wait! His word to whom?! The Hawthornes?

The thought brought reality crashing down around her lust, reminding her who this man was and why he was here.

———

"Well, I wouldn't want to be the cause of you breaking your word." She said righting herself as elegantly as possible using one arm and avoiding touching him at all costs. "I would hate for there to be trouble between you and your employer." He started to speak but she cut him off with a wave of her hand. "No, no need to explain, I get it. They probably warned you about their whore of an ex-daughter in-law that seduced their innocent son. About me using my womanly whiles to convince their son to marry me, despite my sketchy upbringing and inferior looks." She hated it that tears were stinging her eyes, but those people made her furious.

Her breath came out of her lungs in a whoosh. One moment she was standing crying, the next she was being promptly picked up and deposited onto a very hard, very male lap. She stared at Seb's deep green eyes, trying to read what he was thinking.

"There is nothing about you that is inferior." His voice was raw sounding.

Before she could respond, he drew her hard against his chest, she could have let out a small cry from the discomfort of her arm, but the feeling was quickly swept away. Replaced by the softness of his lips as he pressed them to her own, and the feel of his hand burying itself in her hair. With his free hand, he slid it up her thigh, pulling her even closer into his body. She gasped from the pleasure his touch was causing, Seb wasted no time delving into her mouth. His tongue exploring every crevice of her mouth, he tasted of coffee and something that was very distinctly him.

She wanted to touch him, to mimic the pleasure that he was giving her. Delilah went to run her hand into his soft looking silver hair, wanting to know if it looked like it felt. Lost in the magic of his kiss and the feel of his touch, she lifted her right arm to explore him.

The soft cry that she let out against his mouth, broke the spell that they had been weaving around each other.

Seb all but jumped up from the chair, carefully placing her on her feet once more. Every spot that had been touching him, felt cold and it sent shivers up her arms. It had been so long sense anyone had touched her with such hunger, she tried to remember if she had ever felt such passion from Nate. Instantly feeling bad for comparing the two men.

"Look, I'm sorry I did that." He looked at her, studying her, obviously seeing the hurt that she was trying to hide at his apology. "Okay, scratch that, I'm not sorry. You needed to be kissed and I wanted to kiss you."

She hadn't expected the two contradictory statements. Delilah couldn't help but wonder, which one was the truth. Was he trying to be nice and not hurt her feelings, had the kiss not been as magical for him?

Delilah had no chance to ask him, as they both heard the sound of her son's piercing scream at the same time.

Chapter 9

It was impossible to keep up with the agile man, as he sped past her. Every possible fear, both rational and irrational raced through her mind. It seemed to take an unrealistically long time to run through the living room and up the staircase. Bobby's room was the first on the left. When she topped the last step of the stairs, his screaming had stopped and all she could hear were his soft sobs.

Delilah braced herself before walking into the room, knowing that she could not show any of her own fear to her young son. He needed her to be strong and reassuring, not the basket case she felt like she was becoming.

"Mo, it's okay, Rock is here." Seb's voice was soft and melodic.

Worry racked through her as she burst into the room. Seb was looking at her, but it didn't seem like he was even registering her presence, not really. It felt like he was more looking through her. He sat on the bed with Bobby curled up in his lap, gently rocking her son back and forth. Even though what he was saying made no sense, what he was doing was obviously comforting Bobby. Upon seeing that her son was in fact in one piece and safe, Delilah let out a breath that she didn't know she had been holding.

"Mo, I was so worried, I didn't know if you were okay. I shouldn't have left you, but I had no choice." She was shocked to see a tear running down the big man's cheek as he cradled her son.

"Bobby." Delilah was beginning to worry about the stability of the man, that was supposedly going to protect them. As it became clearer and clearer, that he was not there in the room with them. All she could think to do, was to get her son the hell away from him. He wasn't hurting him right now, but who knew where the trance he was in would take him.

"Mommy, I want mommy." Bobby only struggled for a moment, against Seb's grip. A moment that she held her breath, as it seemed to stretch on forever. Finally, much to her relief, Seb released her son, and he came flying off from the bed and into her arms.

She watched over Bobby's head as Seb shook his head and quickly wiped the tear from his cheek. He looked to her; she had never seen a grown man look so sad. Delilah didn't have time to debate what had happened to Seb, her first priority was trying to comfort her son.

"It's okay sweetheart." She picked Bobby up and held him in her arms. "Everything is going to be okay."

"I had a nightmare mommy, I dreamed that the bad man who killed daddy, found us." He was speaking through his gentle sobbing. "I woked up and then Rock came and hugged me."

"I know sweetheart, we heard you scream, and we both ran as quickly here as we could." She wanted to lighten her son's heart, while still validating his feelings. Delilah had given similar advice to many parents of children she had counseled, but it felt so foreign to have to use the technic on her own son. "Do you know what I found out?"

Bobby's tear-streaked face looked up at her. "What?"

"That if I'm going to keep up with Seb, I'm going to need to start running." Her son looked to Seb, who was clearly trying to gather himself, still seated on the couch. "It was like he had wings, and as soon as he heard you needed help, he flew to you."

"Like Superman?" Bobby stared at Seb, his case of hero worship getting worse as the seconds ticked by.

"Yep, just like that. Does that make you feel better, knowing that you have someone like that to protect you from the bad men?" Delilah would have believed in her words whole-heartedly before witnessing the scene she had walked in on. She would need to have a serious conversation with him, and soon. "Now, why don't you and I go downstairs and start making some lunch. You know I need your help spreading the peanut butter."

"Okay." Bobby hesitated, looking back at Seb. "Rock, are you gonna help too?"

Delilah rushed to put some space between Seb and her son, feeling like he needed to collect himself. "I think that Seb needs to walk around the outside of the house, to make sure that everything is okay. Don't you Seb?"

He looked at her, all emotion neatly tucked away again, behind a pure green curtain. "Yeah, that is a good idea."

"Do you want a sammich?" Her son's diction for the most part was excellent for a five-year-old, however the word "sandwich" still gave him trouble.

"Sure, buddy." Seb unfolded his long body from the bed and started to walk past them. "Can I have extra peanut butter on mine?"

Her heart fell when she saw the excitement that lit up her son's face, she prayed that he did not get too attached to his new bodyguard.

"Yep, I can do that." Bobby was now squirming in her arms, to get down and start preparing Seb's lunch.

She couldn't allow Seb and Bobby to form a bond, especially not until she found out what the heck had happened in this room. Because wherever Seb had been when she walked in, he most definitely was not in the room protecting her son. Delilah had to make sure that Seb was safe to be around her son and also that he was psychologically fit to do his job. Her instincts were flashing a whole group of red flags, and she would not rest until she cleared them up.

He tried to focus on the sounds around him, the birds chirping, the snap of the twigs beneath his feet. Nature had always had a calming effect on him, but as the bright California sun beat down on his back, Seb couldn't clear his mind of what had just happened.

In the back of Seb's mind there was a space that was solely dedicated to the memories of his time over-seas. When he was drunk or talking to one of his brother's that served with him, he would dredge up certain memories. But never the ones he had experienced today, no, those stayed buried. He didn't even write about them in his journal that he updated religiously. The only time those danced to the front of his thoughts, was during his nightmares. Even those were getting fewer and farther in between, which he was incredibly grateful for.

So, what the hell happened to me today?

It was a question that Seb did not have an answer for.

He tried to play back what happened, to figure out what had snapped his past to the present.

Seb heard the scream, that effectively squashed his libido, in one second flat. He thought he probably overturned the chair, he got up so quickly and ran for Bobby's room. As he ran up the stairs at a breakneck speed, he knew that he was running to make sure Bobby was safe. At the doorway of the room, Bobby had looked up at him, with his chocolate brown eyes filled with terror. As Seb took one step into the boy's room, instead of his boot sinking slightly into the thickly carpeted floor, it had hit the hard dirt covered roads of a middle eastern village that he had tried to forget.

There in the middle of the dirty crumbling village, stood a small boy, with the same sorrowful eyes, reaching out to him. Seb ran to him, admits the sound of gun fire and screaming. He sunk down onto his knees, daring the danger to be damned. Seb did the one thing in that moment that he had never been able to do in real life, he protected that boy. The boy that haunted his nights and brought the pain that he forced to lay dormant during the day.

He couldn't recall exactly what he had said to the boy, that part was too clouded to recall, but he could remember how good it felt to finally get to right his biggest failure.

That was until Delilah's sweet voice, popped the bubble he had been imagining. The look of distrust and fear that she had given him, made him extremely worried that she could see straight into his thoughts. It was terrifying to think that she knew his failures, and now would never trust him to protect Bobby. He knew that it shouldn't matter, that this was just another job. But this afternoon, it hadn't felt like that. It had felt like, maybe, if he could protect this little boy, he could somehow atone for the past. That by saving Bobby, he would be saving that part of his soul that had died the day he had failed Mo.

Walking back towards the house, Seb tried some breathing exercises to relax his body and focus his mind. They were things that his mother and grandmother swore by, something about your chakra or third eye, or some bull like that. But Seb had to admit that he had used the method several times during his career as a Ranger and during his current job also. Not that it was anything that he would ever share with his brothers at arms, they would never stop giving him crap if they knew.

When he walked back into the house, he could hear mother and son chatting at the dining room table. Trying to appear relaxed, like nothing odd had happened to him, he walked towards the table.

Bobby's shining face beaming up at him, was probably one of the best greetings that Seb had ever received. It made his heart clench, thinking that Bobby had probably greeted his dad the same way, and that his dad would never again get to feel the warmth of his son's greeting.

"I poured your milk." Bobby stated proudly, as Seb sat at the spot clearly set for him.

It did not escape his notice that the chairs were situated so that Delilah sat in between himself and Bobby. Even if that hadn't been a clear enough sign, the slightly reserved look she gave him would have been the clincher. He cursed to himself, knowing that he would have to have a serious talk with Delilah and explain.

"Thanks, buddy." It was not hard to infuse his voice with warmth when talking to Bobby, he was a really great kid.

"Mommy says that big guys don't drink milk, but I told her that you wanted it." He smiled proudly as Seb took a large drink of the ice-cold milk.

"Told, Bobby. Not teld." Delilah corrected her son.

"Right, I told her so." Bobby confirmed what he had said.

Seb watched as Delilah rolled her eyes and sighed, clearly not happy that her son had just basically said "I told you so" to her. It reminded him of the type of exchange that would have taken place between his own mother and a five-year-old version of himself.

"How do you think I got so big?" Bobby shrugged his shoulders, indicating that he had no idea. "I drank a lot of milk."

"Did you hear that mom?" Bobby gave his mother a comically serious look, trying to make her realize the import of Seb's statement.

"Yes, sweetheart, I heard it." Delilah shot him a look, that was not exactly a thank you. "But I don't think that Seb needs anymore milk, especially if it will still make him grow. Don't you think that he is big enough? I mean if he gets any bigger, he won't fit through the front door."

89

"Did you just call me fat?" Seb flashed a fake hurt look to both Delilah and Bobby.

"It's not nice to call names mom." Bobby reprimanded his mother.

"I wasn't calling him a name." Delilah was looking at Bobby defending herself, Seb took the opportunity to wink at Bobby, telling him that he was just joking.

Seb had to keep himself from bursting out with laughter, as Bobby picked up his cue so effortlessly. "I think you hurt his feelings." Bobby's pretend serious face was almost Seb's undoing.

Seb had only seconds to look as hurt as he possibly could while fighting the joviality of the situation.

"I didn't mean to hurt...." Apparently, Seb was not doing a great job at masking his emotions, because a light of recognition lit up her cobalt eyes. She looked with suspicion from Seb to her son, Bobby could no longer hold back his enjoyment at teasing his mom. His laughter was the drop that made Seb's own bucket run over, his own deeper laughter joining the small boy's. "You two, really?"

He watched her as she tried to remain serious, it was a battle that didn't last long. Soon her own sweet as honey laughter joined theirs.

Chapter 10

Lunch had led to a rematch at Go Fish, this time with Bobby. Delilah and Seb made a silent agreement to go easy on Bobby and give him a chance to win. They followed the game by playing the few board games that were at the house, some were skipped because Bobby was a bit too young for trivia. For dinner, they had leftovers from the day before, it was even better the second day. Seb insisted on doing the dishes, leaving her free to give Bobby a bubble bath and get him ready for bed.

Bobby laughed as he piled as many bubbles as humanly possible on top of his head. No, matter what weighed her mind down, Delilah could always count on her son to lighten her heart. His child like enjoyment, forced her to push aside all of her adult sized problems and let go, even if only for a moment. The lord knew she had enough adult sized problems right now to keep her permanently preoccupied.

"Mommy, look." Bobby commanded right before shaking his head and sending his bubble hat toppling both back into the bathtub and outside of it.

He looked adorable with his bright smile beaming up at her, he looked like a miniature version of his father. A thought that made her heart clench, she covered up the feeling as quickly as it came, not wanting her son to think sad thoughts before bed.

"Are you ready to get out?" She expected him to fight her, he usually did.

"Yeah, I'm sleepy." Delilah knew it shouldn't worry her, but her son was not a boy to go quietly to bed. So, his eagerness to go to bed was out of character, and she knew that she needed to watch for changes in behavior due to the trauma that he had experienced.

She was an expert at the whole pre-bedtime routine, wash and dry, brush teeth, and put on pajamas. There had been a time when every new development in her son's life was a new learning curve she had to adjust to, and she knew there would be more to come. But for now, she knew her son's routine and all the arguments he would construct each step of the way. Her worry deepened as she performed each task, with Bobby not putting up any fight. He didn't say he was thirsty or complain about which pajama she had chosen. He didn't gargle his rinsing water after brushing until she had to tell him to spit it out. It was like he was performing everything with only half his mind on it, it worried her where the rest of his young mind had wondered to.

When he was snuggled into the big queen-sized bed, it seemed like it threatened to swallow him up with its size. At home he had a fire engine red sports car bed, that Santa had got him last year. She could still hear his squeals of excitement when he had woken up to the bed in the living room. Delilah and Max had worked all night to get it set up, it had been worth it to see the look on her son's face.

"Goodnight mommy." Bobby smiled but she could tell something was bothering him.

"You know that you can talk to me about anything, right?" Delilah needed him to know that there wasn't any subject that was off limits, she wanted to know anything that worried him.

"Yes." Bobby continued to stroke the fur of his favorite teddy, Mr. Fuzzy.

"Is there anything that you want to talk about?" She was torn between needing to know what was bothering her son and dreading the big burdens that had been put upon his tiny shoulders.

"No." Bobby held Mr. Fuzzy with enough force that it almost made her concerned for his stitching.

Knowing that she needed him to talk to her in his own time, she didn't push any further.

"Okay, how about a story?" Delilah didn't feel comfortable leaving the room, until she knew that he was soundly asleep.

"Can Mr. Fuzzy be in the story?" The innocence in his question lightened her heart.

"Of course, he is going to be in it. He is the hero of the story." She assured him.

"No, I want Rock to be the hero." The statement reminded her that she had a very unpleasant conversation awaiting her. She had to make sure that this man that is supposed to be watching over her son, is no danger to her son. This afternoon's scene still sent chills down her spine, when she thought of how lost Seb looked, rocking her son on this bed.

"Okay, so Rock will be the hero and Mr. Fuzzy will be his side kick." Delilah began to tell the story, but her son interjected one more time.

"Can Mr. Fuzzy be his best friend?" Bobby asked.

"Fine, but who is telling this story?" She playfully pointed her finger at him and then at herself. "You or me?"

He rewarded her with a small giggle, "You are."

—

93

Delilah nodded, finely satisfied that they had the outline of the story ironed out, and now she was free to being her tale of adventure. She made it a point to make this story very lighthearted and as comical as possible. Leaving the good versus evil premise for a day where they weren't actually battling something that was a little too similar.

The day felt impossibly long to her as she made her way downstairs. She knew that it wasn't over yet, that the most awkward part was yet to come.

More awkward than that kiss earlier?

Okay maybe not the most awkward, but definitely a part of the day she would rather avoid. Seb was seated on one of the overstuffed couches in the living room, he was on the phone. She didn't want to interrupt, so she went straight to the kitchen, deciding to make herself some tea. If she was honest with herself, her son was not the only person that was having frazzled nerves. Maybe some herbal tea would help to calm her down.

With her steaming hot cup of tea sending delicious aromas of hibiscus and chamomile, wafting up to her nose, she took a deep breath in. Trying to will the tea to take effect even before it was cool enough to drink. Delilah walked back into the living room, relieved to see that Seb was done with his phone call. She was looking at him through the steam rising from her mug, it was like he was an image from a dream.

She almost snorted, because Seb was the definition of a dream looking man. Most women would not balk about having him stroll into their dreams, take them in his strong arms, and claiming their lips with his soft mouth. A mouth that she could remember as tender and passionate. Delilah shook off her lusty memories, reminding herself that she needed to talk to him and not about the kiss they had shared.

94

"How is Bobby?" Seb's question helped her to come back to the topic they needed to discuss.

She took a seat on the couch that stood opposite from his own, suddenly kicking herself for only making tea for herself and not even offering any to him.

"I don't know how he is, and it is driving me crazy. As his mother I want to hound him until he talks to me about everything that is on his mind, but as a counselor I know that I have to give him space to come to me. If I push too hard, he is liable to shut down completely. Which could lead to a lot of problems." She took a deep breath and remembered her manners. "Did you want tea? I didn't ask because you were on the phone." She lied.

He curled up one side of his mouth, causing the skin around his nose to wrinkle slightly, and shook his head no. Usually, he looked hard and sexy as sin, but the face he made him look adorable. She was prepared for broody, masculine, and gorgeous, not for adorable.

"No thanks, I hate tea." Seb got up, she was unsure what he was doing and for a moment allowed herself to envision him coming over to her. What he would do once he got to her, she couldn't imagine, but the very thought sent chills racing down her limbs. "I'm going to grab some coffee."

So much for anything that she was attempting to picture, Delilah could almost laugh at herself. He had apologized for kissing her earlier, she would do well to remember that. Even though he took it back right afterward, it was his first response. When a man kisses you and then immediately regrets it, that was rarely a good sign. To be fair she hadn't been with anyone since Nate, so maybe she was just rusty.

I will be better the next time.

———

95

She scolded herself immediately for the wayward thought, there would not be a next time!

Delilah was saved from her own rebellious thoughts, when Seb returned from the kitchen. She couldn't help but notice that there was no indication of heat coming from the top of his mug. "Is that coffee from this morning?"

"Yes, it is, you want some?" He raised one dark eyebrow at her, his face once again comically adorable.

She knew her face showed her own signs of disgust, making him chuckle. "No, thanks. I think I will stick to my tea. You enjoy your cold bean juice."

"Oh, I will, and you enjoy your steaming cup of leaf water." His smile was infectious, as he returned to his previous seat on the couch.

It was so nice relaxing after the day they had, she hated to bring up something that was going to completely terminate the pleasant mood. But she knew that she had too.

"Listen Seb....... what kind of name is that anyway?" She shouldn't let herself get distracted from what they really needed to discuss, but she would allow the neutral subject to help them ease into more serious topics.

"It is short for Sebastian." His eyes studied her so intently, she felt like she was under a microscope.

"Oh, I like that, does anyone call you Sebastian?" She asked curiously.

"No." His response was more factual than curt.

———

"Not even your mom or dad?" Delilah pried a bit further.

"I wouldn't know if my dad would call me that because I never met him. My mom is the one that gave me the nickname Seb, I was named after my grandfather. So, in order to not have two Sebastians running around, I became Seb." Seb's whole face softened when he spoke of his family, his green eyes warmed with affection.

Delilah knew it was none of her business, but the woman in her wanted to know. The woman that had sat on this man's lap and been thoroughly kissed. "What about a girlfriend? Does your girlfriend call you Seb too?"

The warmth drained from his face at the question. "Do you honestly think that I would have kissed you, if I had a girlfriend?"

The hurt that quickly flashed in his eyes, made her regret her question instantly.

"You did apologize." She defended her reasoning.

"That's true, but if you recall, I took that back as quickly as possible." Seb looked irritated to be reminded of the situation earlier. "Men don't go around kissing women and then apologizing if they have girlfriends."

"Some do." The response slipped out before she could hold it back.

"No, not real men." There was a finality to his statement.

Delilah was regretting every bringing up the subject, she knew that she needed to switch gears and she needed to do it quickly.

"Who were you on the phone with?" Once again, she was skirting around what she really needed to talk to him about, but this time it was less about strategy and more about morbid curiosity.

She knew that she had caught him off guard, by the telltale eyebrow that shot up.

"You are very direct, aren't you?" If she didn't know better, she would have thought that there was a thread of respect in his question.

"I have been told that I can be, when the situation calls for it." She tried not to sound prideful, failing terribly.

"And you think this situation calls for it?" She was frustrated that she was the one with the questions and yet somehow, he had become the one asking them.

"Yes, I do." Delilah took a sip of her now cooled tea before continuing, needing the time to best formulate her answer. "You show up on my doorstep, saying that you are here to protect my son. Telling me you were hired by the Hawthornes, who hate my guts. I have no way to verify who you are besides calling them, but that is not something I really want to do. Then there is what happened earlier today in Bobby's room, and to be honest with you, I don't know if I can trust you."

She looked at him, for any show of emotions as she spoke, but his face had become the blank slate that she had seen him apply on several other occasions. It was frustrating as hell how this man could shut down and hold everything inside.

"It sounds like we have a long night ahead of us." His tone was flat.

This time Delilah did snort, thinking how ironic it was that she was sitting feet away from a sexy man and their plan was to stay up all night and talk.

Chapter 11

Forcing himself to remain in control of his emotions, he prepared himself to answer any questions that Delilah had ready for him. He knew after this afternoon that she would need to speak with him, but that didn't mean he was looking forward to it.

"No, we don't have all night." She corrected him.

"You have somewhere to be?" He meant it to be funny, she didn't even crack a smile.

"Yes, actually." Delilah raised her chin slightly up defiantly; it was hard to concentrate when she looked so damn adorable. With her shapely legs curled up underneath her, both her delicate hands wrapped around the mug that sat in her lap. At some point she had taken her dark red curls out of the confinement of her ponytail. He noticed when she was nervous, as she was now, she ran her hand through the silky ringlets. Leaving utter chaos in her wake, it made him picture how she would look on top of him, wild curls bouncing rhythmically up and down. He took a long swallow of his cold coffee, trying to curb his pleasure ridden thoughts.

"Where would that be? Because you are not leaving this house." Even though he was trying to keep his voice calm, there was a distinct edge to the warning.

"Of course, I wouldn't leave my son." Delilah cobalt eyes lit with defensive fire.

The unspoken part of that sentence hung in the air like an uncomfortable weight.

Of course, I wouldn't leave my son......with you.

If he was going to successfully protect both mother and son, he would not be able to do that if she didn't have any trust in him.

She broke the silence first. "I just don't want to leave him alone too long; I'm worried he will have another bad dream. It was a very traumatic day for him, I can't imagine losing my father at such a young age."

He couldn't imagine having a father, at any age really. But he did understand about loss, the mental list of faces he would never see again flashed to the forefront of his mind. Some were of his friend's faces smiling or of good times, some were covered in blood-almost unrecognizable. Seb focused on the situation at hand, he couldn't fix the past, but he could help these people.

"Yeah, he took it better than I thought a five-year-old would have, he is a tough kid." Seb didn't even try to keep the admiration from his voice.

"He is, but I don't really think that it has hit him yet." She ran her hand through the crazy curls again, this time leaning back against the couch. The movement thrust her breasts forward, he almost groaned, his mouth longing to taste her.

Is she trying to kill me?

"Maybe, were he and his father close?" Seb didn't need to know the dynamic between father and son to do his job efficiently, but he was curious.

Her lips curled down slightly at the corners; he could see she was holding back tears. Who held this woman when she cried, who listened to the trauma she had been through? Seb felt an urge to go to her and wrap his arms around her, it wasn't the first time the urge had hit him.

101

"They were remarkably close. Nate was a good father. He always worked with me about making sure that for all the important things in Bobby's life he would have both his mother and father present." Her deep blue eyes filled with a tenderness, that made jealousy rear inside of Seb. He told himself that he could not be jealous of a dead man, especially one that hadn't been married to her for four years. His body tensed despite his reasoning skills.

Delilah physically shook her head, sending her curls swaying in many directions, thoroughly distracting him. He longed to just grab one of those soft curls in his fingers, while he let his hands slide up…

"How did you do that?" Delilah's question destroyed his fantasy.

"Do what?" Seb asked.

"I had a bunch of questions for you, and here I am wasting time talking about my life." She eyed him like she was expecting him to admit to some sort of magic trick. The truth was, when someone wanted to talk, Seb found it easier to just let them. Most of the time, people would let their words run wild and they tended to forget all about the original topic. Obviously, Delilah was not one of those people. "You are the one that needs to answer the questions, Seb."

She said his name with such venom, he tried not to take offense to it. "Do you not like my name?" Delilah gave him an angry glare, that he dared to ask another question without first answering any. "Okay, okay, I'm sorry. How about we make a deal?"

"What kind of deal?" She asked warily.

"A question for a question, an even exchange of information." Seb issued it like the challenge that it was, not knowing if he hoped she would decline or accept.

"Fine, but ladies first." He grinned, breaking the blank slate that he had been putting up. After he nodded his head, accepting her terms, he prepared himself for her first question. "What happened this afternoon? In Bobby's room."

Damn! She couldn't start with an easy one!

He took a deep sigh, not wanting to look into the deep blue pools that were her eyes, he chose to look down at his coffee cup.

"I had a flashback. I can't really explain why, other than the fact that Bobby reminds me of someone and for a moment I was in the past. It has never happened before, and it will not happen again." Seb knew that he was making a promise he didn't know if he could keep, but he wanted Delilah to trust him so badly.

"Is that who Mo is?" Delilah asked.

"Who Mo was, and yes, the person that Bobby reminds me of was named Mo." He looked up, trying to prepare himself for whatever emotion he saw on her face. The look of sympathy cut him like a sharp knife, he didn't want this woman to feel sympathy for him. Seb didn't want anyone's sympathy. "Now it is my turn, and I get two questions." He waited only moments for her to nod her head in agreement, before continuing. "First question. Why did you get a divorce?"

He saw the effect of his question, as she sucked in a breath and her cheeks colored the most beautiful crimson.

"I ruined our marriage." The confession looked almost painful, making him regret his question. "I'm afraid I was not very good at being a wife."

Bullshit! He didn't believe that for one second, it felt like she was reciting someone else's opinion, not the truth.

"Is that what he told you, when he left you?" He barely had a grip on the rage that was tearing through him, what kind of man would say such a thing?

"I left him." Delilah was not making eye contact with him, but he could see the shame written all over her beautiful face.

"Why?" Seb's voice was thick with emotion, he felt himself almost leaning forward, wanting to go to her and hold her.

"Oh no, you don't, that was two questions." Her smile was forced, and it didn't come close to making her sapphire eyes twinkle. "It's my turn. Did the Hawthornes warn you not to touch me?"

He wasn't prepared for the question at all, thinking about the kiss from earlier was the last thing he needed right now. Seb was barely restraining himself from going to her and knew that if he did move closer to her, he wouldn't be able to keep his hands to himself.

"No, it wasn't the Hawthornes." Seb's answer was far from complete, but he didn't really want to elaborate.

"Who was it?" Delilah asked, apparently not even trying to adhere to the rules of the game. "Don't look at me like I'm asking too many questions, I don't care."

Good lord she was a ball of fire, staring him down, making him aroused with her passion. He wanted this woman; he had spent two days with her and both days he had managed to touch her. Seb knew himself well enough to know that he was in serious trouble.

"It was your brother." He hated throwing Max under the bus, but when it came to the ire of a strong woman, it was every man for himself.

"You promised my brother not to touch me?" Her tone was one of disbelief.

"He actually wanted me to not even look at you, but I knew I couldn't keep that promise." Seb was not proud at how quickly he broke the promise he had made.

"You didn't keep the other promise either." Delilah's voice seemed to drop an octave, deeper, sexier. "Why did you break your promise?"

Because I want you! Because it is taking all of my self-control not to rip off all your clothing and take you right here on the couch.

"I don't know, okay? It was unthinkably dumb. I can't go around kissing people that I am being paid to protect. I can't let myself feel their silky-smooth legs in kitchens or fantasize about what it would feel like to…." *Good God, have I lost my ever-loving mind?! How about, I can't make embarrassing confessions, to my client. Especially when I am on fire with need for her.*

Her eyes were round orbs as she stared at him, "To what?" It came out as a husky whisper.

She was playing with his last thread of self-control. It had been too long since he had wanted a woman this badly. Hell, he didn't think he had ever reacted to a woman on such a carnal level.

"You know damn well, what I want to do to you." It came out as a growl, the passion that he was holding back, threatening to burst forth.

"The look in your eyes, it's like you want to eat me." Her voice was awed with curiosity.

105

He couldn't help but laugh, she could not be as innocent as she looked right now. She had a child for God's sake, she had to know everything that a man would want to do to her.

"Among other things, yes." Delilah mouth opened in a silent "O", as she realized what he was saying. A bright red blush lit up her face, shocking him.

"Well, it seems like we may have a problem, Sebastian." The way she said his name, melted away the last thread of restraint he had been clinging to.

He rose from his couch and set his coffee cup down. In two strides he was standing before her. Seb used his finger underneath her soft chin to lift her face, wanting to drink in every expression she made.

"Tell me." His voice was rough with need. "What problem do we have?"

"I want you too." She didn't need to say it, once she had looked at him with her bright eyes burning with passion, he was a goner.

Seb dropped to his knees in front of her. He buried his hand deep in her velvety curls, forcing her mouth forward, covering it with his own. This time she opened to him immediately, her tongue meeting his thrust for thrust. Their tongues danced in eagerness to explore each other, she tasted of herbal sweetness, like honey. Good lord this woman tasted as good as she looked.

He moaned as he felt her hands slide up and down his back, Seb broke the kiss, only to trail a path of kisses over her jaw and down her soft neck. He ran his tongue along her collar bone, delving his tongue into the divot that lie in the middle of her neck. She seemed to be melting backward onto the couch, as she groaned and dug her nails into his back.

Running his hand over her pebbled nipple, he felt himself harden to a painful level, his erection pressing against the zipper of his jeans. He slowly traced the outline of each of her needy peaks with his finger, his need to take them into his mouth, only heightened by his delay. When he moved to slip down the strap of fabric, he wondered to see that she wasn't wearing a bra. Her proud perfectly rounded breasts jutted out, as she arched her back under his gaze. The rosy tips calling out for his attention, he bent his mouth to take the sweet pebble into his mouth. Seb heard her cry out as he flicked her nipple with his tongue, as he started to increase the pressure of his sucking, she began to writhe against him.

She unwrapped her legs, he knew instinctively what she wanted, to have less space between them. It was what his body was aching for also, with both hands he cupped her bottom. With a slight squeeze he pulled her forward, needing her small body pressed to his own.

The sensation of warm liquid spreading against the fabric covering his erection, made him stop dead in his tracks. At first, he had almost thought that his excitement had gotten away from him, the level of need he felt, made this almost a possibility. But the fact that he was still rock hard and throbbing with the need for release, meant that the liquid that now soaked him, hadn't come from him.

"Oh, no!" Delilah's exclamation, followed by her movement to right her spilt teacup, made him feel like an idiot.

Chapter 12

He jumped back faster than if the tea had still been hot. Delilah wasted no time, tugging her dress back up, to cover her exposed breasts. Her body was still on fire from his touch. She felt unnaturally cold now, in all the spots that her skin had previously been pressed to his. There was a part of her that wanted to continue despite the minor spill, but she knew that it would not be wise. Most likely the whole intense attraction was brought on by the extreme stress they were under. She had heard that such things could happen. Delilah had always felt like the idea was total bunk, until now.

There really was no other way to explain the tingle in her skin when he touched her. It was like his fingers held secret powers that spoke directly to the sex of her. With a mere brush of his skin, he seemed to bring her body to life in a way that she had never felt before. To counter-act the part of her that wanted to dive into the uncharted water, there was a current of fear. She felt like her body's reaction to him, was too strong, especially considering how long they had known each other.

Yeah, it must be trauma related, there was no other explanation.

"That cooled us off, didn't it?" Delilah wanted to lighten the mood, and also establish that what had just happened, could not happen again.

He turned from where he was standing, looking out the window into the dark night.

"Yes, it did." He ran his hand through his silver hair, her fingertips still longed to feel the silky strands again. "I will have to tell the Hawthornes, and if I'm lucky they will agree to my partner replacing me. If not, then they will most likely find another company to protect Bobby."

She felt guilty for the part that she had played in the kiss. For the part of her that had moaned into his touch, instead of pushing him away and demanding propriety. A thread of panic cursed through her at the idea that Seb would be sent away, and that the Hawthornes would find out that it took less than two full days for her to compromise their employee. It would only confirm everything they thought of her. That she was some sort of master seductress, that could not be trusted with the male sex. Delilah knew that she could not let them find out, no matter what it took.

"Please, don't tell them." She looked into his deep green eyes, knowing her own were filled with genuine pleading. Seb's eyebrow raised as he studied her openly, she tried not to squirm under his intensity.

"Why?" He showed no emotions, the eyebrow his only show of curiosity. "Don't you think that they have the right to know, that I can no longer be trusted to protect you or your son."

"They never wanted you to protect me in the first place, and I think that you are the best possible person to protect Bobby." Delilah was surprised that despite her earlier suspicions she was speaking the truth. There was something so uncalculated about his responses to her questions, a raw quality to the pain that she had seen in his eyes when he had spoken about Mo. Even though she still didn't fully understand what his relationship was to Mo, she had a feeling that Bobby reminding Seb of Mo would only make Seb protect her son with more verve. "I trust you to protect my son."

There was a warmness that softened his emerald gaze, it was fleeting, but she saw it.

"I appreciate that, but do you trust me to keep a clear head around you?" Seb asked.

"We can do better to refrain from touching each other, I'm sure you have protected people prettier than me." A truly sickening idea hit her. *Did he kiss them too, was this a regular thing for him?* "Unless this has happened before."

There was a heat burning in his eyes when he heard her speculation. "No, I have never been inappropriate with a client before. I have been hired to protect gorgeous women before, but never once did I touch them."

She wanted to believe him, she wanted to believe that compared to those gorgeous women there was something special about her. The idea wasn't congruent to the facts though, she knew that she was not a breathtaking woman, Delilah had been referred to as cute and once elfin, probably due to her coloring. But never gorgeous, not even by Nate. She had been to enough society events during her brief marriage to know that when it came to the upper-class women, she just didn't measure up.

It was nice of him to try and make her feel special, or maybe he was just trying to appear innocent of previous wrongdoing. It really didn't matter either way.

"That settles it then, it is a fluke. So, if we ignore it and don't feed into it, it will just go away." Delilah knew that her feelings would not be so easily pushed aside, but maybe Seb's would be more easily restrained.

"Okay, one more chance, but if I mess up again, I'm resigning." Seb's voice was reluctant but firm, a wave of relief washed over her. "And I won't mention it to the Hawthornes, but what about your brother?"

"What about him?" Delilah could feel her anger flare, at the thought that Max had any right to control her sex life or lack thereof. "It is none of his business, whether we jump into bed with each other or not, he is the last person we need to worry about."

"If you say so." Seb did not look convinced.

"I do." Delilah used her firmest tone, to emphasize her determination at keeping her brother out of her love life. "With all of that settled, I think it is time for bed."

"You're right, it's been a long day." Seb sighed; she understood his exhaustion.

"You can sleep in my bed if you want." As soon as the suggestion had made it past her lips, she regretted the way it sounded. The look of hunger that lit Seb's eyes, indicated that he had misunderstood her meaning. "I mean, I'm going to sleep with Bobby tonight, in case he has another nightmare. So, if you want to, you can sleep in my bed……without me in it…of course."

If she hadn't felt like a total fool rambling on, the look of amusement on Seb's face, would have made her feel so.

"As long as you aren't going to be anywhere near the bed, I think that will be safe." She stuck her tongue out at him, knowing that there were far more mature responses to his teasing. It was something that she would have done to her brother, maybe if she started treating Seb more like her brother, she would be less likely to want to jump his bones.

Making her way upstairs, she could hear the gentle rumble of his very masculine laughter. The sound made her feel like tiny bursts of flame were licking up and down her skin. Leaving traces of fire in their tiny wake, efficiently igniting her passion that she had managed to keep dormant for all of five minutes. She moaned in frustration, treating Sebastian like a brother, seemed like an impossible task.

Seb awoke well before Delilah and Bobby.

Could you call it waking up if you never went to sleep?

No, he didn't think you could.

He had spent all night tossing and turning, unable to keep the images of an imp of a woman, half naked and staring at him with more passion than he had ever seen in a woman's eyes. It didn't help that the bed he was fighting to sleep in smelled like being wrapped in her scent. It was still a honey dipped flower that he could not place, but every intake of breath last night had been torture. Seb swore it was the sweetest scent he had ever smelled.

Then there was the memory of the taste of her mouth, and her rosy peaked breasts, how did a woman taste like honey?

He groaned to himself as he pushed the button on the coffee maker to start it percolating, needing caffeine this morning more than he had in a while.

Good lord he hoped that they would figure out who was after Delilah and Bobby quickly, because the woman was a special kind of torture to him. He knew that no matter what Delilah thought, his feelings for her were not willing to be ignored. Seb had finally given up last night and allowed his mind to fantasize about her, putting the two of them in every possible romantic situation and several different positions. Hoping that if he let his imagination run away with itself, that the real thing would dull in comparison. He wouldn't know if it had worked until Delilah woke up, and if it didn't, that meant he spent over half the night with a painful erection for nothing.

Forcing himself to let go of his ever-present fascination with Delilah, he picked up his phone to try and call his partner. He had tried to get ahold of him last night, but Cody's phone had been on do not disturb. Seb knew that Cody could take care of himself, he had been a Marine and seen his share of action. He smiled at Cody's possible reaction to him even thinking the words "had been a Marine", Cody would cut him off faster than he could blink. Reminding Seb that once you are a Marine, you are always a Marine. His volatile reaction to the phrase made it too tempting to not say it incorrectly sometimes, just so you could watch Cody lose his mind.

He waited patiently while the phone rang, Seb knew better than to worry, but he had his own problems he needed to talk about. He had promised Delilah not to tell the Hawthornes, but he had made no such stipulation regarding his partner. Cody depended on him to keep a clear mind and do his job, if he had any doubts about his ability to do so, he owed it to him to come clean.

"What?" Cody's scratchy voice asked.

"Did I wake you up?" Seb couldn't keep the enjoyment at teasing him out of his voice.

"Hell no, I haven't even gone to bed yet. You do know that there is a time difference, right?" He felt like a total idiot, he had forgotten last night that Cody was in England. So, it would be late at night over there right now.

"That's right, so that is why you didn't answer your phone last night." He guessed that made sense, but it was still weird that his phone had been off completely.

Seb could hear his partner and friend sigh, "No, that is not why. My phone was in a certain debutant's tiny sparkly purse. I just got it back about an hour ago."

Cody had been assigned to watch over a filthy rich English woman, Seb couldn't remember exactly but she was something like 27th in line for the crown. He had no idea how the English kept that crap straight; it was enough to give you a headache.

"You let her have your phone?" He asked in disbelief.

"No, I didn't know she had taken it." Cody admitted.

"You left your phone somewhere that she could take it?" This was getting more bizarre by the second, Cody was a stickler for detail. Seb could not imagine him being so reckless.

An even deeper sigh followed by a curse. "Listen she isn't what she seems okay? At first, she is all chestnut brown hair that hangs down to her ass, with amber colored eyes, I swear to you the most innocent damn eyes you have ever seen. Then the next thing I know, I can't find my phone, and she slips out of the hotel room. There is a whole gaggle of weirdos trying to kill this woman, but she manages to lose me, just so she can go to some party. By the time I finally tracked her down, I was ready to throttle her." He hesitated before continuing. Seb knew he looked like an idiot, standing in the kitchen his mouth hanging open, shocked at his friend's tale. "So, all things considered, the fact that I tied her to a chair isn't that unreasonable, right?"

"You have our client tied to a chair, against her will?" Seb asked, not trusting what he was hearing.

"Yeah." Cody sounded ashamed of himself.

"That kind of sounds like the sort of thing bad guys do. Something that the people you are trying to protect her from would do. Don't you think?" Seb tried to keep the humor out of his voice, but he was on the verge of busting out into laughter. The idea that his tightly wound partner, had lost his cool, was inconceivable.

"I know that Rockmiller, I don't need you to tell me that." Cody must have heard how much Seb was enjoying this, and he wasn't happy being the butt of a joke. "But this woman, you don't understand, she is driving me crazy."

"Listen to me West, untie her, and apologize." Seb's voice was stern, trying to verbally shake some sense into his friend. "You haven't done anything else, like anything inappropriate have you." Part of him wanted his answer to be yes, it would make his own confession way easier.

115

"Like what? Isn't tying her up inappropriate enough for you?" Cody asked.

"It just sounds like this woman has managed to…. ruffle your feathers…. I was just wondering if you have let your feelings get involved. Or maybe the way you described her; you might have kissed her." He was fishing, fishing to save his own ass.

"Good lord no! Do you honestly think for a second that I would go that far off the rails? I would never abuse the trust placed in us; you know that." Each word Cody spoke was like a fresh dagger to the heart.

Guilt lay heavily on Seb's shoulders, he knew what he should do, but he couldn't bring himself to do it. Instead, he took the cowards way and lashed out at his friend with anger.

"I'm sorry but the last time I checked, our clients do not pay us to tie them up and keep them hostage from innocent parties." Seb heard his friends soft swear as his words hit home.

"You're right." Cody sounded like a man defeated, and tired. "I need to go clear everything up with Ms. Innocently Wicked, did you need to speak with me about anything else?"

This was his chance, to come clean, to confess everything. What he needed to say was, "You should take me off from this assignment, because when I'm around Delilah I can't think straight. Oh, and I basically mauled her in the living room." What he did say was, "Nope, just checking in with you. Mine is smooth sailing."

Cody snorted. "Well, I'm glad that one of us is doing a good job."

After saying goodbye, Seb reached for a cup and filled it with coffee, wishing it were something stronger.

116

"Is that for me?" He heard her words at the same time that her floral scent hit him.

Freesia, that was the flower! The woman smelt like a bouquet of freesias.

Turning, bracing himself for the jolt of excitement that hit his body whenever he saw her. She was smiling up at him, her deep red curls an absolute mess from sleeping. Her lightly freckled face was clean of the little make-up she usually wore, it looked as fresh as a spring morning. She wasn't dressed, all Delilah seemed to have on was a huge T-shirt, that looked like it might have belonged to an ex-boyfriend. He wanted to rip it off her little body, and not just because he could remember vividly what the top half of her looked like naked. No, the idea of her wearing another man's shirt made his blood boil, an unhealthy jealousy surging in his heart. *How in hell am I going to make it through this?!*

Chapter 13

"Sure, I just poured it." His voice came out similar to that of a toad, but it was the best he could do.

"Thanks for the coffee." She came to him to grab the mug, he set it down on the counter, determined to avoid all possible contact. Using the pretense of getting another mug for himself to explain his sudden decision. If she thought it was weird, she didn't show it.

"You're welcome." He looked out the window and took a sip of the piping hot coffee. "How did Bobby do last night? I didn't hear anything, so I was hoping the little guy got some sleep."

"He slept very well, thank goodness." He could see out of his peripheral, her roll her shoulders while she yawned. "His mother on the other hand, will have bruises from where he was practicing his martial arts in his sleep."

He chuckled at the image she created. "That bad huh?"

"Uhm, worse." Her laugh sounded almost sweeter than her skin tasted. Was there anything about this woman that he wouldn't find desirable as hell? "About our conversation last night."

Seb took a huge gulp of coffee and instead of waiting for it to cool before swallowing, he swallowed quickly, allowing the burning sensation to distract him from his uneasiness. "What about it? Have you changed your mind? Because I can call in someone else." It would be a relief to him if she had, then he wouldn't have to be tortured anymore. At the same time though, he protectively didn't want her to be anyone else's responsibility.

"No, I haven't changed my mind." She stood beside him on the counter, her proximity was distracting at the very least. "I just wanted to say thank you for not giving up on us. I know I was a bit reluctant in the beginning." Seb snorted at her description of her attitude when they first met. "Okay a lot reluctant, but Bobby seems to be comfortable around you, and right now I think that that is the most important thing. So, I'm glad that we can put aside a few kisses, and concentrate on the problem at hand."

A few kisses?! Is that honestly how she thought of their attraction?

It hurt ridiculously to hear her trivialize the pull between them, he knew that it wasn't just one sided. Seb had felt her body's reaction to his touch, she had been a puddle of lust beneath his fingertips.

If she wanted to play it cool, like what was lingering between them was no big deal, so could he. Hopefully.

"You're right, it was just a couple kisses, not a big deal." He heard the falseness in his words, he prayed she didn't. "It's not like either of us are sweet little virgins, that haven't done things a whole lot more exciting than kiss someone."

"Exactly, we are experienced adults." Delilah voice was determined, almost like when someone is trying to sell something that even they don't believe in. It made Seb wonder just how experienced she was, who besides her ex-husband and himself had tasted the sweet nectar of her skin.

"I was thinking that we could go for a walk and then maybe grocery shopping." It was the first time he had addressed her, while chancing to look into her gem-colored eyes. He fortified himself for the hunger that burned inside him. "Unless you would rather stay here? It would be safer for you to stay inside, until this whole thing is over, but most people have a hard time with that."

She nodded her head running her finger around the rim of her coffee cup, just like she had done last night with her tea. "I'm one of those people, I get cabin fever easily. Plus, I want to behave as normally as possible for Bobby. Even though this is all about as far from normal as you can get."

He grinned, "Oh it can get farther from normal." Thinking back to all his "travel", none of it for pleasure, all of it pretty damn far from normal.

Understanding lit her blue eyes, "I guess this is pretty normal for you."

"I don't even know if I have a normal anymore." The words sounded bleak, but to him they were just the simple truth.

"I can't imagine living like that. I enjoy getting out of the house, but only because I know I have a home to come back to. Taking pleasure in the occasional excitement doesn't make me appreciate all the hidden gems of just being at home, safe and sound any less." She said wistfully.

He couldn't help himself. "You are taking pleasure in being here?" The intimate words passing through her velvety soft lips was enough to make his groin tighten.

"Nope, none at all." Seb whipped his gaze to hers so quickly it almost made his head swim.

None at all? Was she honestly trying to say that she felt no plea...?

Then he saw it, the small upturning at the corners of her lush mouth, her blue eyes dancing with laughter that she was clearly trying to hold back. Seb was sure that his reaction to her comment was obvious, by the amount of humor she was finding in it he knew that his shock had shown.

"You little lying imp." She looked the picture of beautiful elfin mischievousness.

Her laughter filled the kitchen. "I had you going though, didn't I." Delilah face was shining with happiness at her joke, she playfully poked him in the arm.

"Yes, you had me going." He admitted.

Seb wished that he found the look on her face and the small contact of her finger hilarious, but unfortunately that was not the feeling that it ignited inside him. He allowed his true feelings to show, knew as he looked at her that his eyes were aflame with the desire that he felt for her. Delilah stopped laughing upon seeing the emotions swirling in his eyes.

"Umm, maybe I should go get dressed." Delilah squeaked out the words.

"That is probably a good idea." Seb decided he needed to work off, some of the sexual energy. "I'm going to go for a run, stay inside until I get back."

"Okay." She all but ran from the kitchen, making him feel like a hungry lion, watching his breakfast prance away. If she thought that standing in the kitchen half naked, teasing him, while looking like she just rolled out of bed was helping him keep his hands off of her. She was dead wrong.

"Mommy I found the biggest one!" Her son squealed with happiness. In his small hand he held up a pinecone, that was so big it dwarfed the hand that was holding it.

"You found the biggest one, so far." Seb's taunting challenge made Bobby laugh. "Don't think for a second that I am accepting defeat."

After a quick breakfast of cereal, they all set out on a walk through the wooded area surrounding the cabin. It was cool and peaceful under the canopy of green, it was almost serene enough to make Delilah forget why they were here and the danger they were in. Almost.

"Why the serious face?" Seb fell into step alongside her, as her son raced ahead searching for an even bigger pinecone. "Don't tell me that you are that invested in our game. I will let him win if I have to." His humor seemed to make him look so much younger, not to mention devastatingly handsome.

"No, you don't have to let him win, being a good loser is just as important as being a good winner." Could she sound more matronly if she tried? "And of course, I am invested in the biggest game of find the world's largest pinecone that has ever been played. People will be talking about this event for years to come. I wouldn't be surprised if it made it into the history books."

"Oh, good, for a moment there I thought you didn't appreciate the importance of the game." His green eyes seemed to be lit from the inside, making them appear lighter than normal. "So, what are you worrying about then?" Seb's tone lost its' humor and became serious.

She sighed, they were having such a good morning, she didn't want to be a bummer. "Everything I guess." She admitted. "What we are going to do without Nate, when will we be able to get back to our normal lives, and of course the biggest issue, who is threatening us and why? You know, just regular everyday concerns."

"I get that, I'm sure that you miss Nate very much." Seb was keeping his voice low, so that Bobby couldn't hear. She found it smooth and soothing.

"Yes, I miss him. We were always very good friends. Even after the divorce, maybe more so after it actually." She had never spoke the words out loud, but she had known for a while that she and Nate had made much better friends than anything else. "I expected Bobby, to wake up this morning, crying, or screaming for his father. My instinct tells me that he is a hairs breadth away from having a total melt down. I feel like I'm walking around watching the person I love the most in this world on the edge of devastation and all that I can do, is wait. It is very frustrating."

"Children are very resilient, I'm sure I don't have to tell you that. You counsel children, right?" It felt like he was trying to keep her mind off her worries, so she let him gently steer their conversation.

"Yes, I work with mostly at-risk children. A lot of them dealing with loss and abandonment issues. Not to mention the anxiety that living in bad environments can cause in a child." Delilah hesitated to delve too far into the reasons she chose her particular line of work, something inside her wanted Seb to know about her, to understand her. "My work brings me a lot of joy. Growing up, let's just say our household was volatile and wildly unpredictable. My father was a cop, and for the most part a good man, but he had a nasty temper when he drank. My mother was a nurse, she worked long stressful hours at the local E.R. So, they both had to deal with seeing children from our neighborhood abused and killed for senseless reasons. I'm not saying that my parents weren't responsible for their actions, but being a parent myself now, I can more so understand their burdens."

"You do that a lot." Seb looked at her concerned.

"Mommy is this one bigger?" Bobby asked jogging back to them holding a pinecone that she could see was a little smaller than his previous find.

"No, it looks like it is a little smaller." Delilah held up the reigning champion pinecone to show her son.

"You're right, I'm gonna keep looking." Bobby said with his soft brown eyes looking determined. "Rock, are you still looking?"

"Yep, I'm just keeping your mom company while I look." Seb responded.

"Good idea, mommy gets lonely." Bobby clearly approved of Seb's plan.

She wasn't sure why her son thought that she got lonely, but before she could ask him, he had skipped off again. Delilah liked to let him have his freedom, but she felt nervous because she could no longer see him.

"Should we let him get out of our eye-line? I don't want to question you about your work but…." She didn't want to offend him, but her son's safety came first.

There was an unceremonious pat on her head, causing her to look up into Seb's laughing green eyes.

"What?" She demanded.

"Well out of my eye-line and well out of yours, are two very different things, shorty." He chuckled, patting her head again, making her feel like a child.

She shook off his hand. "Stop that, I get it okay? You are on top of it, this whole protecting him thing. But just remember that you have been protecting him for a hand full of days, I have been protecting him his whole life."

"I'm not questioning your ability as a mother or a protector. I was raised by a single mother. I know better than to question a woman's capability. I just want you to trust me, when I tell you that I will keep you and Bobby safe." He is looking down at her with such intensity that it drew her eyes to his gaze like a magnet. "Do you?"

"Yes." Delilah response was almost a whisper, the emotions evident in his eyes stole her breath away.

"Good." He looked away scanning the trees, nodding when she assumed he had reaffirmed where Bobby was. "Now, back to what we were saying. I noticed that when you tell me about your past, like your divorce or your less-than-ideal childhood. You tend to make excuses for people's behavior."

"My divorce was a complicated time. I had found out that I was pregnant, Nate was excited and so were our families. Looking back, I think that was the happiest I had ever been. Then when I was seven months pregnant, I was woken one night by a knock on the door, standing there in the pouring rain were two uniformed police officers. My first thought was that something had happened to Nate, he had been out of town. Then they told me that there had been an accident and that my parents were both dead. One day to next, they were gone." Delilah tried to hold back the tears that reliving that night still brought to the surface. Wanting and needing for Seb to understand why her marriage failed and why the blame lay solely on her shoulders. "I shut down; I couldn't deal with the pain. Like a coward I hid inside myself, Nate would try to talk to me, I could barely answer. I stopped being a wife, I was taking in the minimum amount of nutrition, I found food almost revolting, eating only for the baby's sake. The doctor was concerned, and my in-laws were furious. After about a month of me isolating myself, Nate started sleeping in the spare room, we seized being husband and wife the day my parents died. So, the reality of the situation is that I killed my marriage, it doesn't really matter what he did because of how I acted."

She didn't expect the strong arm that wrapped around her waist, pulling her close into the nook of Seb's body. She wanted to press inside the warmth and comfort he was offering and not come out until she felt the sadness ebb away. Delilah rarely let herself hash up the past, she still wasn't good at dealing with it, without wanting to break down. She knew that for proprieties sake, she should not allow him to hold her, especially where Bobby could see.

Delilah let her body melt against Seb's, digging her face into his hard body. Feeling the tears moisten his shirt, she let her emotions flow, unlike she ever had before. Finding solace in this man's embrace, feeling like it was the safest place in the world.

———

Chapter 14

He could tell that both of his companions were drained after their walk through the woods. Bobby was physically tuckered out, after his victorious search for the largest pinecone and his mother was emotionally drained, after her heart wrenching confession. Seb had never before experienced the need to help someone so strongly, he would have given anything to wipe the sadness from her eyes. He had promised himself that he wouldn't touch her again, and promptly broke that promise less than twelve hours later. It was different though, today's contact wasn't about sex, it was about wanting to fix her pain.

Seb's original plan had been to go to the grocery store, but when Delilah suggested that she might lay down with Bobby while he took his nap. He knew that neither of the two were up for a trip to town. His new plan was to order in dinner, have it delivered to the reception desk and walk down to get it after the delivery person left. All things considered It was safer than going to the store.

Sitting down on the kitchen table he rotated his phone in his hand, knowing that it was his day to check in with the Hawthornes and dreading the conversation. He really couldn't decide who he wanted to speak to less, Mr. or Mrs. Hawthorne, it was a toss-up. He waited patiently, praying that his call would go to voicemail, the ringing turned out to be a short-lived reprieve.

"Hawthorne speaking." Came the drawl voice of the man of the house.

"This is Rockwell, calling in for my weekly check in." Seb tried to sound neutral, even if he was inclined to dislike the Hawthornes on behalf of Delilah.

"Ah, Mr. Rockwell, I was wondering if you had forgotten. I must admit that I was expecting a call from you earlier in the day. I trust that everything is okay? No new developments, or surely you would have felt the need to contact me earlier." There was a slight reprimand in Hawthornes tone and words, the man could take a flying leap as far as he was concerned.

"After meeting with Ms. Reyes, that evening I started my protection of your grandson. I had to move him, because there was a shooting and some unfortunate graffiti on Ms. Reyes' car. I have had them in a safe location since that time. There have been no new developments since that evening. The police are no closer to finding who is threatening your grandson, unfortunately." Keeping his tone cool and business like was making him sound like a cold-hearted ass, but he didn't care. It was better than letting Hawthorne know how much he resented him.

"I am well aware of the shooting and the threatening message that was scrawled across the vehicle of my ex-daughter in-law. What I am confused about, is why in the world I had to hear of it through my own connections, instead of from you. The man that I am paying exorbitant amounts of money to keep me updated." Hawthornes accusations that Seb was not doing his job, did nothing to help endear him to the man.

"I assure you that it was not my intention to keep anything from you. I felt that the threat had been neutralized by removing them from harm's way. I do not have the luxury of calling you to ask for your permission every time I need to act. In the future I will be happy to inform you, if I need to move them again, but only after the fact." Not willing or able to act like he gave a hoot about making the man happy, it was the best Seb could do.

"I would appreciate it, if you have to move my grandson to a different location that I am informed as soon as possible. May I ask why you never thought to bring him to our residence? I assure you that it is very likely safer than where you are currently located." Hawthorne was using his high dollar manners to sugar coat the fury with which he spoke.

"I don't think that Delilah would be okay with coming to your house, do you?" Seb was amazed that Hawthorne even thought it was a possibility.

"I am not concerned with whether it would make *Ms. Reyes* happy, my only concern is my grandson's well-being, as should yours be." Hawthorne was one cold son of a bitch. Seb did not miss that he had caught Seb using Delilah's first name, clearly the familiarity did not sit well with him.

"Surely you aren't suggesting that I try to take Bobby, somewhere his mother does not want him to go. There is a word for that, as I'm sure you are aware. And that does not fit into my job description." Seb let his thinly veiled threat sit in silence, wanting the old man to watch himself and his untoward suggestions.

Hawthornes whole tone changed, the fake civility was an ill-fit on the man. "Of course, Delilah is more than welcome to come along also. I would never support taking a child from his mother, unless of course the mother was in some way unfit. But I'm sure that isn't the situation with my grandson, right?"

The twist and turns that Hawthorne had made during their brief conversation were tying Seb's stomach in knots. The man had gone from cold anger, to kidnapping suggestions and now he was fishing, fishing for Seb to come up with dirt on Delilah. Blinding red rage threatened to render Seb speechless, he was a man of action, not words. If Hawthorne had been in the same room with him, he would already have had the despicable man up against the wall. He forced himself to cool before responding, keep your enemies closer, right? If Seb flat out refused to do what Hawthorne was asking of him, he knew it wouldn't make the old man stop. He would simply fire Seb and hire someone with less scruples. So, even though it turned his stomach, he had to play along. He had to make Hawthorne think that he was willing and able to play along.

"Now we are talking about something more within my capabilities." He tried not to sound too eager, but at the same time making it seem like he was willing. "For the right incentive I could be extra diligent, to keep my eyes open to any deficiency that may be present."

Seb heard the older man sigh, clearly relieved. "Trust me, I can provide plenty of incentive, if the deficiency you find is bad enough." He paused only for a moment before continuing. "I look forward to speaking with you again, soon."

As Seb heard the line go dead, a chill ran through him. He knew that he would in no way hand Delilah over to this man, who was clearly used to buying whatever and whomever he needed. But he still felt sick at even pretending to go along with him. The Hawthornes primary concern should be the safety of their grandson and in all honesty their grandson's primary living parent also, but it was painfully apparent that they wanted Delilah out of the way. They wanted primary control over Bobby and his future. The idea that anyone would think that taking a boy's mother from him after that boy had just lost his father, would be in the child's best interest, scrambled Seb's brain.

Delilah and Bobby had slept for several hours, leaving Seb plenty of time to himself. Usually he enjoyed solitude, but he found himself waiting rather impatiently for them to wake up. He tried to write in his journal, it was something that he had started in the military. You always wanted to appear unaffected and undisturbed for your brothers in arms, not wanting your short comings to weigh them down. So, when he felt anxious about something or had doubts about his own abilities, he would write during his precious down time. Half of what he had written during that time was so terribly scribbled that he could barely read it. It didn't matter though; the journals weren't for rereading they were an attempt to get all the bad feelings and ideas out of his head and onto paper. It had helped him, even though when his fellow Rangers had found them, there was some brutal commentary from some. Others however looked jealous, that he had found an outlet for his fears, and they had not.

Four other individuals that are now closer to him than brothers, started their own journal process. Soon whenever there were a couple minutes to spare, they all could be found lying on their cots, writing in their journals. The four others were now scattered across the globe, they still called each other and checked in religiously. You could never be too sure that your buddies were okay, unfortunately they all had their demons that they brought home from the war. The suicide rate among soldiers was too high to be ignored, the country did not do enough to help them, in Seb's opinion. So, it left the responsibility squarely on their own shoulders, to make sure that they were all doing their absolute best to stay positive.

They had all chosen wildly different ways to spend their time after their service had ended. Spencer Day was in the kitchen working as a baker, Mike Williams had taken their journal writing a step further and now was a published author, Trevor Johnston served his community as a sheriff, and Miguel Lopez was back overseas working as a contractor. The five of them tried to get together once a year for a weekend if they could all swing it.

He was busy writing, sitting on one of the couches in the living room, with his phone open to the surveillance cameras. Seb could hear light footsteps coming down the stairs, it was a toss-up whether they belonged to Bobby or Delilah. When the brown-haired head peaked around the corner, with those deep chocolate eyes looking at him uncertainly, Seb's heart clinched.

The look in his eyes, it is like looking at Mo again.

"Hey buddy, how did you sleep?" He tried to keep his normally deep tone light and friendly.

Bobby relaxed and came into the living room, his eyes focused on the leather-bound journal that Seb had set on his lap.

"Good, mom is extra tired, so I left her in bed." Bobby said.

"That was nice of you, she has been through a lot." Seb agreed.

"Yeah, I'm worried about her." The way too grown-up sentence coming from the mouth of the small child, just didn't fit. He was too young to have to worry about his mom, but then again, Seb could not remember an age that he hadn't worried about his own mother.

"That is normal, but if it helps at all, your mom is really strong." Seb didn't really think that his opinion would carry any weight with the small boy, but to his surprise Bobby did look slightly relieved.

"You think so?" Bobby asked.

"Absolutely, I have been in some very dangerous situations, and you find out very quickly if someone has the guts to handle things. And your mom, she is as strong as they come." Seb believed every word that he was saying. It would have been easy for Delilah to crumple, or run to her filthy rich in-laws, but she faced her troubles head on.

"You was in danger? You mean with me and mom?" Bobby looked mildly alarmed, as if there had been additional danger that he had not been aware of.

"No, no, no, not with you and your mom. But you aren't the first people that I have had the job of protecting and plus you know that I was in the military also, right?" Seb waited for the boy to nod his head before continuing. "When I was a Ranger, I found myself in pretty dangerous situations, and do you know what the most important thing to do is?"

"What?" Bobby was now seated next to him on the couch, his eyes staring up at Seb, he was fully captivated in what Seb would say next.

"Stay calm." Seb saw a little disappointment on the boy's face, surely Bobby thought that Seb was going to hand him the key to surviving any dangers. It was clear the boy felt that his advice had fallen well short of that.

"That's it?" Bobby asked not trying to hide his disappointment.

"No, that isn't all you need to do, but it is the first and most important step." Seb explained.

Bobby looked up at him, hesitant to say something, then the small boy took a noticeably big breath and asked a question that floored Seb. "My daddy wasn't calm enough then?"

Shit! Shit! Double Shit! You are an idiot!

Here he was giving his no nonsense guide to surviving a dangerous situation and it never occurred to him that Bobby would relate it to his dead father. Now not only was Seb making it seem like anybody could survive by being calm, he also was making it look like Bobby's father could easily have saved himself. He scrambled for a way to explain or to fix the situation. Bobby was staring up at him with the pain of someone much older radiating from his deep brown eyes. Then it hit Seb like a ton of bricks, Bobby didn't need a child's explanation, he needed a real explanation.

"No, I'm sure he wasn't calm." Bobby nodded his head, a tear running down his cheek, cheeks that Seb had just noticed were freckled like his mom's. "But you can't blame him for that Bobby."

"I can't?" Bobby sniffled his question.

"Let me explain something to you." Seb took a deep breath; he was about to talk about something that he never talked about with anyone. "When you love someone, and you think that that person is in danger, you tend to react on instinct. That means that you act without thinking. Your only thought is to get to that person and protect them, you don't think about yourself and whether you are safe. I have no doubt that your father loved you more than he loved himself, so when the shooting started, he thought only of you and getting to you. It has happened to me too, that is how I got this." Seb rolled up his t-shirt to show Bobby the ugly scars where several bullets had torn through his chest, nearly killing him.

He flinched as Bobby reached out to touch the scars with childlike curiosity.

"Does it hurt?" Bobby had not missed Seb's reaction; it had caused him to draw back his hand.

"No, buddy, at least not on the outside." Seb knew that the next part was the hardest part to share and possibly the part that could help Bobby understand. "It hurts on the inside, because when I saw someone I loved in danger, I ignored all of my training and I didn't stay calm. I ran into the middle of a lot of gun fire, just like your daddy probably did, to try and save that person."

"Were they okay? The person you love?" Bobby asked, but Seb could see in the boy's eyes that he already expected the truth.

"The person didn't make it." Seb felt tears welling in his own eyes, as he pictured Mo's smiling face. He was so young and so innocent, he had had plans of coming to America when he was an adult, dreams that would never be fulfilled. "If I could go back and change the situation, I would have made it, so he survived instead of me. Just like your dad would. I have no doubt that if he had the choice, he would choose for you to live instead of him one hundred times out of one hundred."

"Why can't everyone live?" Bobby's impossible question stumped Seb, he himself was a religious man and he did his best to have faith in God's will. But he had no idea how Bobby was being raised and he felt that it would be very inappropriate to push his beliefs on a small child. He could only imagine Delilah's rage; her freckled cheeks would turn fiery red, and her blue eyes would sparkle with anger. It would be almost impossible for him to have an argument with the woman, when she looked at him all filled with her sexy fury.

Like she popped right out of his head, Delilah entered the living room, Seb immediately wondered how much of their conversation she had heard. He chastised himself for not hearing her come down the stairs, Seb had been too wrapped up in his conversation with Bobby. He couldn't allow his awareness to slip just because Bobby reminded him so much of Mo.

"Because that isn't how life works son." Delilah's voice was somber and sad. He could see that she too had shed a tear or two. So, she had either woke up crying or had heard enough of their conversation to make her emotional. She came to the couch and sat next to her son, the three of them fit perfectly on the couch, with not an inch to spare. She placed her hands on either side of her son's face, the look of all-consuming love that she gave Bobby reminded Seb of his own mother. "Life is not fair, son, but it can be beautiful. Like the love that we have for each other and the love that your father had for you. You are the most precious part of both your father and I, so when you live your life. A part of you will always be your daddy, everything you do, every achievement you make, he will be right beside you. When we love someone with our whole heart, not even death can truly separate us."

Bobby buried his face in his mother and openly wept, Seb felt like her words had ripped at his heart strings, leaving his pain bare. Delilah was not immune to the raw emotions in the room, as her own tears started anew. He reached over to wipe the tear from her velvety cheek. She looked at him with a moment of surprise and then she leaned her cheek into his hand. His breath caught in his lungs; it was such an innocent cry for comfort. Seb rubbed his fingers gently over her cheek as she nestled her face into his palm. The intimacy of the moment was one that he would never forget, he reveled in her needing him to comfort her. His need to wrap them both up and keep them safe from harm, was terrifyingly strong.

Seb knew that somewhere along the line it had gone too far, he cared more than he should. Yet he didn't have the strength to walk away, because in this moment he felt more whole than he ever had.

Chapter 14

Delilah sighed as she waited for Bobby to take his turn, they were on what felt like their one hundredth game of checkers. Seb had walked down to the front office to pick up the pizza they had ordered. She wasn't used to being dormant or feeling useless. Despite her lack of activity each new day managed to bring with it something that ended up being emotionally draining. Even the impromptu nap today had not refreshed her, after waking up to the terror of Bobby missing and then walking in on Bobby and Seb having a heart to heart.

The look that the big man had been giving her small son, tore at her heart. If she had doubted him prior, the compassion that he had shown Bobby, and the genuine care that he had handled his questions with, had endeared her to him. She was now sure that no matter what other motives he may have, protecting Bobby was his primary concern.

She found it comforting to know that she and Bobby were not in this alone, but she was also concerned about the fall out after everything was done. Once the people that were after them were apprehended, and they were safe. What would happen to Bobby if he came to depend too much on Seb's presence? What would it do to her? She would love to say nothing, but the gorgeous man had wormed his way under her skin, in an incredibly short amount of time.

Delilah found herself hanging on his every word and sneaking glimpses of him when she thought he wasn't looking. Occasionally he would be staring off, his mind somewhere else entirely, and she would seize those moments to study his face. She tried to tell herself that she wasn't doing it to try and hold on to his image, for when he was no longer in their lives. Because that's what he was, as fleeting as a ship in the night, not a permanent entity to get attached to.

"Pizza!" Bobby jumped up disturbing the placement of the checkers, he looked down and shrugged not seeming to care. *Of course, you don't care, you were losing!* She couldn't help but laugh at her son.

The smell of the melted cheese and rich tomato sauce made her stomach growl, much to her chagrin, Seb clearly heard her body's call for pizza. He looked down at her with laughter making his green eyes sparkle like the gems they resembled. The small quirk at the corner of his soft mouth, made her stomach feel like it was doing back flips and not from the smell of the pizza. When she pulled her eyes from his smile hiding lips and back to his eyes, the laughter had fled, replaced by an exposed longing. She took a sharp intake of breath, trying to right the sensations that threatened to take over her common sense.

"Hungry?" His eyes had deepened in color, his question that was so clearly for her and so clearly had nothing to do with the pizza boxes he was holding. Sent a blood pumping blush to flourish on her freckled cheeks and stole her ability to form words. At least any words that wouldn't sound husky with the passion that this man ignited inside of her.

"Starving!" Bobby responded, not realizing that the question was addressed to her. She was thankful to her son, for breaking the tension that had been building.

139

Delilah looked down at her son, it seemed like the only safe place for her eyes to rest. "Me too." She smiled at her son who was dancing around Seb, celebrating the man who had brought him food. "I will get the plates and napkins and meet you two at the table."

"Mom, can I eat my pizza and watch cartoons?" Bobby knew that on nights that they didn't eat foods that required forks and knives she would let him eat in the living room. Usually she joined him, which gave her an embarrassing knowledge of all the cartoons that a five-year old watched. Admittedly she knew more about their plot and characters than the average woman, not something you put on your online dating profile.

"Sure, honey." He whooped triumphantly.

Delilah took two slices of the cheese pizza along with a napkin and settled Bobby in the living room, she put on his favorite show that was playing on the cartoon channel.

When she returned to the dining room, Seb had already served himself. He looked up at her from his plate, a sheepish grin forming on his mouth. "I would have served yours, but I didn't know how hungry you were." She could tell by the wicked glint in his eyes that he knew darn well that his statement would remind her of the sizzling connection they had shared earlier.

"That's okay, I can take care of it myself." Delilah wanted to kick herself, as she saw Seb's eyebrow shoot up. Only realizing afterward how her statement could be miss-interrupted. "I mean, that I will get my own pizza." Her clarification only helped to deepen her embarrassment. She might as well have hung a sign on herself, *I am single, celibate, and will remain so the rest of my life!*

Seb was ungentlemanly enough to laugh at her obvious struggle, she shot him a glare, which only resulted in making him laugh harder. She found herself wanting to punch him in the arm and wanting to quiet his mouth in other ways......so many other ways.

Delilah tried to pay attention to getting her pizza and sitting as far away from Seb as she could get. Keeping her gaze on her food, and her thoughts on the delicious food her body was craving. It helped her keep her mind off of something else that her body seemed to be craving, something that she most certainly could not give it.

"What do you normally have on your pizza?" The question was so pedestrian, that it caught her off guard.

"This is good, I'm not very picky." Delilah admitted.

"I can see that you are pretty easy going, well about most things anyway. When you order for yourself though, what do you get?" Seb asked.

Delilah looked at the slice in her hand, it had mushrooms, olives, pepperoni, and jalapeno on it. She had to admit that it was pretty close to exactly what she would have ordered, but there was one thing missing. "I usually just get cheese for Bobby, and then have a couple slices of it. I don't remember the last time I ordered a pizza with just what I wanted on it, but if I did, it would need extra onion."

"Onion, huh, not something that you order when you think that there is any romance in your future." *Was that why he hadn't ordered theirs with onion? Was he planning romance in their future?* "Not that that is the reason I didn't order it, I'm actually slightly allergic to onion."

141

"What?!" Delilah had never heard of someone being allergic to onions. "How do you eat anything; everything has onions in it."

Seb laughed at her reaction, she loved the sound of his throaty laughter, it made her smile to be the cause of it.

"I told you it is a slight allergy, so I take pills for it, because I know that there are onions in the sauce and places that you wouldn't think they would be." Seb explained. "You're okay with the heat from the peppers?"

It was her turn to laugh, "Yes, I can handle heat." This time she was well aware of the double meaning behind her words, as she shot him her best playful smile. She was unreasonably gratified to see passion flare in his eyes, Delilah had never been one to play with fire, but that is what it felt like she was doing and enjoying. "You might not guess it by looking at me, but I am half Mexican."

She laughed so hard that it brought tears to her eyes, as Seb choked on his pizza in surprise. Delilah was used to people reacting with disbelief when she told them where her Latino sounding last name came from, they usually assumed that it had come from her ex-husband. Tiring quickly of explaining to people that she looked like her mother who had Irish heritage and almost nothing like her Mexican father, she started carrying a picture of her parents in her wallet. It was an easier way of explaining where her fluent Spanish and love for spicy food came from.

Delilah got up from the table and went to get the picture that was now well worn from years of her packing it around in her wallet. She handed it to Seb who was watching her like she was crazy. "Oh, stop it, it's not like I told you I was half fairy or something."

He took the picture and studied it. "That I would have believed easily, when I first saw you, I thought you looked like a beautiful impish fairy. I mean if fairies had vicious tempers and looked at you like they wished they could kill you, that is." A wicked grin played on his kissable lips, she was lost in looking at him and in his words. *Beautiful?*

She rolled her eyes, no one had ever called her beautiful before. Cute, pretty, once or twice Nate had said she was adorable, but never beautiful. "Okay, whatever you say."

His brows drew together, "You don't believe me?"

"No, but that's okay, I know you are just trying to be nice or funny or something." Delilah wanted to talk about something else, anything else. The bright pink paper lying underneath the pizza box caught her attention, so she grabbed it. "What is this?"

"I thought maybe that if you and Bobby were getting cabin fever, we could go into town on Sunday." Seb sounded unsure, probably responding to the emotions that she knew she couldn't hide. "Are you okay? You are white as a ghost?"

Delilah fought to hold back the tears, God she was so tired of crying. "Yeah, sorry, I just forgot that it is Mother's Day this weekend."

He nodded his head in understanding, but she knew there was no way he understood, not really. "You miss your mom, I'm sure it is a hard day for you."

"I do miss my mom, but I miss her every day. No, now I have a new reason to hate Mother's Day." Delilah could no longer hold back the tears that ran down her face.

———

She felt him at her side, before she even realized he had moved. For such a big man he was surprisingly light and quick on his feet. With one of his big hands, he cupped her face and turned her toward him. He kneeled in front of her, causing her to be slightly taller than him. His deep green eyes were pools of concern. "Why do you hate Mother's Day?"

"Because it is the reason Nate is dead." She whispered.

Chapter 15

What in the hell was she talking about?

"How do you figure that?" Seb heard the confusion in his own voice.

"I don't want to talk about it, okay?" His heart contracted as her sapphire eyes looked at him, pleading for him to not push.

He couldn't ignore the hurt that she was hiding, Seb needed to help her, needed to ease her pain.

"No, it's not okay." He tried to sound stern yet comforting, as he stroked the petal soft skin of her cheek. "What you just said makes no sense. Nate died because he was shot in a drive by."

She shook her head, denying what he had said. "He would have been safely in the house. The bullets never would have touched him. Or touched me." He watched as she subconsciously reached for her wounded arm.

"You don't know that there is no way you could know that." He was trying desperately to get her to see the untruth in her statement.

"I do." She hesitated, sniffling back additional tears. "Before I put Bobby in the car, I asked Nate to wait, I needed to talk to him about Mother's Day weekend. As always Nate didn't argue, hell the whole conversation wasn't even necessary. I could have just told him over the phone, I should have just told him over the phone, then he would still be alive. We would be home right now."

Delilah broke down, losing the battle she had been fighting to hold back her emotions. He acted on instinct as he pulled her to him, holding her small body against his own. Seb wasn't thinking about the sparks that his body could feel hers giving off, all he concentrated on was trying to take her pain away.

"Shhhh, sweetheart." He spoke softly to her while running his hands over her back, in what he hoped was a soothing motion. "It wasn't your fault; you didn't make those men shoot at Nate and he could have just as easily been shot inside his home. Hell, any number of things could have happened. You cannot punish yourself; you are a victim in all of this." Seb cradled her face in his hands, she felt so small and delicate. "Listen to me Delilah, you are not to blame for any of this."

Even though she nodded her head in begrudging agreement, he could still see the lingering doubt in her eyes.

"Are you just trying to appease me?" He grinned at her softly, not being able to help admiring how strong she was. She gave him a small smile and nodded her head again. "Can I convince you that you are wrong about this?"

She lowered her eyes, barely looking at him through thick golden lashes. "No."

He sighed, tipping her chin back up to look into her blue eyes that were as deep as the ocean and just as liable to drown a man. Delilah had the kind of eyes that made a man want to look at nothing else, and a taste so sweet that would make all future tastes bland in comparison. Seb knew he was staring at her pouty mouth. Her lips were parted as if inviting him to partake of her pleasures. When he looked back into her eyes, there was a storm of passion raging in them, darkening them with desire. He groaned, as he moved to claim her mouth with his own.

"Mommy, are you okay?" Bobby's voice was like a life preserver thrown to Seb, preventing him from losing himself and his self-respect in a moment of weakness.

"Yes honey, I just hurt my arm a little and Seb was checking to see if it was okay." She was quick, Seb had to give her that.

To make her cover seem legit he examined the wound that marred her perfect skin, anger alighting anew within him. If he ever got the chance, he would kill whoever had done this to her and to her son.

"It doesn't look like you did any additional damage." Seb backed away from her, needing to put space between them. "Your mom sure is a quick healer, buddy."

The little boy looked from his mother to Seb, he was not sure whether he believed either of them, that much was obvious. Seb smiled at him, he was a clever boy and very protective over his mother. If he had a son, he would hope that he would be like Bobby.

"You don't believe us, do you?" Seb decided to level with Bobby, which earned him a shocked glare from Delilah. The little boy studied him for a moment more before responding.

147

"Not really." The boy admitted.

"Okay, I will tell you the truth then." Seb pretended to be resigned.

"Seb, please, I don't think that...." Delilah started to protest, apparently Seb was a better actor than he had thought.

He grabbed the pink flyer that Delilah had dropped on the floor and handed it to Bobby. "This is what we were talking about." Bobby looked from him to the paper and back again, still confused. "I found out about the Mother's Day festival they are having in town and suggested that we all go. Your mom wasn't sure it was a good idea, with everything you two have been through. But I think that it would be the perfect way to celebrate what a good mom she is. What do you think?"

Seb looked at Bobby like they were making a man-to-man decision, ignoring the astonished look that Delilah was giving him.

Bobby's young excitement won out over his suspicions about what they had been talking about. He jumped into his mom's lap, placing his small arms around her neck. "Mom, we have to go."

It was like magic watching the one adoring look from her son, melt away the sadness and worry. He knew that it was ridiculous, but he wished he could do that for her. That he had the power to help her forget her worries and feel something pleasant.

"If you are sure that you want to go." Delilah didn't sound completely convinced.

"Yes, mommy, you are the bestest." Bobby kissed his mom, with all the love of an unabashed child. "Can I have more pizza?.......please?"

Delilah must be used to sudden changes in topic because she took it in stride, pausing only shortly before placing another piece of pizza on her son's plate.

"What do you say?" Seb smiled watching the two, going through what was clearly a normal routine.

"Thank you." Bobby beamed up at her.

"You're welcome." Delilah's smile was so bright, it made Seb's heart lighten, even though he wasn't the one receiving it.

"Mom, do you want to watch T.V. with me, it is the last one of Road Rippers. You're gonna miss what happens to Tina, she is your favorite." Bobby stated his argument like a boy much older than his five years.

The blush that colored Delilah's cheeks made her seem so innocent and beautiful, he loved the fact that she was embarrassed about her knowledge of her son's cartoons. Seb found it endearing, he could in fact imagine watching Saturday morning cartoons, with his son and wife. Not something that was in the cards for him anytime soon, but not something that he would ever be embarrassed about either.

"Go, ahead, I have some phone calls to make anyway." Seb tried to give her the perfect out, she took it, with a look of appreciation.

"Okay let's go." She grinned at Bobby, grabbing another piece of pizza for herself before leaving. "Tell me everything that I have missed, did they find Mike? Did he lose his powers?"

All Seb could hear after her shot gun questions was Bobby rattling on, assumedly filling his mother in on the details she hadn't seen. The ease that existed between mother and son, was something to be treasured and envied. He had one of those relationships with his own mother. Sure, she had never had time to sit and watch cartoons with him, but she never missed an opportunity to listen when Seb needed to talk about his life.

All the heartwarming mother son stuff made Seb feel a stab of guilt, it had been too long since he had spoken with his mom. Making a swift decision to ratify that, Seb grabbed his remaining pizza, and headed toward the front porch swing. On his way out, Delilah and Bobby didn't even look up at him passing, they were both cuddled on the couch, eyes glued to the television. He was surprised how much he wanted to change his mind and curl up on the couch with them.

Yeah, he definitely needed to talk with his mom, maybe she could help him figure out the jumble of emotions that he was feeling.

The phone started ringing before Seb even settled down on the swing, and his mother's warm voice greeted him as he sat.

"Hello, there, my handsome son." His mother Margaret had a deep voice for a woman, she contributed it to her years as a smoker. Seb had always just assumed that was how her voice was because his grandmother, an avid non-smoker, had a similar voice. "I thought that maybe you had lost your phone, or possibly your mind."

He chuckled at his mother's usual dry wit. "Well, I can assure you that I haven't lost my phone, as for the other part, not so sure."

"I don't like the sound of that." Her tone had become serious and worried in an instant. "What is going on, Sebby?"

"Nothing mom, I am just on a job, and I felt like calling you." Seb knew he sounded defensive. He really did want to talk to his mom, but he had no idea how to explain what was going on in his head.

"You never call me when you are working." The worry in her voice was only getting worse.

"Yeah, well, this job is a little different." He wasn't trying to seem mysterious or aloof, but he couldn't bring himself to come to the point. "I don't know if I can continue doing this job, mom."

"I thought you loved your job?" She sounded confused; he didn't blame her.

"I did, I mean I do, it's just......shit I don't know mom." Seb confessed.

"Language, Sebastian." Her reprimand made him smile, he could picture her pretty face scrunched up with displeasure. "Now, why don't you tell me her name."

He pulled the phone from his ear and stared at it. *How in the world does she know about Delilah? She can't, right?*

"Delilah." It was as if his heart had moved his lips against his will. He had been all ready to deny that his problems had anything to do with a woman.

"That is a pretty name, does Delilah have a pretty face to go along with her pretty name?" His mother wasn't being unkind if anything he could hear her concern.

151

How did he answer that? With the truth? That Delilah was a small fireball of a woman, who had the softest dark red curls that always seemed to work their way free of any up-do she tried to constrict them to. Almost as if they could read his mind and knew that he would love to see them all down, surrounding her gorgeous face. He couldn't even begin to describe the color of her eyes, the deepest purest blue that he had ever seen. Her pert bow shaped mouth, her skin, oh god the taste of her skin.   Honey so sweet, she would put bees to shame.

His mother's whistle drew him out of his own thoughts, thoughts that he most certainly would not be sharing with his mother.

"Uh, oh." His mother sighed into the phone line. "You are in deep trouble, aren't you?"

"Yeah mom, I think that I am." Seb admitted.

"Tell me what's going on, son." Margaret's statement left no room for arguments, and Seb had no desire to do so anyway. He found himself over the next hour telling his mother everything that had happened to him over the last week. Leaving out the details but confessing enough to where she understood the severity of his missteps. At the end he felt a little better. "You know that you need to quit, right?"

"I know, it's so hard to think about walking away." Saying it out loud made it seem even more ludicrous, it was unbelievable that he had become so attached to them both so quickly, but he had.

"I can understand that, but right now they need someone who can focus primarily on protecting them." His mother's voice was softened by compassion. "Is that person you?"

"No, it's not, I think I need to take a break from all of this for a while." Seb's path seemed to clear in front of him, he knew what he needed to do next. "I'm going to call Cody and tell him, and then I think I'm going to come for a visit."

"I think you are making the right decision son." Margaret sounded relieved.

He was having pain in his chest at the idea of leaving, he tried to tell himself it was heart burn from the pizza. But the emotions he was feeling, were clear indicators that he was no longer the right person to protect Delilah and Bobby. And it hurt like hell.

Chapter 16

Delilah had been feeling lonely all night, it was not something she was used to feeling while sitting and watching television with Bobby. When she watched Seb walk outside, she hadn't thought that he would be out there all night. But they had finished eating, she had put away the food and it was time for Bobby's bath and still no sign of Seb.

"Okay kiddo, time for bed." She tried to not let her unease show.

"I want to say good night to Rock first." Bobby whined, a sure sign that he was tired.

"Let me check and see if he is busy." Delilah relented.

She walked out onto the porch, only to catch the last part of his conversation with someone.

"Fine, I will stay until Monday, but then I'm leaving. I can't do this for much longer." Shock rippled through her; *he was leaving. Why?* "Okay, good, yeah I will, bye."

She was taken aback by the look of guilt that riddled his forest-colored eyes, Delilah was confused and filled with dread.

"Bobby wanted to say good night to you." Her lighthearted tone sounded false to her ears.

Without responding to her, he unfolded his long body from the porch swing and walked past her and into the house. She followed him in, unable to see his face. She watched as he knelt down, there was no hesitancy in Bobby, as he ran up to Seb and wrapped his arms around the big man. If Delilah didn't know any better, she could have sworn that she heard sadness in Seb's voice as he said good night to Bobby. She prayed that her son didn't notice, he had had enough of sadness, for such a little guy.

"Mom, can Rock read my bedtime story?" Bobby's innocent question threatened to break down the fractured walls that were her emotions.

"I don't know if Seb would want to sweet...." Delilah started to make Seb's excuses for him, she knew that it brought back bad memories for him. Even though she didn't know the details, she knew that Bobby reminded him of someone named Mo. So, she worried that Seb would dredge up negative feelings whenever he spent time with Bobby.

"I will read you a story buddy, but only if your mom reads the girl parts. No matter what I do, I can't get my voice to sound like a lady." Bobby burst into a fit of laughter and Delilah found the humor overriding her concerns. At least for the most part.

"That is a good idea, what do you want me.... I mean us to read to you tonight?" Delilah hoped that it wouldn't be anything too long. Seb looking around at her, his gaze unreadable.

"Roddy." Bobby proudly exclaimed the title of his favorite book, Delilah cringed on the inside. It was a story she had read a dozen times; the classic story of boy meets girl, boy finds out girl is a space alien, and helps her save her home planet from destruction. Even though she knew Bobby's favorite parts were the adventure and the author's ability to create a fantastical new planet, she was not looking forward to reading the underline romantic aspect of the story. One that Bobby was most likely completely unaware of.

"Roddy it is!" Seb laughed and swooped Bobby up in his arms.

Her son's giggles of joy caused her the craziest sensations, both mending rips in her shredded heart and piercing new holes at the same time. Her first reaction to the idea of Seb leaving was a troubling amount of regret and sadness, but there was also a part of her that knew they were getting too attached to the gentle stoic man. If it were just herself and her own heart at risk, she might be a tad more cavalier, but she worried about Bobby. Any form of attachment on his part to Seb, could only lead to heart break.

As Delilah snuggled into the bed on one side of her son, she was too aware of Seb's body on the other side. She and Seb were both careful to keep any contact to an absolute minimum. She held onto one side of the book, and he held onto the other. She grinned as Seb quickly realized that being the main character of the book, Roddy the male had much more to read. He shot her a wicked glare as he turned the page and her character had yet to speak more than a dozen words.

Having heard the story what felt like a hundred times, she allowed her mind to wander while Seb read the familiar words. The deep timber of his voice was soothing, and he read with the ease of an avid reader. It didn't surprise her. She had seen him writing something the other day. Seb was so much more than what met the eye, he was so much more than the tough Army Ranger, or the hard exterior he showed the world. The tenderness that he used when dealing with Bobby, the all-consuming passion that he had kissed her with. Seb was a dangerous cocktail of a man, and she would be smart to steer clear of him.

There was a crash somewhere above her loud enough to wake the dead, Delilah threw herself to the floor. She could have sworn she was outside, but when she fell it was onto a softly carpeted flooring.

Crystal shards rained down overhead; it was like looking through a downpour of glass fragments. Lying in front of her was a distinctly male shape, and it wasn't moving. She crawled over the carpet, that hid the glass pieces from view but did not protect her skin from being cut. With each movement the sharp fragments tore at her flesh, she slid on the trail of warm blood she was creating. She had to get to him, no matter what, she shoved her pain to the back of her mind. Determined.

His back was turned to her, as he lay on his side. But the shock of silver hair, marred with the crimson red of blood, told her exactly who it was.

"Sebastian! No, no, please be okay!" She grabbed for his shoulder to turn him toward her.

She fell back as the silver hair darkened to brown and the face that she had been expecting to see turned into Nate's.

His eyes were unnaturally round and his skin a sickly white.

"I wish you had love me like that." He felt each word like a blow to her chest.

"Delilah, Delilah, Delilah." Her name being spoken in a harsh whisper and a distinctly male hand shaking her shoulder, rescued her from her morbid nightmare.

She looked up into Seb's concerned face, it was dark in the room, she wasn't sure how long she had been asleep.

She could sense him moving but was caught off guard as he lifted her off from the bed. While still cradling her in his arms, he reached down to pull the covers snuggly around Bobby's shoulders.

Delilah shamefully melted into his hard body, allowing his strength to support her fully. She nestled her face into his muscled shoulder, inhaling the scent of him. He smelt like a rich spicy woodsy scent, and something so distinctly male, the more she took it in the more it became her new favorite scent.

"I'm going to put you on the bed." Seb's voice was low and husky sounding.

Not being able to stop herself she ran her hands through his thick hair, needing the affirmation that this was no longer a dream and that he was okay. His body stiffened against hers, she could feel the muscles in his arms tighten.

"What are you doing?" Her touch affected him; it was clear in his voice.

"I was making sure you were okay." She explained.

"Why wouldn't I be?" He questioned as he set her down on the soft bed in her room, breaking the brief contact.

"I had a nightmare." She admitted, Delilah tried to ignore the thrill that ran through her, as she felt his weight settle next to her on the bed. Even though she was lying down, and he was seated, the intimacy of the moment excited her.

"Is that why you called my name?" She thanked God he couldn't see the blush that she felt burning her cheeks. *I said his name out loud?!*

"Yes, was it loud? Is that why you came to wake me up?" Her only relief was that she hadn't woken her son with her outburst.

"No, it wasn't loud." She felt him holding back, hesitating to say something. "We both fell asleep, I only planned to close my eyes for a minute."

The image of the three of them nestled in bed, was too painfully like a normal family. It was too much to concentrate on, without losing it.

"I don't blame you; Roddy can be very boring to read." Delilah tried to lighten the mood; she heard his halfhearted chuckle.

"It wasn't that bad, but my lady love fell asleep." Her sharp intake of breath must have scared him because he worked quickly to explain himself. "I mean Roddy's love in the book, the part you were supposed to read."

She could only see his outline but his search for an explanation was so adorable, it made her smile. Picturing his handsome face struggling to cover up his blunder, she reached out to him, needing to have some contact with him. Her hand found the hardness of his knee, not exactly the most romantic body part on a man, but it felt good just to be touching him.

Seb grabbed her hand in his own, she felt his warm breath on the palm of her hand, exciting the flesh there even before he caressed it with his soft lips. It was far from an erotic gesture, but it sent every one of Delilah's nerve endings tiny shocks of pleasure.

"Are you okay now?" Seb asked, still holding her hand.

"Yes, I'm okay." She wasn't, she was so far from okay, it wasn't even funny.

Delilah wanted to scream at him, that she was not okay. That she was confused as hell, because she had just had a nightmare that she couldn't begin to understand. Because the terror that she had felt rip through her like an earthquake at seeing him hurt, had felt more real than anything she had ever felt. It was like watching her own heart exposed and bleeding on the floor, all she could think about was rushing to it and putting it back into her body where it belonged, where he belonged.

"I'm going to let you get some sleep." Seb let go of her hand and started to get up from the bed.

"Don't leave." Her voice was steady, while her heartbeat was an erratic mess.

"I can't stay, Delilah." She could hear pain in his words.

"Can't stay in this bed, or can't stay here with us?" Either way the answer would tear a hole in her.

"Both." Seb answered.

"Why?" Delilah whispered the question, she wanted to cover her ears like a child would, not wanting to hear the answer.

"Because I can't trust myself around you." He sighed. "In this line of work, you have to be alert at all times, on your guard. But when I get around you, I lose all perspective. When I should be thinking about possible dangers, and security measures. I am busy thinking about the feel of your skin, the taste of you, and the look in your sea blue eyes when you want me."

His honesty was raw and the torment in his voice made it apparent that it was not easy for him to admit. She longed to go to him and wrap her arms around him, to confess that she felt all of that and more. Tell him that she knows it is crazy and inappropriate but that her feelings were too strong to ignore. She wanted to be the one to bandage all of his aches and kiss away all of his fears. But she knew he was right. She couldn't put her feelings, no matter how strong they were, in front of her son's safety.

"When do you leave?" Each word burnt like bitter acid on her tongue.

"Monday, my partner Cody will come and relieve me. He is in Europe right now, but he should be wrapped up this weekend and then he will be the one looking out for you and Bobby." Seb's words were wrecked with a sadness that her heart mimicked.

"I understand." She replied.

"Well, I'm glad you do, because I sure as hell don't." His frustration was clear.

———

"I understand why you are leaving, and I understand that whatever this is between us, could be distracting." She explained.

"To put it lightly, yes, it is extremely distracting." He agreed.

"So, you have called your partner and told him to come and take your place." She was trying to tread lightly knowing that she was walking on thin ice.

"Yes, that was who I was talking to before you came out on the porch." Seb sounded exhausted and resigned to his fate.

"You have done your job, and the responsible thing. Now I don't see any reason why we can't spend the night together." Delilah could feel the shock resonate in Seb at hearing her wanton suggestion.

Chapter 17

"Delilah, don't." Seb's head was swimming with the images of what making love to Delilah would be like. The very idea made his heart beat double time as his body harden at the thought. "I'm trying so damn hard to keep my hands off of you."

"Well, you haven't been very successful so far." The painful reminder of his various failures made him flinch.

"Don't you think I know that? Which is exactly why I can't make love to you tonight. But maybe I could...." Seb hesitated, not sure that he could do what he was about to suggest.

"You could what?" He envied how fearless she sounded, almost daring him to go against his better judgment.

Seb walked around to the opposite side of the bed, sliding off his shoes. He knew that if he had any prayer of restraining himself, he had to leave every article of clothing that he was wearing on. He slid under the covers, Seb could feel Delilah freeze, waiting to see what he was going to do.

There was a virtual war going on within him, his body wanted him to ravish the beautiful woman practically offering herself to him. His mind was telling him that making love to her would be ethically wrong and he knew it would be hard to live with himself afterward. Since his mind and body could not come to an agreement, Seb decided to follow his heart. His heart just needed to be with her, needed her by him, making it impossible for him to leave her.

He tucked her small frame into his, once she realized what he intended she snuggled back into him. Rubbing places on his body that threatened his resolve and his sanity. Seb clenched his jaw, trying to fight the urges that her innocent movement was creating. She reached back and took his hand, bringing it forward and wrapping it around her.

Delilah sighed. "This feels nice."

Seb's face was lying in a bed of her dark red curls, they smelt like honey dipped freesias, no doubt the freesia was her shampoo, but he knew that the honey was a scent that was entirely her own. Pushing his body's limits he placed a kiss on her exposed neck, feeling her body tremble from his touch was intoxicating.

"You feel nice." Seb continued to place kisses on her neck, moving down toward her shoulder. He could hear her breath become more rapid and he knew he was playing with fire.

"Sebastian, are you going to keep doing that?" Delilah voice was husky with need, a need for him, a need that made him hard as a rock.

"I'm going to try and stop." Seb explained.

"Good, because it is impossible to fall asleep while you are kissing me." Delilah didn't sound like she really minded his kisses.

"You're right." Seb used every shred of his will power to rest his head back on her soft curls, pulling her as close as possible, relishing in the feel of her body. "I just want to hold you, it's all that I can offer you."

"I understand." For some reason it felt like she really did understand. "I want you; my body reacts to you more than it ever has to anyone, but I know you're right. If you ever did make love to me, I wouldn't want you to regret it, I wouldn't want to regret it." He could feel her relax into him, her breathing getting steadier and deeper. "I can't remember the last time that I was held, it feels so safe to be in your arms."

Her voice had taken on a drugged like quality, it was clear that she was losing the battle with sleep. There was a certain level of satisfaction that Seb could give her this, if he couldn't give her anything more intimate, at least he could be here for her.

"A woman like you was made to be held and cherished, if you were mine, I would spend every day of my life worshipping your body and warming your heart." His confession went unheard, as she began to snore softly. It was for the best; they were things that he shouldn't say or even feel. He had nothing to offer a woman like her.

His job, if he decided to continue in the private security business, did not make one the ideal family man. Seb spent most of his time traveling and was constantly in situations that he could not be reached or counted on. He would never make it to soccer games, or school plays, and you could forget making plans on anniversaries. No, there was no room in his life for a serious relationship, and he couldn't see Delilah any other way.

Whether he liked it or not, in such a short period of time, his feelings had become involved, and he could not start something casual with her. Even if she thought it was what she wanted. If they did have some sort of adrenaline-fueled romance, she might be able to walk away unscathed but he sure the hell wouldn't. Leaving her and Bobby in the care of Cody, someone he trusted with his own life, was already painful enough. If he let his walls down and made love to her, leaving would crush him.

Bobby's soft calls for his mother, woke Seb up. He was honestly surprised that he had been able to fall asleep, Seb pressed a soft kiss to Delilah's shoulder before removing himself from the bed. He tried to rush without waking her, his first priority was making sure that Bobby did not walk in on them in bed together. The little man had been through enough, he did not need to try and figure out why a man was in bed with his mom.

It had been risky and inappropriate to spend the night with Delilah in his arms, but he didn't regret it. It had taken awhile for him to fall asleep, but once he did, it was the deepest, sweetest sleep he could ever remember having.

He ducked out of the room just in time to see Bobby's little head poke into the hallway. The little boy's eyes lit up once he saw Seb, catching at Seb's heart. Between awaking snuggled up to by Delilah and Bobby's unbidden joy at seeing him, Seb could not help but be envious of Nate. It was ridiculous to be jealous of a dead man, and he knew that the reality of the situation was that Nate never had mornings like this. He and Delilah had split up well before Bobby could even walk. But the fact that Nate could have had this, and gave it up, bewildered Seb.

"Morning buddy, how did you sleep?" Seb asked.

"Really good, I like the big bed." Bobby smiled up at him. "Let's wake up mommy."

"Do you think we should let her sleep in?" Seb was reluctant to disturb her, when he had left her, she had looked like an elfin angel curled up in bed.

"Oh, sure." Bobby nodded his head enthusiastically. "She always tells me to wake her up, she says that we should not waste time being apart when we could be together."

The too grown-up words were obviously something that Bobby had heard numerous times. The sentiment made Seb wish for things that could not be, for a life that did not belong to him.

"After you then." Seb motioned with his hand for Bobby to lead the way, which the young boy did like it was second nature.

Either Seb was getting slow, or they were making boys faster than they used to, because Bobby seemed to catapult himself into bed the moment, they entered the room. Eliciting an "Oof," from his mother, most likely because he knocked the air out of her.

"Careful buddy." Seb could not hold back his first instinct, which was to protect Delilah. Not only was she a petite woman, but she also had a healing bullet wound to contend with.

Delilah sat up in bed, wrapping her arms around Bobby.

"It's okay, it didn't hurt." Despite her comforting words, he could see the pain that her son had caused her, clearly evident on her face.

"Are you sure mommy?" Seb could see the concern in Bobby's chocolate eyes as he looked up at his mother.

"Absolutely, but I do have a serious problem." Delilah looked down at her son, love radiating off her like a light in the darkness.

"Oh, no!" Bobby began to giggle, even though the boy seemed to guess his mother's problem, Seb was very much in the dark.

"That's right." Delilah licked her lips, Seb watched as her pink tongue ran along her pouty lower lip. Feeling like a complete ass, because even though he couldn't guess what her problem was, he was finding himself with a problem of his own. "I'm hungry! Hungry enough to eat a…. horse…. or a….boy."

She rained down kisses and play bites all over the giggling boy, Seb wanted to join in their fun, but it wasn't his place.

"Rock run." Bobby managed to wiggle out of his mom's embrace, colliding with Seb right leg and wrapping himself around it. "Now you can't get me! Rock will protect me." The little boy taunted his mom playfully. Seb saw a look of sadness cloud her blue eyes, he felt guilt stab him as sharply in the heart.

Delilah got off the bed and threw her arms into the air. "Fine you win, but maybe I can persuade Sebastian to make us some of his delicious pancakes." She looked up at him, batting her eyes and smiling.

His heart did a gymnastic move good enough to win him the gold medal, he smiled down at her, unable to hold back the feelings that were pouring out of him.

"If my options are finding you a horse to eat, sacrificing poor Bobby, or making pancakes, then I guess I only have one question." Seb looked down into her oceanic eyes, wanting to dive right into her world.

"What question?" Delilah placed her hands on her small hips, trying her best to look tough.

"What do you prefer, Clydesdale or Mustang?" Seb's laughter was shortly joined by Bobby's, and eventually Delilah's, after she stuck her tongue out at him.

Chapter 18

The first part of their day flew by. Making breakfast had turned into a group project, Seb had made up the mixture and she and Bobby had been in charge of cooking them. Seb had leaned his long frame against the kitchen counter and sipped his coffee while watching her try to instruct Bobby on the basics of pancake flipping.

Having his dark green eyes follow her every move, made her unreasonably nervous. Which made her a bit scatter brained when telling her son what to do. The results were messy and ugly, but all things considered, breakfast was still delicious. She tried to sneak a peek at what Seb put into the batter mix, because they were the fluffiest pancakes she had ever eaten. But he had blocked her view and distracted her, so she knew that there were at least a couple ingredients that she didn't get to see go in. He smiled at her wickedly when she asked for the recipe and refused to give it to her. Claiming it was a family secret.

Seb had walked down to the front desk, the woman that they had met on their first night here was apparently willing to let them use her car to run to town for groceries. Delilah tried not to think about the busty blonde's willingness to let "Foxy" use her vehicle. For all she knew, it was something that she did regularly, but remembering the way she had looked at Seb, she doubted it.

Bobby was doing the one and only puzzle that was at the house that was not way above his age range, while Delilah hopped in the shower.

She stood under the hot stream of water, willing it to cleanse her of her urges and desires. Last night had been both the most frustrating night and also the most beautiful night that she had ever had. Delilah blushed as she remembered how she had basically offered herself to Seb and he had turned her down flat. Sure, he had claimed that he wanted her, that the only reason he held back was because he was on the job, and she really did understand. But there was still this nagging voice in the back of her mind, telling her that maybe he was just using that as an excuse.

Delilah had tried to be nonchalant and understanding about it, but it still had hurt her ego.

She had to admit though, the consolation prize of him holding her all night long had been almost as good as sex. Nate had hated cuddling and only ever did it for a few minutes shortly after they had made love. Delilah had lied last night when she had told Seb that she couldn't remember how long it had been, she knew exactly how long it had been since a man had held her like that, her entire life. Seb held her like she was the most precious thing in the world, at least that was how it had felt. In a way she was glad he had held back, because what he gave her last night was exactly what she had needed. Delilah had woken this morning feeling refreshed and ready to handle whatever life decided to throw at her today.

She had toweled off and started to put her clothes on, humming to herself, when a knock came on her door. Without thinking she answered. "Yeah?" Knowing that it was Seb, thinking that he would simply reply through the door of the bedroom.

"Hey, I just wanted to let you know that I have the keys, and we are all ready to......" As he talked Seb had appeared in the doorway of the bathroom. She was acutely aware that she had only got as far as putting on her panties, in vain she wished that they had been a pair vastly more exciting than the white with purple bunnies that she had on.

"Seriously, you just walk in on someone?" She grabbed her towel from the counter and covered her body the best she could.

His emerald eyes glowed with anger and enough desire to make her bones feel like they were melting. "The door wasn't shut, and you answered me. I thought you were just in here doing your hair or something."

"The door was to shut." Delilah raced to remember if she had made sure the door was in fact shut. She was so used to living alone and with him being out of the house, was it possible that she hadn't shut the door? Crap, maybe he was right. It was like he could read her mind, as she watched his kissable lips curve into a smug grin.

"You sure about that door?" She would give anything to be able to wipe that smug look from his handsome face.

"You know damn well that I'm not sure." Delilah glared at him.

"Has anyone ever told you that you are adorable when you're angry?" Though she could still see passion light his eyes, his words acted like a cooling agent to her own desires.

"Yes, I get that a lot, cute, adorable, and every other thing that you can say to a woman that isn't all the sexier words." She hated the tears that she was fighting back, he had hit a very raw nerve with her. Delilah just wanted him to leave the bathroom and quit reminding her that she was not the type of woman to inspire lusty thoughts, no matter what had happened between them in the past. If last night was any indication, his attraction to her was something that he could turn off and on like a faucet. If only her own were as easily controlled.

"Did I upset you?" Seb's look softened with concern.

"Just forget it okay?" Delilah turned around and wrapped the towel more securely around herself. "We are both adults, it's not like I have anything you haven't seen before. Please close the door on your way out, I will only be a couple more minutes and then I will be ready to go."

"Delilah, I think there has been some sort of miss understanding. You are..." Seb started to explain, but she really couldn't take him repeating anything that she had heard before.

"Sebastian, please just get out." He must have heard the desperation to be alone in her voice, because without further argument he walked out of the room.

Delilah held in her tears until after she heard the door click. As she slid down the bathroom wall and into an emotional puddle on the floor, she hated herself. After Nate had cheated on her and cast her aside, she swore that she would never again care about what a man thought of her. Her ex-husband had once referred to her as safe and comfortable. When he confessed his affair to her, he had told her that she was what he had thought he wanted in a woman, until he had met Rebecca. Nate had begged for her forgiveness, trying to get her to understand that he had never felt like he did for Rebecca for anyone else, including her. Sure, he didn't say it exactly like that, but that was the general idea. That Rebecca was too beautiful and exciting to turn down, she was not the type of woman that you chose to cuddle with. Oh no, she had no doubt that if Seb had been in bed with a woman like Rebecca last night, nothing would have stopped him from having his way with her. Where with Delilah he had found the strength to refuse her embarrassing advances.

She picked herself up off the floor and dried her eyes, she sighed as she looked at her puffy reflection in the mirror.

Crazy emotional basket case, great! This is apparently my new go to look.

There was no fixing it now, the damage was done. Slipping on her dress, she winced as she forgot herself and raised her arm too quickly. It still caused her pain, but she felt like it was healing well. She would always have a small scar as a reminder of this whole ordeal. As if she would ever be able to forget this messy painful scenario. Delilah wrangled her curls onto the top of her head, into a bun, the type that Nate had absolutely hated.

174

She looked at herself in the mirror and nodded at the image looking back at her. Delilah had to be happy with herself, it was the only way she knew how to be okay with the events that had happened in her life.

Delilah tried not to glare at the hot-pink fuzzy dice swinging from the rear-view mirror of the cherry red Mustang. She still didn't quite understand why they hadn't taken Seb's car, when she asked him, he said that it was simply precautionary. He didn't want to take a chance that the person that had vandalized and shot her car had seen his vehicle parked at her apartment.

This car smelt like Dolly, which Seb informed her was the name of the blond from the hotel. It was like vanilla mixed with bubble gum, the combination was making her a little nauseous. If these were the scents that drove men's passion wild, she didn't think that she would ever have to worry about having wild men on her hands.

She hadn't said more than a couple words to Seb sense the bathroom incident, she wasn't mad, so much as she was embarrassed. Much to Delilah's relief he hadn't pushed conversation on her, deciding to focus mainly on conversing with Bobby. The two of them had had a steady stream of dialogue from the house to the car and now nearly to the store.

The grocery store was a good size, and Bobby was very enthusiastic to be out in the world again after almost a week of seclusion. He beamed his thousand watts smile up at her, she did her best to fake a matching one. It was thankfully enough to appease him, but the frown that Seb flashed her, made it clear that she hadn't fooled him.

At the front of the store stood a blue glittered airplane, that would take its passenger on a two-minute ride for the meager cost of four quarters. She groaned internally when she saw it, knowing that her son would plead for one go round. However, the idea of a little time to herself appealed to her greatly, so when Bobby started his campaign, she relented quickly. Followed by the quick suggestion that she go in the store and get everything they needed while the two of them stay outside for a ride. Even though Seb did not look like he liked the idea, Bobby's adorable face made the strong man cave.

Delilah pushed the cart around the grocery store when she started getting a tingling sensation. Her skin was crawling, with the feeling that someone was watching her. She sped up slightly and abruptly turned down an aisle that she didn't even need anything on, her heart was beating against her chest. She tried to tell herself that it was nothing and to stay calm, the pep talk wasn't working. She looked over her shoulder casually, making sure to keep her eyes on the shelves, not making it obvious that she was looking for another person in the aisle.

Her breath caught as she accidently made eye contact with a tall man following her, he smiled, but it felt wrong. She quickly took an assessment of him before turning back around. He was tall, with dark hair and eyes that were almost black they were such a deep brown. Delilah wouldn't say he was a bad looking man, but she didn't like the fact that he wasn't even trying to pretend that he was shopping for something. His eyes were fixed on her unapologetically.

She took a chance and stopped pretending to be deciding on the right cleaning product, amongst the plethora of choices. Praying that he would be unable to justify hanging behind her, making his only choice to continue walking down the aisle past her.

"Did you catch me staring at you?" The man's voice was deep and sickly sweet, when she looked up at him, he had a fake innocent smile on his face. He was a good-looking man, but that did nothing to help the fear that was coursing through her.

"No, not at all." She lied, not wanting to make him think that she had suspected him of much worse than staring. The last thing that she wanted was for him to feel backed into a corner, like she did.

He laughed, placing his hand on her shoulder, she went rigid under his touch. His grip was firm but not abnormally tight, still the fact that he was putting his hands on her sent all of her alarm bells ringing.

I never should have left Sebastian! Where is he?

At the same time, she fervently wished that he were here to protect her, but she was also glad that he was somewhere else with Bobby. If something did happen to her, at least her son would be safe. The man looked down at her, with a predatory gaze. She had no idea what to make of the man, and she wished he would just go away.

"That is sweet of you, trying to pretend like you didn't see me." The man started rubbing her shoulder gently. He was either the most forward man she had ever met, or she was about to be thrown over his shoulder and kidnapped. "Obviously, what I have heard about red heads isn't true."

Did this guy almost scare me to death to hit on me? This was the last damn thing she needed!

———

177

Delilah put her hand on her hip and prepared to rip this guy a new one, the man's eyes shot a wary look over her shoulder. It was the only warning that she received before a large hand wrapped itself around her midriff, pulling her firmly backward until she hit a familiar hard frame. His hand burned through the light fabric of her dress; her body came alive everywhere that they were sandwiched together. The man that had had his hand on her shoulder seized to exist for her, as she reveled in the protection of Sebastian's embrace.

"If what you heard, is that they have fiercely jealous boyfriends, then it is indeed the truth." She felt the fabric that once lay smoothly over her stomach bunch under his hand, the strength with which he held her, excited her to no end. "If you don't believe me, I would be happy to demonstrate."

Delilah had to hold back the laughter as the previously well bronzed man that stood before her turned white as a ghost. Served him right for hitting on someone so forcibly in the grocery store. Really, what was wrong with him?

"Calm down man, I was just..." The stranger started to explain but Seb gave him no time.

"Leaving? Glad to hear it." There was a chill in Seb's voice that she had never heard before, the man must have recognized it also because without saying anything else he turned and left the aisle.

She allowed herself a couple more seconds to delve in the feel of the unexpected contact, before she pulled away and turned to face her "boyfriend". Looking up at him, he was staring down at her, the hunger in his eyes left little doubt about what he was thinking.

"Was that really necessary?" Delilah said what she thought that she should, but not how she really felt. Propriety and being a self-respecting independent woman meant that she should be wildly offended that he thought she needed him to jump to her aid. Then there was the other side of her, that felt like swooning from him chivalrously riding in and grabbing her like she belonged to him. To say that she was conflicted was an extreme understatement.

"He was touching you." It was a matter-of-fact statement and one that he obviously found self-explanatory.

Movement from beside Seb drew her eye, as she saw Bobby slowly unwrap himself from around one of Seb's legs. Seeing the arm that hadn't been on her, draped around the shoulders of her son, made her feel like an idiot for taking his chivalry so personally. Of course, he jumped in to protect her, he was being paid to do it. Well technically just to protect Bobby, but she was quite sure that her brother and he had worked out some sort of payment arrangement for her as well. Here she was getting all hot and bothered, when in reality he was just doing his job. *Was she the reason he was leaving because he could see how much she was starting to care for him?*

"Did you say it was okay for that man to touch you, mommy?" Bobby's question caught her by surprise.

"Did you?" Seb looked as if he had never even considered that she might have wanted the man's attention. Emotion darkened his forest green eyes, her heart leapt at the idea that he might be jealous.

"No, of course I didn't." Delilah bent down and placed a kiss on her son's forehead.

"But Rock touched you, did you say it was okay for Rock to touch you?" Bobby was clearly trying to figure out the puzzle of when to be concerned about someone touching his mom and when not to be. That was a maze that she really didn't not relish the idea of helping him navigate today, or any day soon, so she took the easy way out.

"Yes, I did sweetheart, and do you know why I did?" She asked Bobby, but she couldn't help but catch the surprise that lit Seb's expression.

"No." Bobby admitted.

"Because we trust Seb, he is here to protect us, right?" Delilah felt like a coward for such a simple answer when the real explanation was so complicated that she couldn't begin to describe it.

"That's true." Bobby shook his head in agreement and threw his arms around her. She rubbed his back and avoided looking up at Seb, she could feel his eyes on her. But she didn't want to know or see what he was thinking, afraid that he would accept her answer as the truth and not know it for what it was.

After the grocery store episode, Seb had suggested that they pick out a couple movies from one of those box rentals they have outside stores. Then Bobby begged her to make mile high nachos for dinner, his favorite. She was grateful when Seb suggested that he and Bobby kick around a soccer ball that he had bought at the store. He tried to suggest that maybe she would like help with dinner, she quickly declined. The last thing that she needed was to be moving around the kitchen, trying to avoid contact with Seb.

The Carne Asada was done, the veggies cut, and the guacamole and fresh salsa finished. She stood back and took a deep delicious breath in, letting her mind wonder back to her childhood. When her grandma Rosa had bounced her on her knee and sung Spanish ballads to her, while she helped press the tortillas. Her grandmother had been like a mother and father to her, because her parents worked so much, she was either alone or with her grandma. That is up until she had died of a heart attack when Delilah was ten, cooking her grandma Rosa's food always made her feel nostalgic and a little heart sick.

Delilah walked out of the house, forcing her mind to return to the present. Walking onto the porch she was right in time to see her son kick the soccer ball hard, it flew in the direction of the porch. She gathered by their exclamations that she hadn't been his original target. She covered her face and felt the ball whack her in the forearms. An involuntary wince scrunched up her face, from the sting that the ball left.

They both came running up to her, Seb reaching her before her son could. He took her arms rubbing her forearms, which were both over sensitive due to the sting of the ball. Her breath caught in her throat, and she tried to keep the passion that his touch ignited from showing on her face. He didn't meet her eyes and she was thankful for that.

"Mommy, are you okay?" Bobby had finally made it to the porch and was looking at her wary of getting in trouble, but also concerned for her welfare.

She smiled down at him. "Yes, I will be fine. That was one heck of a kick."

He beamed. "Thanks, rock said I'm natural."

"I said you're a natural." There was laughter in Seb's voice as he corrected Bobby.

"Right, I'm a natural." Bobby repeated correctly. "He thinks that I should sign up for soccer."

"I don't think that is a bad idea." Her heart fluttered at the easy comradery between the two of them. "I will look into it when everything settles down, I promise."

"Do you need a kiss better?" Bobby's suggestion was expected, in their household they used kisses like others used Band-Aids. She did not look forward to the day that her kiss no longer held the magic to wash away his hurts.

"Yes, please." Delilah said, smiling at her son.

There was a tiny glint of something she didn't recognize in her son's eyes. "Rock should do it." A smile lit his face, as if he was enjoying his own suggestion.

Delilah looked down at her arms, they were still being held by Seb's firm hands. She was about to change her mind and refuse the magical kiss of healing when her arms were unceremoniously dropped. Her son's smile faded at the same time that her heart fell to her feet.

"I don't think so buddy." Seb sounded jovial and light, Delilah felt like crawling into a hole. "If you are the one that hurt her, you are the one that needs to kiss it better. Those are the rules, right?"

Seb was trying to wriggle out of an awkward situation and avoid having to kiss her forearm. She could make it harder on him by telling him that they had no such rule in their house, but what would be the point? If he didn't want to kiss her, she sure as sugar was not going to make him.

"That is true." She held her arms out and plastered on a pretend pout. "Where are my magical healing kisses sir?"

Bobby laughed at the face that she was making and placed light as a feather kisses on both her arms. She raised both of her arms into the air, trying not to wince as she felt the pain from her bullet wound.

"So much better." She allowed her arms to fall to her sides, careful not to jar her shoulder again. "Now, that I am healed, it is time for dinner you two. Which movie are we going to watch first?"

"Mine." Seb and Bobby answered at the same time, then they both stuck their tongues out at each other. It was so perfect that it could have been planned.

She fought back the tears that the moment threatened to bring to the surface. Seb and Bobby had grown close in the last week, they had an easy way around each other, and she knew that it would be painful for her son to watch him walk away. Seeing the two of them also brought to the surface a reminder, not that she needed one, that Bobby no longer had a dad to joke around with. A reality that she didn't think had really sunk in for either her or her son.

Chapter 19

The little boy's weight in his arms, felt too familiar. Taking each step one at a time, trying to concentrate on the present, fighting back the memories of the past. He focused on the feel of the carpet beneath his feet, noting that it wasn't sand crunching under his boots. Looking at the knots of wood in the natural walls, instead of the dust covered walls of the middle eastern homes. The smell of Delilah's dinner still lingering in the air, erasing the scents of gunpowder and dirt.

By the time he reached Bobby's bedroom and had been able to remain in Napa and not flash back to Iraq, he was relieved and proud of himself. He had learned the visualization technics from the psychiatrist that had cleared him after returning home. Seb had not ever been able to successfully utilize them though, not until now.

Maybe because you are finally somewhere that you want to be, with people you want to be with.

He hated to admit it even to himself, but he knew that it was true. Knowing that he only had a couple days left with Delilah and Bobby, he had spent the whole day savoring every memory with them. But the fact that doing something as simple as carrying a tired boy to bed threatened to overwhelm his senses and send him right back overseas, was proof that he was no good for anyone. In order to be the provider and protector of a family you had to be stable and consistent. Neither of which he felt like he was at the present time.

The thought of his reaction and behavior with Delilah was a good example of that. Since the moment he met her almost, he had been in a personal war with himself not to step out of line, and still he had failed several times. Today in the grocery store he had been ready to snap that slimy stranger's arm in half for touching her. It had taken every bit of self-control that he possessed not to physically remove his hand from her delicate shoulder. Seb had done the next best thing, to take her and bring her abruptly against his own body. He still worried that he might have been a little too rough with her, and lord knew he had no right to touch her at all. But it was instinctual to show the man that she belonged to him, even though she didn't.

When she hadn't fought his embrace or even shown any discomfort, it sent pleasure roaring through his body. Then when she relaxed back into him, it had almost been too much to handle.

Seb closed the door quietly, not wanting to wake up the sleeping boy.

It had been a whirl wind of emotions today; he had made memories with both Bobby and Delilah that he would hold onto for the rest of his life. Playing with Bobby brought a longing up inside of Seb that he never had experienced before. Bobby made it easy for Seb to laugh and joke, the more time he spent with the little boy the less he reminded him of Mo. Which was a particularly good thing, because for the most part the flash backs had been held at bay. Despite the fact that Bobby called him by the same nickname that Mo had, they were clearly two different boys. He cared for Bobby and was reluctant to give over his protection to anyone, even Cody. Yet at the same time he knew that if a situation arose that he could only save one of them, his mind would be too clouded with emotion to make a levelheaded decision.

You are no good to them. You aren't what they need.

185

Walking back down the stairs, the words rang true in his mind, in more than one way.

Seb planned on calling the Hawthornes tonight, to tell them about the switch on Monday. He would have to tell Cody of the situation, and the need to keep the Hawthornes in the dark about personal matters. He wouldn't be able to leave them thinking that Cody might inadvertently give Hawthorne information that he could use to break up mother and son. Cody would agree with Seb. He was almost positive.

Her back was to him, she was sitting on one of the couches, resting her auburn curls on her arm. His fingers could remember the feel of her silky strands running through them, before he could stop himself, Seb realized that he wasn't remembering he was doing. He looked down into Delilah's surprised upturned face as she looked at him, clearly not understanding why he was running his hands through her hair.

"I love your hair." *What the hell are you doing?!*

"You do?" There was an endearing shyness in her question.

"Yes, very much." He admitted against his better judgment.

"I like yours too." Delilah's fingers were playing with the hem of her dress, drawing his attention to her creamy white legs.

He laughed despite the passion coursing through his veins. "You don't have to say that. I know my old man hair is not something that women usually desire."

She shot him another shocked look.

"What? You look like I just told you that the curtains match the drapes and invited you to a private showing." He didn't think that her azure eyes could get any bigger, but they managed.

"I never thought of that. Do they?" The open curiosity was adorable, he wished that he found it adorable, instead of sexy as hell.

Seb pulled his hand back from their silky haven. Deciding that an ice-cold beverage might do his internal body temperature some good, he started walking to the kitchen. Last minute remembering his manners. "Do you want something to drink?"

"No, thanks." He didn't look back at her, just headed to the kitchen, needing to put space between the two of them desperately.

Seb buried his face in the fridge needing the coolness to wash over him. He felt her approach before he withdrew from the fridge to look at her. Not trusting himself to be alone in the kitchen with the woman that fired up his libido faster than anyone he had ever met. Finally, he grabbed a sparkling water from the fridge, wishing that it could be a beer or even something stronger. But he was on the job, which he needed to keep reminding himself as he looked into Delilah's eyes.

"Did you change your mind?" Seb would have welcomed another excuse to open the fridge again and drag his eyes from her petite body. She looked so fragile and small compared to him, he wanted to do unspeakable things to her and at the same time cherish and protect her.

"Yes, I did." There was a twinkle in her eyes, that made him think that she meant more than she said.

"What do you want?" Seb cursed himself as he heard the need deepened tone of his voice. His control was slipping, it always felt like it was slipping around her.

"Well, that is complicated." Delilah seemed hesitant to say something, she bit her lower lip in contemplation, and he had to hold back a groan. He wanted to bite her pillow like lips, and lick, and suck, and hell everything that could be done, he wanted to do it. "I want the truth, but at the same time I'm afraid of it."

Her vulnerable statement made him feel like a Creighton for the things he was imaging doing to her. "Don't be afraid, you can ask me anything." It was the truth, something about her made him want to stop holding back and holding things inside. She made him want to share every part of himself, even his heart and that scared the crap out of him.

"If the circumstances were different, would you have turned me down last night? If you weren't here working, would you have made love to me?" He cringed inside when she said that he had turned her down, *is that how she saw what happened last night?*

"First of all, I did not turn you down." Seb could see doubt cloud her eyes. "Really, I wish you didn't see it that way."

"I don't know how it could be looked at any differently." She shrugged. "I wanted to make love to you, and you only wanted to hold me. How can that be construed in another way?"

"The way you explain it, makes it sound like I don't want you." Seb was astounded that after his many slip ups with this woman, she could be so oblivious to the way he wanted her.

"Don't, not didn't. That sounds like present tense." Delilah looked up at him, he could see the raw emotion, raging in her oceanic eyes.

"It is very present tense." Seb moved closer to her, his body doing what it wanted, what all of him wanted if he was honest. "I wanted you in the past, I want you this moment, and I am one hundred percent certain that I will want you in the future. But none of that changes the fact that I have no right to want you at all."

"Because you are here to protect me?" Delilah was searching his face, he wanted to look away but couldn't. Maybe he wanted her to see him, with all of his flaws, and still want him. Could that even be possible?

"Because I'm me, and you don't need a broken man in your life." Seb knew he was trying to drive her away with his words, at the same time his body was inches from hers. "You have been through a stressful situation and are grieving, the chances of me making love to you and you not hating me in the morning are slim to none. It would be me taking advantage of you, while you were vulnerable."

"What about today in the grocery store?" Delilah ran her fingers up his forearms, making him swallow to force moisture back into his mouth.

"What about it?" His mind was working overtime to stay focused on their conversation and not on her hands that had made their way up to his biceps. His muscle flexed automatically under her touch; he clenched his fist to keep from touching her. He wished that he had water bottles in both hands instead of just one.

"You called yourself my boyfriend, in front of that nice gentleman." Her hands were now flat on his chest. He was sure she could feel his heart beating wildly in his chest.

189

Wait, what?!

"Nice gentleman my ass, I saw the way that man was looking at you." Seb froze as she came to the hem of his shirt, needing her to slide her hands underneath, praying that she would. She took her time, her eyes never leaving his own, as she slid her fingers over his stomach.

"Was it anything like the way you're looking at me right now?" Delilah looked at him with a challenge in her words.

"No." Seb dragged out the word, his mind almost completely past coherent thought. "He looked at you like an innocent schoolboy, compared to how I look at you. Compared to how I want you."

It was all that Seb could take, he was past the point of holding back, past the point of thinking about propriety. He dropped the water bottle not caring where it fell, needing his hands on her more than he needed his next breath. Thrusting his hands into her fiery curls he leaned her head back, dipping his own down to capture her sweet mouth with his own. He had meant for it to be a gentle kiss, but his need to show her how wild she drove him, also drove the kiss. Seb plunged his tongue into her mouth, exploring, tasting, reveling in the soft velvety texture that was Delilah.

My Delilah......

The possessive thought made his body freeze momentarily, the war between what he wanted and what was right, reared its' ugly head inside of him.

Delilah must have felt his body go rigid, she started coyly flickering his tongue with hers. While running her hands over the muscles on his back, she nipped at his lower lip. The exact thing he had been daydreaming about doing to her, all the sensations he was feeling overwhelmed his restrain. He slid his hands down to her shoulders, along the curvature of her slim back, finally finding that roundness of her bottom. Seb cupped the softness, gave it a squeeze that made her moan into his mouth.

With one swift movement he lifted her, pressing her into himself, so they were connected all the places that he longed to be. She fit so perfectly against him; her butt fit so perfectly in his hands. He felt her lock her legs around his hips, she was a marvel, he hadn't thought her legs long enough to do that. But she clung on to him tightly, the pressure it created was exquisite torture.

He needed more, to see more of her and taste all of her. His need was blinding. Seb took one hand off her butt, to reach for the strap of her thin dress. He slid the strap down her shoulder, she helped him by lowering her arm, so the dress strap slipped off. He broke off his kiss, wanting to see the treasure he had uncovered. He sucked in a sharp breath when he saw that she hadn't been wearing a bra, at any time in the day, he could have reached out and touched her bare breast under the thin covering. The thought drove him nearly mad with passion.

"All day, you didn't wear a bra?" He asked the question while gently suckling her ear lobe, allowing his hand to play across her exposed breast.

"Sometimes I don't." Her words were breathy and heavy with her need, sending shock waves of pleasure rippling through him.

191

"You never should." Seb was not joking in the least, but her husky laugh speared his passion past the point of self-restraint. "We need a bed."

She shook her head no, while returning his nibbles on his ears, running her tongue along his neck. Basically, making it impossible to think clearly, if she wanted to stop, she had an odd way of showing it.

"Too far." Delilah into the hollow of his throat, he buried his face in her curls as she explored him with her mouth.

Knowing that she was right, and that if he didn't find them something quickly, he would take her right here in the kitchen. The thought made him harden, pushing against his zipper to an almost painful level. Seb started walking out of the kitchen, holding her while she worked her magic on him. It was a miracle that he managed to stumble them onto the couch without crushing her small body. Her legs still clung to him, but he wanted desperately to remove his clothing and free his need for her.

He played with her lips, nipping, and gently sucking them, as he pulled away, he felt her legs tighten. "Listen my little imp, I need to get up." The fear that crossed her passion deepened blue eyes, tore at his heart. "I want to take my clothes off. I need to feel my skin against yours."

Her desire fueled the fire that lit her eyes, making his urgency double. Seb got up tearing his shirt over his head, he heard her sharp intake of breath, he had heard it before. Without looking he knew that she was seeing his scars, he was lucky that all of his marks from the war could be covered with clothing, he knew many who were not so lucky. The realization of what he was about to do, who he was crashed down around him.

Before he could pull his shirt back on and put a halt to their love making, she was there, running her hands over his scars. When she started to kiss them, he was lost once again, in the magic she wove inside of him. She made it possible to forget the world around him and focus on her, her touch, her taste, the passion that she gave him.

His eyes flew open as he felt her nipples brush his abdomen, as she reached up to kiss a scar inches from his heart. Seb looked down and saw that she had discarded her dress and stood in front of him in only her panties. He recalled the purple bunnies with extreme clarity, thinking how he had thought they didn't really fit her personality. This woman wiggling almost naked against him was not the cute undies kind of woman, she was lace and satin, and all sexiness.

When she flicked his nipple which bore no scar, his pulse shot up and he knew that his limit of enduring her sweet torture was at its end. He picked her up and laid her down on the couch, with no warning, she let out a small cry of surprise.

As she lay on the couch, the shock of color from her hair and expressive eyes, was a huge contrast to the creamy whiteness of her skin. He could feel her eyes watching him as he unzipped his pants and shrugged the rest of his clothing off with one swift movement. A devious smile lit her angelic face as she surveyed him, he had never wanted any woman to like the way he looked more than he wanted her to.

After seeing his war-torn body, the fire of lust still blazed in her sapphire eyes, he felt relief and his own desire wash over him.

He reached down and hooked his fingers inside the sides of her underwear, "I hate your underwear."

He had meant for it to be playful, but from the sad look she gave him he knew he had missed the mark. Seb cursed himself, he had never been good at verbal foreplay, apparently nothing had changed during his stint of celibacy.

"They were a gift from……. someone told me they suited me." The idea of a man buying her underwear made him see red, but that was dumb, she had been married. Of course, her husband had bought her underwear, he wanted to buy her underwear himself.

"They don't." He stated, playing his fingers along the elastic top of the offending article of clothing. Enjoying the catch in her breathing every time he dipped his fingers further under the material. "I would buy you satin in shockingly bright colors because that is what you are. Soft as silk, and as sexy as sin."

As he spoke, he stopped his game, and drew her last piece of clothing down her legs. Exposing all of her to his eyes. "You're perfect."

Chapter 20

"You're perfect." The raw honesty in Seb's words sent her mind reeling, no one had ever said that to her. The craziest part was that she believed him, she believed that he found her perfect, and it made her want to cry. She held back her tears, knowing that crying was not usually a turn on for men.

It wasn't hard to focus on something else, as Seb kissed his way up her legs, taking his time. She squirmed with desire, her body pulsating with its' need for release, she didn't know how much more she could take. She wanted to reach down and pull him up, to force him to end this torture and give them what they both wanted, but the idea of her being able to budge him was laughable.

All thoughts of laughter fled her mind, as she felt him pause over her most private spot. Her eyes flew open. She hadn't even realized she had closed them. First his fingers brushed her, then they dipped inside, running down the length of her. Until they finally entered her, she stared at him, wanting to put a stop to it, but not wanting it to stop.

"You don't need to do that." She struggled for the words, needing to explain to him that she didn't actually like that. Her ex-husband had tried it a couple of times, but it really didn't feel good to her. *God this is awkward.*

"Yes, I do." At first, she thought he meant that he needed to do it for her, she was about to explain to him that he really didn't, when he continued smiling up at her ruefully. "I need to feel and taste you, everywhere."

He didn't break eye contact as he dipped his tongue into her, the look in his eyes as he tasted her. It was the most intimate, shocking experience she had ever had. He snapped the eye contact like a rubber band as he buried his face in her, there were too many sensations at once, she couldn't focus or concentrate.

He fondled her with his fingers, while his tongue had found the most amazing spot to play with. Seb started to suckle the spot that was driving her wild, she felt her whole body tighten, she had never felt anything so amazing in her life.

"Come for me love, let go." Her body seemed to hear Seb's words and react in turn, as she felt a climax rip through her.

"Oh yes, Sebastian." She felt her liquid passion warm her body, the aftershocks seemed to go on and on, she never wanted them to stop.

He left the spot where he had brought her so much pleasure, as he trailed kisses up her stomach. She felt his erection against her leg, knowing that she had reached her end, but he hadn't, made her feel guilty. That was until his mouth found her aching breast, with one hand he toyed with one nipple, mimicking what his mouth was doing with the other. Her need which she thought had been satiated flared back to life, she began to arch her back, the passion he was creating making it impossible to lay still.

"I love it when you call me that." He spoke while making love to her breasts with his mouth. If he thought she was capable of having a conversation while he did that, he was crazy. "No, one calls me Sebastian but you. I don't want anyone to ever call me that but you."

Through her passion clouded mind she heard his words, and they were more potent than any physical act he could have performed. He was giving her something of himself that was for her alone, she reached down running her fingers through his silver hair.

"Sebastian, please, I can't wait any longer." She heard him moan, when he moved further up her body, she could see the strain on his face. "I don't think you can either."

"You drive me crazy, my angelic imp." He spread her legs with his knee, she returned the nudge by wrapping her legs around his back, feeling him line up with the place she wanted him the most.

Seb crushed his mouth to hers, gone was the gentle exploratory kiss, in its place was a kiss filled with blinding raw need. She had just grown accustomed to the roughness of the kiss when he filled her in one swift motion. Delilah cried out, as her body had to stretch to accommodate him. He went still, breaking away from their kiss, and staring down at her in horror.

"Did I hurt you? Oh god, I'm sorry, it's been so long. I shouldn't have been so rough." Seb started to pull away, the fear that he was stopping gripped her heart in ice.

She tightened her legs around him, arching her back to pull him fully inside of her. His eyes looked at her questioningly.

"I haven't…. you know…since before my divorce." She was shy to tell him something so personal, but she needed him to know, that she just needed a moment to get adjusted to him. Delilah would die if he stopped now, she clenched around him, trying to show him her need for him.

His emerald eyes drove into her, there was a storm raging inside of them, of passion, and something else that she couldn't quite understand. Protectiveness? Possessiveness? Love? No, he didn't love her. It was in that moment that the truth hit her like a ton of bricks, she was head over heels in love with this man. That's why after all of these years of waiting she had yearned to give herself to him and to have him, if only in the physical way. She would take whatever she could get of him and hold it with her always.

He withdrew only to plunge back into her, with every motion he drove her need higher and higher. Seb watched her the whole time, she was having a hard time keeping her eyes open. They found a rhythm together that was driving her crazy. Until finally, she felt her whole-body shatter into a million shards of pleasure. She seized to exist as a single person, Delilah was in every way an extension of this man that had sent her to heaven.

Her eyes opened when her orgasm cascaded over her, she was just in time to see Sebastian come apart inside of her. His muscled shoulders rippled, and he threw his head back and called out her name. Then he brought his mouth down to capture her own, in a kiss that was like a summation of everything that she was feeling. He seemed to pour out all the emotions into one kiss, longing, belonging and something so much deeper.

When he withdrew from her, she was scared that he would just get up and get dressed. She prepared herself for the aftermath of what they had just done. Instead of leaving, he slid next to her on the couch and pulled her into the crook of his body. She snuggled back into him and allowed herself to imagine that this was her reality, that she had no worries in life but this man and her son. The simplicity of such an existence almost brought tears to her eyes, why couldn't life be that simple?

"I could stay like this forever." Seb echoed her own thoughts out loud.

"Me too." She admitted, "But we can't."

She said it lightly, but she suspected that they both felt the heaviness of her words. Not only could they not stay curled up naked on the couch, but they couldn't even stay together. They had tonight and tomorrow, and then neither of them knew what the future would bring. The tears were working their way to the surface once again, she refused to give into melancholy thoughts when she had just had the most amazing experience with the man holding her.

"I'm going to bed." She got up from the couch, stretched as if she were tired, well aware that Seb's eyes were taking in the back side of her. Delilah looked over her shoulder and smiled. "If you are too worn out, you can sleep on the couch."

Seb grinned, his eyes sparkling mossy gems. "I will show you how tired I am."

Delilah was always surprised by the speed of Seb, for a large man he was very quick. Before she could make it around the couch, he had caught up to her, and lifted her off the floor, into his arms. She couldn't help but laugh, thinking that this must be what it felt like to be swept off your feet, both literally and figuratively.

Seb drowned the humor out of her thoughts, nibbling on her neck and kneading her legs with his hand. Delilah planned on making this a night that she could hold onto and remember always, she refused to waste one moment.

There were whispers coming through the door of the bedroom, Delilah awoke to her son's giggle. She stretched, welcoming the morning with a full heart and a sore body. Her body reminding her of the magical night she had spent with Seb, and her heart making her acknowledge the fact that she had fallen……. hard. There was no denying it, she had not just given her body last night, she had given everything.

It had been the most foolish, wonderful thing that she had ever done. Delilah couldn't regret it if she tried, which she wasn't.

The door opened, the first thing she saw was her son trying to balance a cup of orange juice that was sloshing dangerously close to the edges of the cup. The pride in his eyes, when he looked at her, quieted any words of warning that she might have said. Seb was grinning down at her, holding a tray loaded with food, her heart skipped at seeing the open affection in his eyes. She would hold onto that and keep it. The fact that even though her feelings might be deeper, he made no effort to hide the fact that he does care for her. At least that's what she thought she saw in his emerald eyes.

"Happy Mother's Day!" Bobby yelled out, Seb just barely reaching for the juice in time to prevent her son from spilling it.

"Go ahead and give your mom a huge, good morning hug and I will arrange breakfast, okay buddy?" Seb was walking the tight rope of trying to keep Bobby from making a gigantic mess, but still trying to make him feel like he was part of the preparation. She knew how difficult that could be, and she loved that he cared enough to do it.

Bobby nodded to Seb before catapulting himself onto the bed with all of the energy of a five-year-old. After the hug had subsided, Seb set the tray down and handed her a cup of coffee. She closed her eyes and inhaled the unique smell of freshly brewed coffee, opening them to him studying her. When he saw her catch him looking at her, he put up a wall, so quickly that she was shut out from whatever he had been thinking.

Her son was hungry and started directing Seb what he would like on his plate, not allowing her to dwell on Seb closing off his emotions from her.

There was fresh fruit, homemade muffins, bacon, and eggs, enough to feed more than just three people. Bobby sat next to her on the bed and Seb made himself comfortable at the foot of the bed. She soaked in every moment of the breakfast, Seb and Bobby making fruit involved faces at each other across the bed. Seb picking out the blueberries from one of the muffins, after Bobby decided he did not like cooked blueberries. The patience he showed with her son, was another tug on her already smitten heart.

Seb caught her looking at him again, she was surprised it didn't happen more often, because she was always looking at him. "How was your Mother's Day breakfast?"

She moaned and rubbed her belly playfully. "It was the best Mother's Day breakfast I have ever had."

"Wait, what?" Bobby looked at her, betrayed.

"I'm sorry honey, I mean besides last years' cereal in bed, of course." Delilah tried to keep from laughing as her son nodded his approval that she remembered his efforts last year. "Where did you learn to cook so well?"

She knew that he wasn't exactly comfortable talking about himself, but she had a burning curiosity to know everything that she could about him.

"My mother and grandmother, they love to cook, and it was especially important to them that I know how to cook also. So, from a young age I was in the kitchen, working with them." Seb paused, a handsome smile lighting up his face. "My sister however was banned from the kitchen. I think she still might be."

"Banned, that sounds serious." Delilah laughed. "Tell me about her."

"Her name is Melanie, and she is 29 years old." She was relieved when he expanded on his description of his sibling. "She almost burnt down the kitchen when she was ten and ever sense then, she has not been allowed back in. I don't see her as often as I should or would like to. It's funny you know. When I was overseas, all that kept going through my mind was how when I got home and out of the military, I was going to make a point of seeing my family as much as possible." He looked distant as he drifted from talking about his sister to speaking about himself. "But life happens, you make decisions that pull you away from the people you most love."

She felt that statement like a stab in the heart, she wanted to scream at him that life didn't have to be like that. That if he made a decision to stay near her, she could love him. The words almost forced themselves out of her mouth, it would have been disastrous if she had let them escape. No matter what she felt for him or could possibly feel given more time, Seb had not changed his mind, tomorrow he would be gone. Nothing she could say would change that.

"You don't have to be away from the people you love." It was all she would allow herself to say, even that made her feel dangerously close to exposing too much of her emotions.

His eyes were sad when he looked at her. "Sometimes you don't have a choice. The military for example, they don't ask you whether you want to be away from your family. Whether it will hurt to miss birthdays, weddings, graduations, and sometimes even the death of a loved ones. The only way that you can get through it is by leaning on people in the same situations, brothers that know your pain and understand."

"Is that how you got through it?" Delilah asked, trying not to pry, but not being able to stop doing exactly that.

"Yes, I relied heavily on four of my fellow rangers specifically, we are still close." Seb hesitated, looking down at his hands. It made her think of the scars on his chest and back, she recalled running her fingers over them, wishing she could take away the pain of them. "That and also writing, I found that writing helped quite a bit."

"You mean like a diary?" The look he shot her was priceless. Outrage, until he saw that she was joking, then her reward was a wicked grin.

"No, not like a diary." Sebastian threw a piece of muffin at her, it hit her in the middle of the forehead. Bobby had been ignoring their conversation until he saw the food fly, then he burst out in laughter. "Men have journals, not diaries."

She laughed shaking her head. "I don't know. Dear journal does not quite have the same ring to it as dear diary. You might want to reconsider the name of your diary."

The look that he gave her, made her blood burn with desire inside her veins. She knew that if Bobby weren't in the room their conversation would have taken a turn towards lusty about then. "You are lucky there is a chaperone in this room." He once again seemed to read her mind.

"What's a chaperone?" Bobby asked, now fully invested in their conversation.

"It is someone who watches you and makes sure that you don't do anything naughty." She couldn't hold back the giggle that bubbled up, knowing that her son's definition of naughty and her own were two different things. If she had to guess, she would say that Seb's was closer to hers, than to her sons'.

"Mommy doesn't need a chaperone. She never does anything naughty." Her son was so innocent with his statement that it made her feel a little bad for her less than appropriate thinking. Until she saw Seb wink at her, with his devil may care grin on his handsome face.

"I'm sure you are right, buddy." Seb looked at Bobby very seriously, but she could only imagine what was going on in that head of his. She would like very much to know.

"Can I go watch T.V.? Or do I need to help clean up?" Bobby was clearly not eager to help clean up, but he knew that he needed to at least offer. She could see him praying that Seb would turn down his aid, she decided to help her son out.

"You go ahead. I will help Seb with the dishes." Relief flooded her son's face, as he hopped off the bed. He ran out of the room before she could change her mind, or Seb could contradict her in any way.

Delilah felt his eyes burning into her skin before she turned her head towards where he sat on the bed. Seb's emerald eyes were alive with passion and a little humor as he stared at her.

"Your chaperone is gone." Seb smiled at her. "I dare you to call my journal a diary one more time."

She had never been caught between laughing and longing so much in her life, but somehow Seb made sexy so much fun.

"I would never insult a man's…. diary." She squealed as he grabbed at her and pulled her onto his lap.

Chapter 21

Seb had surprised himself by being able to walk out of Delilah's room after one long lingering kiss. He only managed to accomplish that by reminding himself that he needed to be downstairs with Bobby. He might have thrown all professional integrity out the window last night where Delilah was concerned, but he could at least still watch out over Bobby sufficiently.

Sufficient? Maybe, but who are you kidding? You are emotionally invested in both of them.

How had his emotions gotten so far out of hand so quickly? Maybe it was because this is the first case he had worked, that involved a child? Seb would like to think it was that easy, but he knew that the reason ran much deeper than that. He wanted to protect both of them with a ferocity that went way beyond the professional realm. He sighed as he plopped down next to Bobby on the couch, after depositing the dirty dishes in the kitchen.

Seb had told Delilah to take her time getting ready, the Mother's Day festival didn't start for another hour or so. He was excited about getting them out of the house, he suspected that both mother and son needed a tiny bit of normalcy infused back into their lives. And Seb wanted to be the one to give it to them.

"We can watch something else, if you want?" Bobby looked up at him, his case of hero worship was going to take a blow when Seb left tomorrow. He forced the unwanted thought from his mind, *focus on today, you still have today with them.*

"Nah, this is good, what is it?" Seb tried to follow what was happening on the television screen, but it was all strange animals and large eyed human characters to him. The last time he had watched cartoons had been when he was a child, so he was not up on the latest ones.

Bobby delved into a strange and foreign world, explaining the differences between their world and ours. Almost like it was a real-life place, Seb suspected to Bobby it was close enough. He just kept nodding his head, but truth be told he had been lost from early on in the explanation.

Bobby must have noticed. "You don't like it." Seb was not happy with himself when he saw tears well up in the boy's eyes. He knew that Bobby would be over emotional for a while after everything he has been through and the loss he has experienced.

"No, it's not that buddy." Seb wanted to reassure him that there was nothing wrong with his show. "I just don't understand it."

"I thought grown-ups understand everything." Bobby seemed to contemplate Seb's confession with a profoundly serious face.

"I can't even begin to tell you how much we don't understand." Seb shook his head as if disgusted with his own short comings.

"Like what?" He could sense that Bobby needed something real from him, maybe so he didn't feel as alone in his own confusion.

"This show for example." The little man did not hold back his look of disappointment at Seb's response. Like his talk previously with Bobby, Seb knew that he needed more than just easy answers. Bobby was trying to understand very grown-up problems and he needed insight into an adult's mind. "I don't understand why my father didn't want to stay and see me grow up. When I was younger, I used to think that I had done something wrong that had made him leave, but that my mom loved me too much to be mad at me. As I got older, I knew that I had been wrong to think that, but to this day I still don't understand why he left."

Seb had never spoken to anyone about his father's absence in his life, maybe he had chosen Bobby because he was safe to talk to. Or maybe because Bobby would be going through his own missing father issues, and he didn't want him to feel alone. Either way, he didn't think it was a wholly appropriate conversation for them to be having. But at this point the appropriate-professional wagon was way off the tracks, might as well burn the thing to the ground.

"I know why my dad is gone." Bobby's statement was full of quiet sorrow, Seb wondered if he actually did understand.

"You do?" Seb was quite sure that Bobby had no clue why Nate had been shot and killed, but maybe it was enough that the little boy understood that his father was gone.

"Yes, the bad man, with blue tears shot him." Bobby sniffled trying desperately to hold in the tears that were threatening to escape. "He shot mommy too."

Blue tears? What in hell does that……. oh no…. oh god no……

"Bobby, did you see the man that shot your father?" Seb felt a cold ice grip his heart, praying that he was wrong.

The little boy looked up at him, but for the first time Seb didn't see him as anyone but Bobby. Mo was gone, he knew that he was beyond Seb's reach or aid. But Bobby was sitting here, next to him, looking to him for help and guidance. He was so scared that he would fail Bobby the same way he failed Mo.

"Yeah, I saw him." Bobby voice was so small and so scared sounding, Seb grabbed his hand, wanting to lend him all of the strength he could. "Is that good……. or bad?"

"It's going to be okay; I promise." Seb pulled Bobby into a hug, the boy hid his face against Seb's chest and let the tears burst out.

That was how Delilah found them forty minutes later, Bobby had fallen asleep in Seb's arms. He had thought about moving him, but he didn't want to wake the boy, and he found comfort in how at ease Bobby felt with him. He looked up as he heard Delilah enter the living room, she looked stunning, but she always looked stunning to him.

She had left her red curls down. They were already drying in silky soft ringlets around her face. Seb's fingers itched to touch them, remembering how soft they were against his roughened skin. Delilah wore a little make-up that only accentuated her natural beauty, it covered the light spattering of freckles that were usually visible on her cheeks, he found that he missed them. Her dress was tight over her generous breasts and flowed out at the waist, it was a dark purple color that looked beautiful on her.

"You look gorgeous." A light blush colored her cheeks, he could look at her forever and never get bored.

"Thank you." Her gaze softened even more when she looked down upon her sleeping child. "Is everything okay with Bobby? It's a little early for him to nap."

Seb sighed, wishing that he didn't need to tell her what he needed to tell her. No sense in pro-longing the inevitable. "We were having a little talk about his T.V. show and somehow the conversation took a rather serious turn." She looked alarmed and he rushed to his point. "Anyway, I told him a little about my past and he started talking about what happened to Nate."

"What did he say?" It was barely a whisper, as she sat down next to them on the couch. They were both speaking quietly to try and not wake up the sleeping child in his arms.

"He told me that he knew that Nate was gone because the bad man with the blue tears shot him." Seb waited for it to sink in for her, she just looked at him clearly puzzled.

"I don't understand, blue tears?" Delilah asked.

"Delilah, Bobby saw the man that shot Nate. He must have had a tattoo on his face, from the sounds of it a possibly distinct tattoo." Seb was torn between not rustling Bobby and wanting to hold Delilah as the truth hit her. She pitched forward, her elbows resting on her thighs and her face buried in her hands. Her reaction was reasonable; this was not good news.

If the people that shot Nate Hawthorne were after them before, they would double their efforts if they knew that Bobby could identify one of them. Right now, only the three of them knew, but he had little hope that it would stay that way for long. He didn't plan on telling anyone, that was not in his job description. If he ran to the police and told them that Bobby was a witness, instead of just an innocent victim. It would only put the person he was trying to protect in further danger, the opposite of what he was being paid to do. The ball was firmly in Delilah's court.

"What are you going to do?" He couldn't help but ask, he was too worried not to.

She looked up at him, her expression one of exhaustion. "What do you mean, what am I going to do? What choice do I have? If I don't tell the police, they may never get the man who killed Nate, we may never be able to go home again. It's not really much of a choice, is it?"

"That's true, I guess." Seb was reluctant to voice his opinion, knowing that he would be speaking from a place of selfish fear, fear for their safety. "You don't have to tell the authorities, only the three of us know."

He hated the shocked look that she gave him, seeming to judge him for even thinking such a thing.

"What kind of example would I be setting for Bobby? He will grow up knowing that he knew something that could have brought his father's killer to justice and that I didn't go forward on his behalf. He would never forgive me." Her expression had gentled into sad resolve. "In a perfect world the police would catch the man responsible and put him away for life and then we would go home. Life would go back to normal......well the new normal......the normal without Nate."

Seb refused to feel hurt that in her picture of a perfect world, she hadn't even bothered to fit him in. It shouldn't hurt, he didn't want it to hurt, but dammit it did!

"Even if they catch the shooter, with or without Bobby's help, the likelihood of you two going back to life as usual is nil." Seb tried not to sound bitter or angry, even though what he was saying was the truth, the reason he was saying it was because he was hurt. "If this is gang related, which it seems that it is, there may be no going back for you."

The thought obviously hadn't crossed her mind. He knew she had grown up in a gang infested neighborhood, she knew what he was saying was the truth. He watched her mind work through her options, as her face grew grimmer and grimmer, he knew that she was not enjoying what she was envisioning. He felt like the lowest of the low for making her face the harsh reality of her situation. But this was his last day with her, he wouldn't be here tomorrow to talk about it. All his thoughts seemed to hurt him worse than a thousand desert scorpions.

"Fine, you're right." He watched as she physically squared her shoulders, she looked like some sort of fairy queen, readying to do battle. Seb marveled at the way she was able to look both indestructible and delicate at the same time. "We have no real ties to where we live, not anymore. I can get work as a counselor anywhere, maybe even in a school or something." He sat fascinated as she built their future from the ground up right in front of his eyes. "Yes, maybe this is for the best. A new community, a new apartment, if change is forced on you, the best thing you can do is ride the change. Make it yours, don't let life force you down a path, choose your path."

She was the picture of strength personified, and he wanted desperately to be on the path that she chose to go down. He could only imagine what life would be like, going through it with a partner that was as strong and capable as she was. Seb was not the man that would get to walk alongside her, he was filled with envy for that man.

"Well, it sounds like you have it all figured out." There were bitter notes in his voice that he couldn't help.

"We should probably wake him up, so we can get going to the festival, but first I need to call the detective and tell him what Bobby said." Delilah looked a bit reluctant despite her brave bravado. "I will be right back. Do you want me to take him off you first?"

Seb pondered just sitting there for a few minutes longer, but he decided that it would be better if he started to distance himself as soon as possible. "No, I can set him down on the couch. You go make your call; I have to make one of my own."

Delilah nodded and then headed upstairs, she probably wanted privacy. That suited him just fine, because he would need privacy for his phone call as well.

He slid Bobby from his lap and placed him on the spot that Delilah had just vacated. Seb was not looking forward to the phone call he had to make. In truth he had planned on putting it off until that evening, or even possibly the next day. Hawthorne made his skin crawl, and he was dreading telling him that he was leaving.

Seb walked out onto the porch, he wanted privacy, but for safety reasons he didn't want to go too far. He took a huge breath in, willing the fresh woodsy air to strengthen him to make the conversation with Hawthorne bearable. He listened to the ringing of the line, until the familiar voice greeted him.

213

"Hawthorne speaking." What once had sounded like refinement, now just sounded cold to Seb.

"Mr. Hawthorne, Seb Rockmiller here." He tried to keep his tone void of emotion.

"Aww, Mr. Rockmiller, I hope everything is all right. This is earlier than your scheduled check in. Unless of course something useful has happened." It was disgusting to Seb how the older man's voice sounded pleased at the idea that Seb might have some dirt on Delilah. It took everything inside of him not to curse the man out and tell him what an expensive piece of trash he thought he was.

"Nothing useful has happened, but there will be a changing of the guard, so to speak." Seb hoped that Hawthorne wouldn't raise a big stink about it, he wasn't in the mood to explain why he was leaving.

"Really?" He could almost hear the old man's gears turning, trying to figure out what exactly was going on. "That is unexpected, can you please inform me as to why a new guard will be protecting my grandson? I hope that nothing untoward has happened."

Shit! The old asshole is anything but dumb, you must at least give him that.

"No, sir, I assure you that everything is fine." Seb had to sell what he said next, he needed Hawthorne to believe him one hundred percent. "It is something that we do at some point in every protection detail. You see people in high stress situations can form unhealthy attachments to the people paid to protect them. Children are especially susceptible to this, so to ensure that that doesn't happen, we switch the person protecting them."

The silence hung between the two men; he wasn't sure if Hawthorne would buy that it was because of Bobby that he had to leave. In his experience the best lies, held some truth and he was honestly worried about Bobby forming an attachment to him. What he left out was that he was even more afraid of his own attachments to both Delilah and Bobby.

"I see, so this has nothing to do with Ms. Reyes?" Hawthorne did not sound convinced, *Shit, shit, shit!*

"No, it doesn't." Seb heard it, the defensiveness in his voice, he knew that Hawthorne wouldn't miss it.

"The problem Mr. Rockmiller is that I don't believe you. I think that you are holding information back, maybe information that I could use. I do not like being toyed with, and I am especially familiar with how manipulative Ms. Reyes can be. So, if your company would like to keep my business, you will give me every scrap of information that I need to get my grandson." The old man's voice was steel, unfortunately for him Seb was fired up hot enough to melt steel.

Seb wanted to rage against the man. Tell him that he didn't have a damn clue when it came to Delilah. That if Seb had anything to do with it, he would never get his grandson. Last of all, he would tell him that he could take his business and shove it where the sun doesn't shine, but he couldn't say anything like that. Because no matter how mixed up he was, he wouldn't screw over Cody, or the business. Plus, he could not trust the fact that if they stopped protecting Delilah, Hawthorne wouldn't hire someone shady as hell to watch her every move.

"Whether or not you believe me Mr. Hawthorne, does not change our protocol when dealing with someone so young. Bobby is especially vulnerable because of the added trauma of losing his father." *Keep calm, keep it about business, don't sound like it is personal.* "As to Ms. Reyes being manipulative, I have not been able to find any evidence of that. I will assure you that my partner Cody West, will be taking over for me tomorrow and he will be more than willing to watch out for anything useful to you."

There was only a small silence before Hawthorne's reply, giving Seb hope that he had sold him on his explanation.

"I can see your point, regarding Bobby, and the last thing that we would want would be for him to get attached to a paid employee." It felt like Hawthorne was deliberately trying to goad him. "As long as you are sure that Mr. West will go along with our previous arrangement. Then I don't feel like there is any need to terminate your services, at least for now. But I do warn you Mr. Rockmiller, I don't like surprises, unless they are beneficial to me. So, I suggest that Mr. West surprise me with something I can use, sooner, rather than later. Am I understood?"

"I guarantee that if there is any dirt to be found on Ms. Reyes, Mr. West will be able to find it for you." Seb was seethed with barely controlled hostility, struggling against lashing out at the vile old man.

"Very good." With that Hawthorne hung up, Seb sat there for a moment, wanting to throw the phone into the trees. Needing to be able to take his frustration out on something.

Seb ran his hand through his hair, cursing at the sky, wishing that this whole situation was different. He turned to go back into the house, and was met with a steaming mad redhead, standing in the doorway. Looking like she was going to murder him where he stood.

Chapter 22

What in the world?!

Delilah's head was spinning, betrayal tasted bitter on her tongue, as she tried to formulate what to say and what to think. She had only caught the end of his conversation, but it was enough for her heart to clench and her blood to run cold in her veins.

Dirt on me? Manipulative? Had Sebastian been digging up dirt on her this whole time?

Oh lord, had he told Hawthorne that they had slept together?

No, surely, he wouldn't have told him that. That would end up looking just as bad for Seb's company as it did for her. Wouldn't it? Or would there be a way for Hawthorne to turn it so that it was all her fault? If anyone would be able to, it was Hawthorne. She had never met a man that was sneakier, or more heartless in her life. The idea that she might have handed him a tool to rip her son from her loving arms, made bile rise in her throat. She felt sick.

"I can explain." She had almost forgotten that she was busy glaring at Seb when she had gotten lost in thought. Hearing him speak, sharpened her anger, reminding her that she would deal with Hawthorne later. Right now, she had to deal with the man standing in front of her, looking guilty as sin.

"Please do." Even though she invited him to speak she didn't actually give him time to. "Please explain to me how I was right all along. That you were some sort of G.I. Joe spy sent to get information about us for the Hawthornes. I knew that their offer of help was not without strings attached, strings that they would like to attach to my son and use to pull him away from me."

"You're right." His confession was soft, but it stopped her dead in her tracks. She hadn't realized until that moment how much she had wanted him to convince her that she was wrong. It felt like her heart was shattering into a million crushed pieces. "But you're also wrong."

"How is that?" She asked.

"At first it was just me protecting Bobby, nothing else. Then when I called for my first progress report, Hawthorne not too subtly suggested that there would be good money in it if I noticed you do anything that could make you seem unfit to care for Bobby." Seb looked her straight in the eye as he spoke, she found the intensity of his gaze uncomfortable, but she couldn't look away.

"So, you seduced me, for what? How could he possibly use that?" She honestly had no idea what his end game was, how could her sleeping with him help the Hawthornes get custody?

She almost felt the heat from the flare of anger that lit his green eyes, it made her regret her questions instantly.

"Is that what you think that was?" Seb ran his hand through his hair, he looked frustrated and mad. "No, you're way off base with that, what happened between us has nothing to do with the Hawthornes."

"Why are you yelling?" It was clear on their faces that neither she nor Seb had heard Bobby come out onto the porch. She immediately felt ashamed that their elevated voices had woken up her son, he didn't need any more chaos in his life.

"Didn't you notice that Seb had bad hearing? I was yelling so that he would be able to hear me." Bobby looked at her doubtfully, a small smile playing on his mouth. "Really, apparently his ears are as old as his hair." She smiled and winked at her son, to indicate that she was joking.

Bobby burst out in laughter, "Is that why the army men called you old man? Not just your hair?"

To Seb's credit he caught on quickly to the fact that she wanted keep Bobby in the dark about them arguing. "Not just that buddy, but when I walk you can hear the bones in my knees crunch. Like an old skeleton." To prove his point, he swung one of his legs back and forth, Delilah was surprised that you could in fact hear a crunching noise.

"Oh, cool." Bobby looked at Seb like he had pulled a rabbit from his hat, eyes filled with wonder. "Rock is the coolest, right mom?"
"Yes, he is the coolest." Hollow was how her response sounded; it couldn't be helped. She did not have many good feelings about Seb right now, and she really didn't like that her son did either.

From the moment that the conversation had resonated with her, she knew that she needed to get herself and her son away from Seb's "protection." There was more than one way to be unsafe. They were in danger from the man that had murdered Nate, of that, she was positive. But now she felt like if they stayed under the surveillance of Seb and his partner, they might be in danger of being split up. That was something that she could never let happen. It wasn't like she had anything to hide or did anything that she thought the Hawthornes could use against her in a court of law. The impropriety with Seb notwithstanding, but for enough money people would and could lie. She was almost ninety percent certain that Seb wouldn't make up lies about them, but she had no idea about his partner Cody West. Maybe that was why Seb was so fired up to leave, maybe Hawthorne was leaning too hard on him for useful information.

She was confused, her head hurt, and her heart ached. Delilah watched as all her imagined scenarios, where her love for him could have blossomed into something shared, something real, floated away.

"Are we ready to go to this Mother's Day festival, or what?" Delilah looked only at Bobby, feeling like if she looked at Seb, he would be able to devise her plan. A plan to get herself and her son, somewhere safe, away from the Hawthornes and their watch dogs.

"Yeah, let's go." Bobby jumped up and down.

"Are you sure you still want to go?" Delilah ignored the genuine concern she heard in Seb's voice and avoided looking him in his too knowing emerald eyes.

"Of course, I do, it is Mother's Day after all." She tried to sound lighthearted, needing Seb to forget that she was ever mad or doubtful of him. Delilah needed him to let down his guard just enough so she could get away. "First let me go get my stuff."

"What stuff?" Damn, there was suspicion in his voice.

"I was thinking that we might have a picnic after the festival, maybe at a local vineyard or something." She braced herself to look at him and smile and lie. His intense green gaze was studying her, evaluating her explanation. "So, I want to grab some cutlery, maybe a couple toys for Bobby, and a sweater just in case it gets cooler. You know normal picnic stuff."

He nodded his head, but still appeared a bit wary. "Okay sounds good."

Delilah rushed to put one change of clothing for both herself and Bobby, she grabbed his favorite stuffed animal Mr. Fuzzy, the one that he could not sleep without. Her hands were shaking while she shoved things into a big bag that had held everything, she had brought for herself. Bobby needed his things more than she cared about her own. She was riddled with doubt and unsure if leaving Seb was the right thing to do, but he was leaving her anyway, right?

She rushed down the stairs and into the kitchen just before Seb poked his head in the door, he eyed her as she pulled open the utensil drawer and blindly grabbed forks.

"Do you need any help?" Seb asked.

"Nope, that was the last thing I needed, I'm ready to go." Delilah felt a twinge of pain, with every lie or untruth she told him.

As they walked down the path that led to the parking area, she looked one last time over her shoulder at the log cabin they had been staying at. It pained her to know that the experiences she had had there, the way she had felt there, that was all coming to an end. She had to let go, the part of her that had just been awakened by the man walking next to her son. It was a doomed idea from the start and now it had become nothing more than a fantasy.

Seb walked up to his Camaro; they hadn't used it since the night they had fled her apartment. He looked at her and must have seen the surprised confusion on her face.

"Dolly is using her car today; she had a day spent with her mother planned. So, it looks like we need to take this old thing." Seb looked sheepishly from her to his car, almost like he wanted her approval of his beautiful classic car. Surely, she must be reading him wrong.

"I like your car better, even though the other car smells like candy." Bobby assured Seb.

"It did smell like candy, didn't it?" Seb looked down at Bobby, as he hopped into the car. "To be honest with you, it was making me sick to my stomach."

"It was?" She remembered well the sweet smell of Dolly's car, she positively vibrated with pleasure at the idea that Seb didn't like the other woman's smell.

Stop that! He is not yours! He is going to leave you, and now you are going to leave him first.

His eyes burned into her, the blatant desire as he roved over her body, making her skin feel alive with tingles. "I much prefer freesia mixed with honey."

Honey? Was he talking about her? Did it even matter?

She looked away from him, as she walked to the passenger side of the car, she avoided any further eye contact with him. Delilah set the bag between her legs, on the floor of the car.

"Do you want me to throw that in the trunk?" Seb asked.

"No, it's fine." Her response came out sharper than she had intended, she cursed herself. *Act normal. You, idiot!* "It has personal, female things in it that I need."

She almost groaned out loud, good lord she was bad at the fine art of subterfuge. Delilah prayed that Seb didn't see straight through her ridiculous insinuation that she had started her period. For goodness sakes, they had been intimate last night.

"Really?" Seb asked as he drove the car towards the main road.

"Yes, it started this morning." Delilah blushed, discussing this kind of thing with him, even if it wasn't even the truth. She figured that would shut him up, men usually avoided talking about woman's menstrual cycles, at all costs.

"Do you have everything that you need? We could stop and get something, for cramps, or extra supplies." He winked over at her. "Maybe something both sweet and salty, should the craving arise."

She stared at him stunned, that was the most she had ever heard any man discuss the needs and wants of a woman who was menstruating. God, he would make some woman an excellent husband, a pain of loss shot through her like an arrow to the heart. It was a loss she had no right to feel, he wasn't hers, he never had been.

"No thanks, I'm fine." Delilah didn't have to fake sounding grateful, she was grateful for how well he would have cared for her, had the situation been real.

He let it go at that, much to her relief. Silence in a car with a five-year-old was almost unheard of, so as they made their way to the festivities, Bobby rattled on non-stop. Most of his questions and comments were directed towards Seb, she had to give the man credit, he was a good sport when it came to the incessant chatter. Answering every question with ease and humor that had resulted in Bobby laughing several times and had even forced her to crack a smile despite herself.

He turned off the main road and waited in line, to pay for parking, the festival was at the local fairgrounds. She was surprised to see that. She would have assumed that it would have been at one of the vineyards. Still, it looked to be a rather popular idea for a Mother's Day outing, the parking lot was full and there were crowds of people making their way towards the pinkly decorated grounds.

They pulled into the first available spot, which was a good walk from the actual festivities. It provided her with the perfect excuse to hang onto her bag, telling Seb that she didn't want to have to come back out to the car to get it. He didn't look pleased when she wouldn't even let him carry it, Seb looked at her like he was trying to solve a puzzle. She held her breath until Bobby saved her by tugging on Seb's hand, pointing at the clown making balloon animals.

She suggested that they hold off on the balloon animal until later, reminding Bobby that if there were any rides, it would only get in the way. Her son relented with only a momentary pause for sadness.

The afternoon flew by, as they played silly games and ate horribly delicious food. She relaxed into the day, wanting to soak up the feeling of them all being together before she walked away. Delilah got the feeling that Seb was doing the same thing, he denied Bobby nothing that he asked for and she kept catching him looking at her with the oddest expression. Almost like he was looking at her like he was trying to memorize her.

She watched the two of them throwing balls at goofy faces, trying to knock them down. They would both throw a ball at the same time, but Seb would pretend that it was Bobby's ball that knocked down the face instead of his. The pride and love that Bobby looked at Seb with tore her heart apart. He needed this; Bobby was too young to be without a father figure. But for the life of her, every time she tried to picture a man in that role, she pictured Seb.

It was outrageously unfair to Nate, who should be the one throwing those balls and laughing with his son. But the reality was that Bobby having Nate in his life was no longer an option, and neither was Seb. Both realizations, were as painful as the bullet that had ripped through her arm, maybe more.

"I think it is almost picnic time." Delilah tried to sound upbeat despite her immediate plans to betray Seb.

He looked back at her, his eyes shining with humor. "You cannot tell me that you are hungry."

"Okay, fine, I won't tell you." She smiled at him and looked over at the food stands longingly. "But that doesn't make it any less true."

Seb laughed and grabbed Bobby off the booth ledge that he had been throwing balls from.

"How about the grassy patch over by those trees?" She suggested the spot because even though they could see it from where they stood, it would be completely concealed when you were in the food line. "We will get everything set up and you grab the food."

Seb's eyebrow raised slightly at the idea of them splitting up. "But I don't know what you want."

She waved off his concern, trying to seem nonchalant. "We aren't picky, just get whatever you want, but enough for the three of us."

"I will go with Rock." Bobby suggestion made fear shoot through her like a bullet.

"No!" She forced herself to relax, cursing herself for how fierce her response sounded. "I'm sorry sweetheart, it's just I don't like the idea of you being out of my sight."

"Your mom's right Bobby, you stay with her." Even though Seb agreed with her, she saw doubt clouding his eyes. "If you are a good helper, I will bring you a surprise with dinner."

Her son's eyes lit up in excitement. "I love surprises."

"So do I." His words sounded weightier than she thought such a lighthearted statement should.

She couldn't decide if it was because she had a surprise planned for him that he most definitely would not like, or because he himself was trying to send her some sort of message with his statement. Either way she knew that she was about to hurt him.

Chapter 23

Delilah moved like every moment counted, because she knew that she had to be well out of sight before Seb came back. There was a voice in her head, screaming to her that she shouldn't leave the protection that Seb provided, but she drowned it out with the thoughts of losing her son in a custody battle.

"Where are we going mom?" Bobby asked her as she practically pulled him toward the parking lot, she really wasn't sure where they were going, or even how they would get there.

"It is a surprise." Delilah felt like a horrible person for the pain her son would feel, because of what she was doing. She had to remind herself that Seb planned on leaving tomorrow anyway. She was just leaving before he had the chance to. "Seb likes surprises, remember?"

"Okay." Bobby didn't sound sure. She couldn't blame him.

She rushed past the smiling faces of families enjoying the day, swallowing back the tears that the images conjured up. Why couldn't her day be that simple? Delilah would never have a day with the man she loved, and her child, all three of them spoiling each other with their love for one another. Every step she took, took her further from the man she loved and that impossible dream.

"Mrs. Hawthorne?" Delilah froze in her tracks. It had been so long since anyone had called her that. She felt the smallest sliver of hope that maybe her ex-mother in-law was there, but quickly decided that that would be much worse than simply being recognized by someone from her past.

She turned around and a flood of relief washed over her, standing waving at her was a young Hispanic girl. Maria Vasquez had been a small scared twelve-year-old when Delilah had first met her. Her mother and only guardian had been the victim of domestic violence, that had elevated until her mother was eventually killed. Maria had lived in Santa Clara at the time, and after the loss of her mother had been sent to live with her aunt in Fairfield. Delilah's job had been to get the girl to open up and help her make the transition through her grief. She considered Maria one of her success stories, there were far too few children that she really felt like she reached, but Maria had been one of them.

"Hi, Maria." She couldn't spare the time to stand around and chat with the girl, even though she would love to know how she was doing. "It's nice to see you, but I am in…………."

Oh God! Oh God no!

The hand she held gripped hers harder than she thought her son was capable of, and she knew that he had seen the same thing that she had. Standing next to Maria, with his hand possessively on her arm stood a man. There was nothing overly intimidating about him, until her gaze swept carelessly over his face. We wore a cold smile, a triumphant smile, running from the corner of his left eye were two blue tears. The sight of the tattoo stopped her heart from beating and constricted her lungs from pumping in oxygen.

In her mind, she had run away. Physically she was unable to budge an inch. The two of them started walking over to her, he whispered something to Maria that turned the girl as white as a sheet. Any hopes that the man hadn't recognized her name or face, flew out the window when the girl's eyes filled with despair. She could see it on the Maria's face that she didn't want harm to come to Delilah, but she also knew that she probably had little say in the matter.

Wait! They had seen her, but had either of them even looked at Bobby? Was the crowd blocking him from their view?

Without looking down, Delilah spoke to her son. "Bobby, do you remember where Rock is?"

"I think so." Bobby didn't sound as sure as she would have liked, but it was her best shot at getting him to safety.

"Good, I want you to run to him, can you do that?" There was urgency in her tone, she could feel her son's eyes on her, trying to figure out what was wrong with her.

"What's wrong mommy?" Bobby, cursed to herself, they were wasting precious moments. Still her son's worry for her tore at her heart, she needed him to leave, she needed him to be safe.

"Nothing, sweetheart…." She started to lie to him when her heart dropped down into her stomach. Delilah watched as the man with Maria finally registered Bobby holding on to her hand. His eyes squint, and a truly sinister smile spread on his face. She looked down at Bobby, allowing him to see all the terror in eyes. "Run, Bobby, tell Rock the man with the tear found us!"

"But I can't…" Her son started to protest, but they were out of time, the man was almost upon them.

———

"You can, you have too." He looked up at her, his fear turning in front of her eyes to determination. *God, he is so strong.* "I love you more than anything, now run!"

Pain and relief hit her as she watched her son run away from her, she found it hard not to take off after him. But she knew they would follow her, if she ran, her only hope was that they would let a child go. It was a possibility that they didn't even know that Bobby had been in the car. It was a slim chance, but it was one she clung to.

"Mrs. Hawthorne." His voice matched his face, arrogant and mean. "Where have you been? I have been wanting to talk to you."

He looked at her like he was some grand gangster from a movie, like he had orchestrated this whole meeting. It was clear that he thought that the universe bent to his will and shined down on his existence. Well, she might not be able to run from him, but she sure as hell would wipe the smug look from his face.

"Really? I thought you said everything that you needed to say on the side of my car." She was gratified when she saw the slimy smile slip from his mouth, replaced by a thin line, an angry line. *Shit! Maybe that wasn't such a good idea.*

The look in his eyes hardened with anger, along with his eyes. "Trust me, we have plenty to talk about." He approached her as casually as if they were friends. Wrapped his arm around her waist and pulled her flush with his body, he grabbed her jaw with a roughness that made her wince. He bent down, any passerby would think they were in an intimate embrace, they wouldn't be able to see the brutality of his hands. He whispered in her ear, sending prickles of fear running down her entire body. "Fuego, I think Javier will teach you a lesson personally."

Her eyes shot to Maria for help, maybe if they worked together, they could overpower Javier and she could help the girl get away from him as well. But when her eyes met Maria's the last of her hopes were squashed, the girl's eyes were alive with what looked like jealousy. Instead of looking at her with any sympathy, she was looking at Javier's hands on her, shooting daggers at Delilah. *Seriously?! Could she really think that I am enjoying this? Did she enjoy treatment like this?!*

"We're going." Javier didn't let go of her, he turned toward the parking lot, maintaining his grip around her waist.

She wrestled against him; he had a wiry strength that made his arms feel like bars of steel. Delilah felt helpless, it was a cold realization that she was going to be going with this man no matter if she liked it or not. Closing her eyes, she focused on images of Bobby and of Seb. Wishing that she were with them, losing hope that she would ever see either of them again.

Run! Run! Find Rock!

Bobby's little legs pumped as hard as they could, he wasn't even sure he was going the right way. He tried to see clearly, but it was hard, he was crying hard. Fear threatened to stop his legs from moving. He looked around him, for any sign of Rock. Looking for his silver head above the crowd, knowing that reaching him was his mom's only chance. He couldn't lose her too, he couldn't.

He was whipped off his feet when a strong grip grabbed his arm. It jarred his body as he flew back, terror made him let out a cry. With the cry he took a huge breath in, a breath that smelt like sweet candy. Hope burst inside of him. His eyes darted up, Dolly.

"Bobby, what's wrong? Where is your mom?" This Dolly sounded different than the woman he had met before, she sounded serious and worried.

"The man, I left her, with the man that shot my daddy." He felt the tears streaming down his face, Dolly pulled him into a hug. "You have to help, please."

"I will, but my first priority is to make sure you're safe." He pushed away from her comforting hug, looked up at her, *she must help my mom first.*

"I'm fine, we need to get my mom." She smiled down at him, he hated it when adults smiled at him like that. Like he was cute, but he had no idea what he was talking about. He knew exactly what he was talking about. "My uncle would want us to find my mom."

"Bobby!" *Rock!* Bobby spun away from Dolly's hands that were on his shoulders. He watched as Rock ran to him, he was off his feet and in Rocks arms so quickly his head started to spin. "Oh, thank God, you're okay……. Wait, where is your mom?"

He could hear it. Rock was just as worried about his mom as he was. It was too much to take, worrying about his mom had been his job alone for as long as he could remember. Now there is someone else that loved his mom and knew how special she is. His sobs were coming so violently he couldn't speak, he let Dolly explain.

"He said that the man that shot his father has her." Dolly explained.

"What?!" Bobby felt Rock tense, but he couldn't stop crying to look at him. "I have to go after her." He was being transferred out of Rock's arms, passed to Dolly's like a baby. Normally he would have fought it, but he didn't care, he was too upset. "Bobby."

"Bobby, look at me son." Bobby turned his face, so he could look at Rock. He saw in Rock's serious green eyes that he needed Bobby, he needed him to be strong. "I'm going to get your mom back, I swear it, but I need you to stay with Dolly and be brave. She will protect you." Bobby nodded his head, still unable to speak. "Good, do you remember which way she went?"

Bobby wasn't totally sure, not until he saw the balloons that the clown twisted floating above the crowd. He remembered that when his mom had stopped walking, he had been about to ask her for one. They had been standing close to the balloons when he had left her. Raising his hand, he pointed in the direction that he had last seen his mom. Rock was gone, without another word.

Dolly held him and rubbed his back, he prayed, prayed for his mom and for Rock. They were all he had in the world; *God please don't let me lose them too.*

Chapter 24

He could feel his heart pounding in his head, he ran in the direction that Bobby had pointed. Desperately scanning the crowd, he was trying all his well-used technics for staying calm and reigning in his fears. His heart didn't give a crap about all his efforts, it felt like it would explode if he didn't find her soon.

Near the balloon making clown Seb spotted her bag, lying on the ground, with no sign of Delilah. At least he knew that he was headed the right way.

As he ran, he realized that he was heading in the direction of the parking lot. That made sense, if you wanted to abduct someone, you would move them quickly to your vehicle. Even if you wanted to just get rid of someone, you wouldn't be able to do it in a crowd of people. You would need somewhere much less populated. He didn't know what to wish for, either scenario felt like a knife to the heart.

He passed the gate of the fairgrounds, every step he took without seeing her, the chances of him finding her dwindled.

Seb raced through the center of the parking lot, sweeping his head from side to side searching down every lane. He was almost to the end of the parking lot, it felt like he was moving in slow motion. Something steered him further towards his car. Normally he would search the parking lot and then double back, to make sure that they hadn't in fact stayed at the festival, but his instincts and his heart were driving him to his car. He knew that if he had to get in his car and search for her the odds of finding her were very slim. He paused when he reached the Camaro. It was the first car parked, in almost the last row of cars. Grabbing for the door handle he took one last look around.

He had to shield his eyes as the setting sun gleamed off the chrome covered El Camino that was driving slowly down the lane, he was standing in. Seb knew before he saw her, he felt her near him. Seeing the back of her curly red head, through the rear window, simply validated what he already knew in his heart.

Seb ducked into his car, and started it as quickly as possible, knowing he had precious little time to follow the El Camino.

By the time they reached the first stop light he was two cars behind her, and one lane over. He was happy with his positioning, as long as they didn't spot him, he would be able to follow them anywhere. Seb's last concern was washed away when he saw Delilah turn her head to look at the woman sitting next to her. When he had first seen her curl covered head it had been motionless, and he had worried that they were just propping her up. Seeing her move of her own free will, lightened his heart, as much as was possible in this still rather dire situation.

They stuck to busy roads, then moved onto a residential area, just outside of Napa. They pulled into a suburban type of neighborhood, nothing new or overly fancy. The streets were lined with houses, Seb dared not follow them down the road, he would surely be spotted if he did. So, he continued to drive past, he caught a glimpse of the driver looking in his direction. He reached for his phone, pretended to push a button and held it to his ear, as he continued to drive by. Hoping that the man didn't find him suspicious in the least, he needed them to be at ease, and let their guard down.

He turned down a different road that was three streets from the one that the El Camino had parked on. Seb killed the engine, and this time dialed his phone for real, Max picked up on the first ring.

"About damn time." Max's voice sounded strained.

Seb was not surprised that Dolly had contacted Max, in fact he was counting on it.

"I trailed her to a suburban area outside of Napa. In the car with her there was one man, presumably the one Bobby can identify and one younger woman." Seb wasted no time filling Max in on all the information he had. "He was driving a dark blue El Camino, heavy with chrome."

"I want you as close as you can get without detection, you're to hold off on acting until I can get someone there to back you up." Max's tone invited no argument, which was fine with Seb. He had his own plan, and he didn't give a shit what Max thought of it.

"Understood." It was true, Seb understood what Delilah's brother wanted him to do. There was just no way on earth that he was going to sit around and let something terrible happen to Delilah.

He was going to throw protocol out the window, and when that happened people usually got hurt. Seb would do his best to make sure that person wasn't Delilah.

"Go, try to get eyes on my sister, I'm counting on you Foxy." Seb groaned at the nickname.

"Nothing will happen to Delilah." He sounded more confident than he felt.

He knew from personal life experiences that you couldn't always save the people that you loved. Seb also could recall with vivid detail the immense pain of holding a limp Mo in his arms, watching him take his last breath. There had been nothing he could have done, everyone had said as much, but that didn't take the pain away. The thought of holding Delilah in his arms and watching the wild spark of life that lived within the woman die out. Seb didn't think he would live through that.

Seb popped his trunk and quickly strapped on his back up piece, he was licensed to carry and rarely left home without his 45, but just to be on the safe side he wanted all the fire power he could get. He was qualified to shoot any weapon and enjoyed shooting them all, but in a situation like this he missed having his M-240B. It wasn't his plan to go in the place guns blazing, this was a residential home. For all he knew there were kids in the house, he wouldn't take unnecessary risks.

Pulling a hat on to cover his silver hair, he took a deep breath to center himself. From this point on he would think about nothing but the mission, the extraction of Delilah Reyes.

"Maria, please." Delilah tried to get the young woman to come to her senses. "You don't want to be a part of this, kidnapping? Really?"

"Stop talking I'm trying to watch this, Javier said to keep you quiet while he made a call." Maria looked at her with what Delilah was sure she thought was a hard expression. It made Delilah want to laugh, the girl was too soft for this type of world. "I will hit you if you can't shut up."

She might hit her. Delilah could see her maybe be able to manage that level of anger. Especially because she seemed to be pissed at Delilah for the way Javier had been looking at her. He had made insinuations that he might enjoy having her around, for a while at least. If she stayed here, she knew it would not end well for her. She tried to not think about Seb and Bobby, she wished in vain that she had seen her little boy run to safety. The thought of him lost amongst the crowd made fresh tears well in her eyes, better there than here, was her only comfort.

"I have a son to care for Maria, I'm all he has in the world." Delilah tried to pull at her sympathy.

"Don't try that sappy shit on me. You got yourself into this." This time Maria's words were venomous with anger.

It was all Delilah could take. "How exactly did I get myself into this? By marrying a man that I thought I was in love with, then there was the divorce, which was clearly my fault. What did I do next, oh that's right, Nate took a bad case and I assume he lost it? Defending one of your boyfriend's friends, which I'm sure was innocent of all crimes. Then I had the audacity to pick up my child from his father's house and got shot in the arm for my trouble. Forced to go into hiding, after an attack on my home." By the time she was done, she was breathing heavy with exasperation. "Did I cover all the ways that this is completely my fault?"

Maria looked at her, the doubt in her eyes, reminding Delilah of the young girl that she had known. That girl would have helped her, that girl didn't want a life of crime, with a thug boyfriend. She wished the old Maria were here, but as she saw the angry curtain draw back over Maria's eyes, she knew that wasn't going to happen.

"I'm not listening to what you say, you are a lying Gringa." Not the first time that she had been called a Gringa by someone with more visible Hispanic traits. Usually, she would whip out her picture of her parents and prove that she was no more a Gringa than the girl sitting next to her, but she really didn't care what Maria thought of her.

"Do I hear a cat fight in here?" Javier walked into the room, he had discarded his over-shirt and only wore a white tank top that clung to his torso and a pair of pants that drooped down low enough that you could see his boxers. There was nothing sexual in her look, but he caught her looking and took it the wrong way. "You like what you see, Feugo?"

How the hell was she supposed to answer that without thoroughly pissing him off?

Maria came to her rescue, even though she knew that the girl didn't mean to.

"You don't need her, Papi." She stood from the couch and sauntered over to Javier; his eyes never left Maria. She wrapped her arms around his neck and pressed herself snugly against him. "We can have a good time without her."

"We could have a better time with her." She felt the bile rise in her throat at Javier's suggestion.

Maria brought one hand down from around Javier's neck, Delilah heard the crack of the slap before she had registered what happened. Did Maria just hit him? Fear for the young girl's safety rushed through her, she knew it was asinine, but she couldn't help it. Javier did not strike her as a man that would be slapped and let that go unpunished.

"You little bitch." Javier voice was stone cold, as he grabbed Maria's arms. She could see the white in his knuckles, as his hands dug into her arms. "You need to be taught some manners."

Delilah was completely surprised when she heard Maria laugh, apparently, she was more concerned for her than the girl was for herself.

"That would take a real man." She challenged him, none of Maria's actions or words seemed like a good idea to Delilah.

"You don't think I'm man enough to handle you?" His face changed slightly, now mixture of anger and there was also what looked like desire. He didn't loosen his grip, and he pulled her hard back to him. "I can see that I need to get you under control."

Maria actually looked to be enjoying Javier's rough treatment and unflattering words. Delilah felt like an unwilling bystander to the weirdest flirtation she had ever witnessed. She cringed as Javier moved one of his hands from Maria's arm and grabbed her breast in a none to gentle manner. Maria moaned.

Are they going to have sex right in front of me, or am I going to witness something violent?

The whole situation confused and worried her; she didn't want to see either scenario played out in front of her eyes. And surely didn't want to take part in it.

The two were in their own world now, ignoring her existence, which was fine with her. Even though she did wish they would take it in the other room.

As if Maria read her mind. "Not in front of her." She tore herself from his grip, Delilah could see the marks that he had left on the girl's arms. They would be ugly bruises on Maria later. She watched as Maria walked out of the living room, she assumed there were bedrooms down the hallway.

Her breath caught as Javier hesitated, he looked at her, desire still raging in his deep brown eyes. He drew his tongue over his bottom lip, biting down on it for a moment while eyeing her up and down.

"You stay right there, Papi will take care of you next Fuego." With that he followed Maria down the hallway.

She immediately got to work. Even though her hands and feet were tied with zip ties, she was trying to remember a video she had seen on the internet. Then she cursed as she remembered that you needed shoelaces, she looked down at her sandals, and cursed again. Okay that idea was out the window.

Delilah spanned the room for anything sharp that she could use to possibly cut her restraints, she sighed as she saw nothing.

It took her what seemed like a lifetime to try and maneuver onto her feet, her thought was to hop towards the door. She took her first precarious hop and started to sway in the direction of the sharp looking coffee table. Scared, she over corrected, causing her to plop back down onto the couch. Face in the cushions, she took a moment to wallow in her failed attempt.

She was frozen in fear as a strong arm grabbed her around the waist, pulling her to a standing position. Had they changed their minds, were they back to make her part of their weird sex games? Delilah felt like screaming, she opened her mouth to let out the loudest blood curdling scream she could manage.

Chapter 25

He covered her mouth with his hand, "Shh."

Seb felt her relax against him, she had been so rigid when he had first picked her up. Clearly, she had thought he was someone else, he didn't want to even think about what she thought was going to happen to her. He reached down with his knife and snapped the ties binding her feet and then the one binding her hands. Seb saw the nasty red rings left by harsh zip ties, his first instinct was to rub them and kiss them and make her pain go away. But now wasn't the time and it sure as hell wasn't the place.

She looked up at him, "Bobby?" she whispered.

Seb shook his head trying to convey to her that he was safe, he saw the relief wash over her.

He grabbed her hand and started leading her down the hallway that led to the bedroom that he had snuck in.

She stopped and tugged on his arm, he looked back at her in confusion. Not willing to risk having a conversation that might draw attention to them, he inclined his head to her, questioning.

Delilah pointed down the hallway, then held up two fingers, she brought the hand to her mouth and started kissing it. He smiled despite their dire situation, he was witnessing the funniest tactical hand signals he had ever seen, and he had seen some creative ones in his day.

When she caught him smiling, she glared at him, almost making him laugh.

From what he could guess from her warning, there were two people down this hallway, possibly kissing their hands. He wasn't concerned, his plan was to leave the way he had come in. She would have to trust him, if the people did hear them, their first instinct would be to head for the front door. They would not start by looking in the back rooms, plus when they were outside the house, the window he had chosen had good cover.

He continued down the hallway way, she was tense, but she wasn't fighting him. He was thankful for that. This would have been much harder if she fought him. Seb never trusted any situation when it was going too well, which this one was. He had found his entry point, cleared the room, and then made his way down the hall. Seb hadn't bothered to clear the other rooms, not wanting to rouse the entire house. His objective was stealth, to sneak in and out no matter how many people occupied the residence.

Now that he had what he had come for, the only thing on his mind was extraction. As they swept down the hallway, making little to no sound, moaning and Spanish could be heard from one of the bedrooms. He smiled into the darkness; those would be the sounds of hand kissing he presumed. Good, that should distract the asshole that took Delilah long enough to get her out of this house.

Seb put his hand on the doorknob that he had come in through, checking to make sure the small piece of paper that he had slid in the door was still in place. It was not big enough to attract attention, but if someone had come through the doorway it would have fallen. Giving Seb advance warning that there would be an unwanted distraction in the room. Since his paper was still in place he relaxed only slightly, as he started to turn the handle.

He felt her stiffen moments before he himself heard the sound of sirens ripping through the air. *Shit! Shit! Shit!* Even if they weren't headed to this house, which he doubted that they were. He hadn't given Max the exact address of the house, to allow himself more time to get Delilah out of harm's way. It wasn't that he didn't trust the local authorities, but with someone so precious to him.......... he trusted no one else.

Picking up their pace, he started to run through the room to the window. He threw up the window at the same time he heard the bedroom door open and someone curse. Seb's hope was that they would check the living room first, but he hadn't closed the door again and he was worried that that would catch their eye. No one appeared at the doorway, he sent up a silent thank you.

"Go." He whispered to Delilah.

God, he loved this woman, she didn't hesitate, not one second. She launched herself out of the window, he doubted she knew how to fall correctly, which made him worried that she might hurt something. But he couldn't help but swell with pride at the trust she placed in his direction and the fearlessness of the woman.

Then he heard the last warning he would receive; a loud curse came from the living room. Seb looked down to make sure that he wouldn't crush Delilah with his jump, she had moved a little out of the way to make room for him. He was through the window and had hands on her in a flash. The moments that he had to let go of her in this dire situation, felt like tearing out his heart and leaving it aside. He knew that he wouldn't survive without her close to him, he knew he didn't want to be away from her.

They were standing between the bush and the house; they would both have plenty of scratches from the bushes unforgiving branches.

Footsteps came from the back of the house, he sighed, he almost allowed himself to believe that he would get her out of here with no conflict. They could start running toward his car, but he would not take a chance at the kidnapper opening fire on them. Stray bullets killed people all the time, he wouldn't risk Delilah or any innocent person on the residential street. No, he only had one choice, he needed to take care of whoever was coming.

"Stay here." Delilah shook her head and clung to his hand; tears were rolling down her cheeks. "Yes, love, I will be right back."

It broke his heart to force his hand from hers, but he knew that neutralizing at least one of the people in the house, would be their best bet at getting away.

She remained silent, as he snuck away from the bush, she hid in.

Whoever was looking for her was not concerned with her hearing them, as they turned things in the back yard over. In moments Seb knew that the person would be coming through the gate that separated the back yard from the front and he needed to be ready. Despite being heavily armed, Seb wanted to avoid using guns if possible. It would only serve to draw the attention of whoever else was in the house, and that he didn't need.

He had made his way to the where the gate would open. Crouching, blending into the darkness, he waited. Whenever he had been in situations like this, seconds seem to stretch into minutes. The anticipation of action, alerting every cell in his body, that they would be needed soon. It was a great and exciting feeling, one that he knew that some people got addicted to. This time it felt differently, because standing only feet away from him, was someone more important to him than life itself. The pressure was like an elephant sitting on his chest, he stood by the fence while his heart hid in the bushes.

The click of the gate broke through the silence of the night sky, a figure shrouded in shadow walked by Seb. Seb saw the glint of a knife in the man's hand, he was relieved, no gunfight tonight.

The man paused and looked towards the bush against the house, Seb's breath froze in his lungs. He saw it as soon as the man did, her vibrant red hair barely visible through the bushes. *Damn her gorgeous fiery hair!*

"Fuego, why did you run away? Were you jealous?" There was a sickly-sweet tone to his voice, *was he flirting with her?!*

If he didn't feel enraged before, he sure as hell did now.

Seb was on the man in a split second.

His first priority was to get the knife away from the man. With expert precision Seb knocked through the man's elbow, dislocating his arm, causing him to drop the knife. Seb wasted no time, wrapping his arm around the man's throat. He ignored the tear of the man's nails on his forearm as he struggled for breath, this was the man that had dared to take Delilah from him. Rage filled him, he had fight himself to just put the man to sleep and not cut off his ability to breath ever again.

The man slackened in Seb's arms, and he dropped him to the ground, much harder than he probably had to. A small smile of satisfaction spread on his lips. He wiped it away by the time he had returned to Delilah, not wanting her to see how much he had enjoyed disabling the low life. She would think he was a monster if she had known how badly he had wanted to truly hurt the man, hell part of him felt like a monster.

She rushed out of the bush and into his arms before he had even taken two steps towards her. Part of him was alarmed that she had left her cover, but the other part could not think straight with the feeling of holding her taking over his better judgment.

This is how people get killed, you care too much!

He knew that the small voice of warning, came from his past, but it still jarred him into action none the less.

Seb unwrapped his arms from around Delilah, they didn't have time for hugs, who knows how many more people are in the house.

Taking her hand once more he directed them through the available cover that the yard provided. Once they came to the edge of the property, and there was no sign of anyone else coming out of house. Seb felt like their best option was to run for it. His car wasn't far, and they couldn't get there soon enough for his liking.

"Javier!!!" A scream pierced the silence.

Delilah stopped. "Maria."

"Damn, Maria, we need to go." He steeled his voice, to try and relay how serious he was.

Seb didn't wait for her to agree with him, he tightened his grip on her hand and ran. He kept his pace down, knowing full well that even if she were an avid runner, his long legs would easily out pace hers. He found out quickly that she was not an avid runner when he heard her struggle for breath. They were already moving slower than he would like, he didn't even waste time thinking about it. He stopped wrapped his hands around her waist and flung her over his shoulder.

He fought down memories of feeling a similar weight on his shoulder, as he ran for all he was worth. Fleeing danger, bullets flying, trying to listen for a familiar call or voice, that would lead him to safety. There would be no call, there were no bullets, this was not Iraq, and she was not a small child. If he was honest the fear that gripped his heart was one that came from immense love and the fear of losing that love.

Sliding Delilah from his body, he flung open the door and guided her with a firm hand to get in. He hustled to the driver's side and jumped in; he didn't allow himself a breath of relief until they were well away from the neighborhood. He chanced a look over at Delilah, needing to know that she was okay. She wasn't saying anything, it worried him.

"Are you alright?" Seb asked tentatively.

She snorted, he smiled at her sometimes so un-lady like behavior. He loved the way that she wasn't always concerned with being the perfect image of femininity, but more concerned with just being herself.

"That is a very dumb question." Delilah response had not been what he was expecting. He didn't know what he had been expecting, maybe *I am now that I am with you.* or *Thanks to you I am.* Not, a comment insulting his intelligence, that he had not been prepared for, and it irked him slightly.

"Which part was dumb exactly, that I worry about your well-being or that I care enough to ask?" He didn't try to disguise the hurt that he felt.

Seb could feel her eyes on him, studying him. "I'm sorry, you're right." Delilah sighed and rubbed her wrists. He looked down at the red circles that stood out against her pale skin and cursed.

"No, I'm sorry." She looked at him in surprise. "It was a dumb question, a very dumb question. Of course, you're not alright, how the hell could you be. You were just kidnapped and separated from your son in the most horrific way, who in their right mind would be okay?"

She laughed. "Okay, so we have established that I have every right to be not okay and you have a right to inquire into my well-being. Especially because the only reason that I am sitting in this car, instead of.........somewhere much worse, is because you rescued me. Thank you, I don't know how you did it, but thank you."

"The odds were not in our favor, the fact that I was able to track you, was nothing short of a miracle. A miracle that I am very grateful for." Seb tried to hold back the emotions and confessions that wanted to burst forth. Now wasn't the time to discuss his feelings, but now that he had come to the realization of the depth in which he loved Delilah. His heart urged him to tell her and to reach out with all his love and pray that she felt the same way.

"Where are we going?" Delilah asked.

"To get Bobby, then we are headed north." Seb explained, handing her his cell phone. "Call your brother and tell him that you are with me. Lord knows he has probably called in the National Guard by now."

She laughed, while she took the phone. "Who needs the National Guard, when you have your own personal Ranger."

Chapter 25

Delilah was surprised when they turned down the now familiar road that led towards the cabin the had been staying at.

Surely, he hadn't had time to drop Bobby off here. Did he?

She started to get out of the car, but Seb placed a hand on her arm. There was an electric warmth to his touch, that always made her body want to melt into him.

"Stay here, I'm going to run in and get him. We need to make this quick just in case they know where you have been staying." Before she could argue he was out of the car, it irritated her that he just thought she would follow his directions so easily. Delilah needed to see her son; how dare he ask her to stay in the car.

Then a fresh horror struck her, what if Seb had contacted the Hawthornes? Her actions today would be the exact type of thing they could use against her. She had sent her son off unsupervised into a crowd of strangers, anything could have happened to him. It was a small miracle that he had found Seb.

What if Seb had lied to me? What if he never did see Bobby, and he was only trying to keep me calm? No, he wouldn't do that. Would he?

Just when her mind was truly starting to imagine every possible scenario, relief flooded every other emotion from her mind.

Seb came walking out of the building, a sleeping child draped against his chest. He carried one bag in the other hand. The porch light bounced off a head covered in golden hair, bobbing to the right of Seb, Dolly became visible holding two other pieces of their luggage.

Who had packed all of their things?

Before she could start up her myriad of questions, Seb opened the car door and carefully set Bobby in the back seat. She watched as he wrapped the seat belt around her son, he used such reverence with him that it made her heart ache. He would make a great father someday. Once Seb pulled back out of the car, she heard the trunk pop, he must be loading the luggage. She took the moment when the interior light of the car was still on to look at Bobby. He was curled toward the middle of the seats, asleep and tucked into one of his favorite blankets. One that he had had since he was a baby, one his father had bought for him, one she had not been able to bring with them during her attempted escape this afternoon.

Oh God! What if that is where Seb is taking them? The whole reason that she was going to flee his protection this morning came rushing back to her. She had been so grateful to him for rescuing her and protecting Bobby, that she had forgotten that he was nothing more than the Hawthorne's tool. No matter how she felt about him, it didn't change the fact that he had been spying on them this entire time.

Where had he said he was taking us? North? They don't have a house in Northern California, do they? What about out of California? Did I escape one kidnapping just to be thrust into another?

She glared at Seb in the rearview mirror, well she glared at the trunk that was still open, but she imagined him behind it. To her satisfaction the trunk was lowered giving her a perfect view Seb…. and Dolly…… hugging. *What in the hell?*

She glared harder, how long had that been going on? As their embrace ended, Seb turned and walked back towards the car and got into the driver's side seat. Dolly continued up the front porch of the building, turned to wave at them as Seb pulled the car out of the driveway. Delilah continued to glare at the woman, that smelt like candy, looked like an angel, and for some reason had had her son.

"I don't think she deserves the look you are giving her." Seb's comment wasn't a reprimand, but it was close enough to light her ire.

"So protective, I'm sure she would be very pleased with you defending her." She sounded childish and bitter, and she didn't care.

"Yes, she probably would be." Seb grinned, it was small, but she was looking at him so closely that she caught it.

She stared at him slack jawed. "So, you admit it? Just like that."

"Why wouldn't I admit it. She helped keep Bobby safe, and that is something that she would most likely expect us to be grateful for." Seb looked at her quickly, his forest eyes filled with concern. "Are you okay, honey?"

Delilah chose to ignore the endearment and ignore the feeling that it blossomed inside of her, hearing it. "How exactly did she help keep Bobby safe?"

"I'm sorry, I forgot that you have no idea what happened after you were taken. Of course, you didn't know that Dolly helped, how would you?" He sighed. "I had walked towards our picnic spot to ask you a question, when I didn't see you there, I feared the worst. There was a voice in my head trying to keep me calm, so I started running in the direction of the balloon guy. Thinking that maybe Bobby had simply talked you into getting him one. Then I saw Bobby, standing with Dolly, but you were nowhere in sight. I left Dolly to care for Bobby and came running after you. I found your bag not far from the entrance, and then I started checking the parking lot for any sign of you. I got lucky spotting you in the back of the El Camino and followed you. I think that about sums up everything you missed."

His explanation was exact and to the point, he didn't mince words. She couldn't help but think that he had learned that in the military.

"How did you know that you could trust Dolly? You took a big risk leaving him with her." Her priority was her son, Seb was being paid so that that was his priority too. So why had he left Bobby to come after her?

"Not really, Max told me I could trust her completely, and I trust Max, don't you?" Seb challenged her.

"Of course, I trust him. I trust him more than any other person on this planet." She couldn't be sure in the darkness of the car cabin, but it looked like he winced slightly. "If you trust my brother so much, why didn't you follow his orders earlier?"

Now she definitely saw him wince.

"Not happy with me, is he?" Despite the physical reaction, he almost sounded amused at the possibility that her brother was pissed at him.

"No, he isn't. When I spoke with him earlier, he was very surprised to hear from me. He said something about a damn rogue fox under his breath." She looked at Seb with surprise as he burst into laughter. The rich tone of his laughter permeated every fiber of her body, she could relax and listen to it all day. *No, you can't!* "What's so funny? Why didn't you wait like he told you to?"

Suddenly she needed to know so badly, why he had come after her, when his job was to secure Bobby. Why had he rushed in and not waited like Max had told him to? Hell, why were they even still with him? Was he taking them to the Hawthornes?

"I didn't think that you had the time for me to wait." She could feel his body tense in the close quarters. "Judging from that bastard's comments outside of the house, I was right."

She shuddered as she remembered Javier's words, his promise that there was enough of him to go around. "Did you…. I mean…. is Javier dead?"

His body tensed further, he felt like a bow string sitting next to her, ready to explode.

"Is that what you think of me?" He sounded hurt; she was instantly sorry she had asked. For one thing she couldn't bring herself to even care, as far as she was concerned the man deserved to die. He had gunned down Nate and would have done unspeakable things to her.

"It was dark and all I saw was you choking him and then him crumbling to the ground. He looked dead to me; I wouldn't judge you if you did." Delilah knew that he would look differently at her for her confession, but it was truly how she felt.

"I didn't kill him." He flexed his hands on the steering wheel. "I have enough blood on my hands, I didn't need his too."

He sounded so pained by his explanation, her first instinct was to wrap herself around him and comfort him. She wasn't sure that she could trust him, but that didn't stop her heart from longing for him.

Delilah decided to change the subject, not wanting to hear the pain in his voice. "Where are we going?"

"I'm taking you somewhere I know is safe." His answer was vague and not at all what she wanted to hear.

"Are you taking us to the Hawthornes?" It took all of her bravado to ask the simple question, but she needed to know. How deep was Seb indebted to the Hawthornes, how much power did they have over him?

"Hell no! Why in the world would I take you to that manipulative prick?" There was venom in his tone, and she could feel the anger radiating off him.

"You work for them. It isn't that crazy to think that you might be paid to deliver us to him." Delilah defended her assumption, even though his reaction had told her how wrong she had been.

"I know that you overheard me speaking with Hawthorne earlier today, and I know that we never got a chance to talk about it, but surely you don't think that little of me?" He sounded even more hurt than before, she wasn't meaning to, but she just couldn't stop hurting him.

"I don't know you, not really." Delilah almost whispered the words, it was true. She didn't know him that well, but it hadn't stopped her for falling for him. Her feelings were the part she left unsaid.

"That may be true, but please believe me when I say that Hawthorne will get Bobby over my dead body." The ice in his voice sent shivers running down her body. In that moment she had absolutely no doubt that whatever skeletons Seb still held in his closet, he was no puppet to the Hawthornes.

"I believe you." Delilah said looking at the stony face of the man sitting next to her. He was all sharp masculine lines, the road lights gleamed off his silver-grey hair. She wished she could see his beautiful green eyes. They could be so expressive when he let them be.

Not listening to her brain, she followed her heart and reached out a tentative hand. Running her fingers through his hair, down the side of his handsome face, until she reached his lips. She started to retract her hand, feeling foolish as he sat as still as a rock during her exploration. Delilah let a soft gasp as his hand reached out and took hers before she could pull away.

He placed a feather like kiss to the palm of her hand. She knew that your hand was full of nerve endings that led to all over your body, but it had never been more real for her than in that moment, because she felt his kiss to the ends of her body.

"Get some sleep, sweetheart. We have a while still to go." There was something raw in his voice that she couldn't place, the endearment on his lips made her want to curl up against his strength and take comfort in his protection. She draped her body over the center console lying her head against the firmness of his muscled shoulder. Breathing in the scent of the woods that still clung to Seb, she let her body relax as she drifted off to sleep.

Chapter 26

"Bobby, would you like more French toast?" Seb looked at his grandmother with open affection, she was tiny and getting smaller every year. Despite her advanced years, she had met them at the door at nearly three in the morning with a smile and a welcome.

"No, thank you, Meema." Bobby looked up from his third helping of French toast, with the look of a child who was thoroughly stuffed on his face. Seb smiled at the little boy, it had taken him all of three seconds to get used to calling Seb's grandmother by her preferred name, Meema.

"Such polite manners on your boy Seb." She turned her beaming smile on Seb, it amazed him how so much love was packed into such a small package.

The thought made him think of Delilah, he wondered what it would be like for her to turn her love on him. It was a foolish thought, one that he shouldn't be torturing himself with. She was going to correct her statement that Bobby was in anyway his boy, but he didn't want to inadvertently hurt the boy, so he refrained.

"Thanks, Meema." Seb was rewarded with Bobby jumping off from his chair at the table and throwing his small arms around his waist. He returned the hug and held Bobby. He rubbed his hand over the boy's back in what he hoped was a comforting gesture, he had been through so much for someone so young. It broke Seb's heart that it wasn't his place to help fix Bobby's shattered world, he longed to be the hero for him and his mother. He woke up this morning without a job, and no clue what his future would be. Not exactly a life that you can offer to a woman and child, even if she would have him.

Is that what I want?

Yes…. if I could have it, that's all I want.

Even though he only spoke the words to himself they still rocked him. Nothing was simpler yet more complicated than loving and being loved. The loving part was easy, he loved them both. It was the return of that love that he had little to no hope for, at least where Delilah was concerned.

He looked up from the boy in his arms, just in time to catch Meema wiping a tear from her cheek. Seb looked at her concerned, and she smiled and waved him off. He would have to make sure she was okay, the older she got the more constantly he worried for her. Growing up the only man in the house, he had always had three ladies to take care of. Even when he had been a small boy, their honor and happiness were his responsibility, at least as far as he was concerned. His mother would have probably argued the point with her ten-year-old son, but that wouldn't have changed the weight he had always felt on his shoulders.

"Bobby, do you want to join me in coloring? I have some old books of Seb's that you might like to doodle in." Meema's suggestion was spurred by the entrance of Seb's mother, Margaret Rockmiller.

Bobby looked up at him, questioning whether or not to leave his arms. Seb smiled down at the boy, knowing that he needed to have a private conversation with his mother.

"You go ahead and have fun." Seb leaned forward and whispered into Bobby's ear. "If you stay here you have to do the dishes." The boy looked at Seb's look of utter disgust at the idea of cleaning, he laughed and flew to Meema's side. Bobby's complete abandonment at the mention of doing chores should have hurt Seb's feelings, but instead it made him smile.

259

He watched as Meema led Bobby out of the room, he knew they would be headed for the family room, where all the books in the house lived.

"It looks like you have gotten rather close to the boy." His mother poured a cup of coffee and joined him on the table. It was unnerving to have eyes that looked so much like your own, studying you. It was the only way that he looked at all like his family members, everything else he had inherited from his father. The three woman and himself all had remarkably similar eye color, but he towered over all three women. His mother and sister were not short women, compared to Delilah they would probably look tall, but compared to him they were midgets.

"Yeah, Bobby and I get along well, he is a great kid." Seb couldn't help the pride that he spoke with.

"And the mother? Is she the reason that you called me and that you are all mixed up?" His mother never beat around the bush, he usually loved that abut her, but now it made him uncomfortable.

"It's not anything that she has done, it's me. I started wanting things that are not possible." Seb sighed; he knew that he was doing a shit job of explaining himself. He wished he could write it down and just let her read it. It was so much easier for him to write his feelings, he had written in his journal this whole time, but the detail would shock his mother. He couldn't let her read that.

"What things did you start to want?" His mother's voice was soft but stern.

"I don't know, just more. More of a life, more peace than my job affords me, more...." He searched for the right words.

"More love?" He closed his eyes as if that could block out the truth in his mom's words. "And why do you think that you can't have those things? You deserve to be happy son, you can't spend the rest of your life protecting people, paying for the lives that you couldn't save."

"You think that is what I am doing?" He asked the question, but he knew that she was right. It is why he had jumped on board with Cody to start up their business, to pay penance for the ones he had failed.

"You know it's true, I can see it in your eyes." His mother grabbed his hands that had been resting on the table. "So, what are you going to do about it?"

"I already did it, I all but quit the business. I will speak with Cody when he gets here, he can either buy me out or hell I don't really care. I will let him decide." Trying to explain where he would go from here felt exhausting, or maybe it was the two hours' sleep he had gotten, probably both.

"You know darn well that I am not talking about your work, your main problem is one of the heart." Again, her truth cut him to the core.

"There is nothing to do mom, she has been through so much. She just lost her ex-husband, she was kidnapped, and whoever is after her will most likely not give up. Anything that has happened to us is a result of extreme stress, of her needing me for comfort, nothing more." Seb felt sad, his own truth sliced at his heart.

"Is that what it is for you? Just some trauma induced passion?" His mother asked.

"No…." Seb admitted.

"Then you owe it to yourself to say something to her, you can't let her leave without knowing how you feel." She made it sound so easy, confess your feelings, but it wasn't her that had to deal with the heart ache of rejection.

The sound of the doorbell rang throughout the house, he cursed at whoever had rang it, he wanted to let Delilah sleep a little longer.

His mother rushed to the door, with Seb close behind her.

"Where is she?" As soon as his mother opened the door, Max let his question fly.

"Young man, I'm sure that you are tired and stressed but that is no excuse for bad manners." He smiled over his mother's head at Max's abashed face. "Try again."

To his credit Max took the brow beating like a man, he squared his shoulders and grinned at Seb's mother.

"I apologize ma'am." His face took on the innocence of a schoolboy and Seb had to bite back a laugh. "My name is Max Reyes, and I am looking for my sister Delilah and my nephew Bobby. I have reason to believe that Foxy….um…I mean Seb here has them and I would like to see them, please."

"Of course, come in please." His mother stepped back straight into Seb. "Son, don't loom in the doorway, show Mr. Reyes to the kitchen and get him something to drink. I will go and see if Delilah is up yet."

"I will go get her." Seb wanted to have a few moments alone with Delilah before she saw her brother and he whisked her away.

262

"No, you won't. I would very much like to speak with you, man to man." Max's blue gaze was hard and stony.

"Well, that is settled then, you boys go and talk, and I will get Delilah." His mother ignored his request and sided with Max, it irked him that no one gave a hoot what he wanted.

"This way, Maxie." Seb smiled at the irritated look on Max's face.

"I'm right behind you, Foxy." Seb growled as he turned and led Max down the hallway.

Delilah felt like a warmed-over piece of dung, there was a knocking in her head that told her she had not slept enough. She looked around the room that she was in, it looked like a teenage girl's dream. All explosions of pink with a lot of contrasting colors, she couldn't imagine this was Seb's room, but the possibility made her want to laugh. Did he have a deeply buried feminine side? No, she was pretty confident she had seen most of him and it was all one hundred percent male. The thought brought a blush to her cheeks, as the knocking came again, but this time it was clear that the knocking was on the door not in her head.

"Come in." Her voice sounded hoarse and unused.

A woman walked through the door, she was probably in her fifties, with shoulder length jet black hair. Once the woman made eye contact with her, there were no doubts as to who she was. Seb's green eyes looked at her, maybe a little less bright but they were the same.

"Good morning, Delilah." Her voice was deep and raspy, it fit her dark beauty.

"Good morning, you must be Sebastian's mother." The older woman's eyes lit and grew wide, Delilah realized her mistake in using Seb's full name. He had told her that no one used it, it would probably sound very odd to hear her say it.

"Sebastian? It is nice to hear that, I'm not surprised he lets you call him that." Seb's mother came to sit on the bed. "My name is Margaret, but most people call me Maggie."

"It's nice to meet you, Maggie." Delilah felt odd, meeting Maggie for the first time while tucked into bed. "Is Bobby awake?"

"Yes, he is coloring with my mother in the family room." Maggie seemed to hesitate for a moment before continuing. "You are a mother, and from what I have seen of your son, he is an excellent boy. So, I hope that you will forgive me when I behave a little intrusively."

Delilah's heart sank down somewhere near her feet. *What had Seb told her? Did she know that he and I have made love?!* She feared what Maggie would have to say if she did indeed know what had happened between the two of them, but she couldn't deny a mother's right to be protective of her son.

"Go ahead." Delilah didn't sound as confident as she had hoped that she would.

Maggie laughed and grabbed Delilah's hands; her skin was rougher than Delilah had thought it would be. It made her wonder what Seb's mom had done for a living, what had turned her hands from soft to weathered?

"Dear, please don't look like you are lining up for the firing squad. I promise you that no matter what that son of mine has said, I am virtually harmless." Something that the woman kept behind her eyes told Delilah that the woman could indeed be harmful, if the situation called for it. It was something her son had obviously gotten from her. Delilah tried to relax. "Okay, that is better. Now, do you love my son?"

"What the......?" Delilah hadn't meant to exclaim out loud, but Maggie's question had knocked her through a loop.

"Language please." Maggie said, while rubbing Delilah's hands in a soothing manner. "I can see you and my son have at least one thing in common." Seb's mother grinned at her and waited for Delilah to respond.

"I......well....it just isn't that simple." Delilah sighed, she had barely said a dozen words to the woman and Maggie wanted her to bare her heart.

"It never is." Maggie's warm grin never wavered. "If love were simple, then we would all be paired up like doves in love and the world would be full of happily-ever-afters. Unfortunately, for most of us, that isn't how it happens."

"Tell me about it." Delilah tried not to let the conversation dredge up bad memories of her short comings as a wife.

"So, can I take it that you didn't have a great marriage the first time around?" She found Maggie easy to talk to.

"That is putting it mildly." Delilah fought the tears that threatened to come up.

"In my experience when a relationship goes bad it is rarely a one-sided affair. Most of the time both sides could have done more and worked harder. Was yours something like that?" There was not a trace of judgment in the woman's question.

"Yes, that about covers it." Delilah felt like Maggie could probably fill in all the blanks by herself.

"If you had met Seb before your first husband, would you be hesitant to follow your heart?" She had never thought of that, it was a good question. Were all her reservations left over from her first marriage, or were any of them based off her feelings for Sebastian?

"My first marriage proved to me that I couldn't be a good wife, I don't think that I am cut out for it." Delilah was saddened to admit her short comings out loud, especially to the mother of the man she was in love with.

"Well, that is bullshit." Delilah looked up at Maggie, surprised at the steel in her words, along with the profanity. Maggie smiled, disarming the last of Delilah's defenses. She started to confess to Sebastian's mother, feeling the weight lift from her shoulders, as she shared her worries and dreams.

Chapter 27

"Tell me what in the hell is going on, Foxy." Max hadn't touched his coffee. He had barely sat in the chair before demanding an explanation.

"Your sister and nephew witnessed the murder of Nate Hawthorne, you directed us to a fine establishment in Napa...." Seb was taking great pleasure in how red Max's face was getting.

"Cute, really cute." Max stared at Seb with what he was sure would be his best attempt at being intimidating. "I got a call from a Mr. West this morning, telling me where you had taken my sister and that he was on his way to take over the protection of her and Bobby. Would you like to tell me, what in the world is going on?"

"It sounds to me like you know what is going on." Seb continued to be obstinate, not just because he enjoyed making Max into a human tomato, but because he had no intention of sharing his feelings with Max before he had told Delilah.

"Why is West replacing you?" Max was practically throbbing with anger. "Did you touch my sister?"

"He is replacing me because I am quitting. I am done with the private protection business. He will be buying me out of the business, I think. I don't have an exact plan on what I will be doing for a career in the near future, but I have to tell you I am touched at your concern for my future." Seb tried to keep his face sincere, even though he wanted to snarl at Max's audacity to ask him about his personal life. Like he had any right.

He is Delilah's brother......what if it were Melanie?
Would you be as angry as he is?

Angrier! The truth smacked him in the face, Max
is just as upset as he would be, if the places were
reversed. Truth be told, he might even be handling it
better than Seb would have.

Before Max could rage on further about Seb
avoiding his second question, Seb took a deep breath and
confessed as much as he was willing to. "As to your
second question." Max literally leaned forward; Seb could
see how tense the other man was. "Yes, I touched your
sister.......and yes that is one of the reasons that I am
leaving."

"How dare you, to take advantage of her, during
such a traumatic time. You are a real low life. You know
that?" Max was clenching and unclenching his fists, Seb
curiously wondered if Delilah's brother was going to
punch him, it was probably the least he deserved. "You
didn't force her....to...uh.... you know, do anything against
her will, did you?"

Now it was Seb's turn to become enraged, he
stood up fast enough to send his chair flying. He
slammed his hands down upon the table, leaning forward
inches from Max's face, to his credit Max did not budge
an inch.

"I might have crossed every professional and
moral boundary that I have for myself. I might have let
my emotions cloud my judgment and gotten way to
invested for my own sanity. But if you think for one
fucking second that I would force myself on any woman,
let alone the woman that I...." Seb cut himself off before
he could speak the words out loud, they were not for
Max, and he would be damned if Max would be the first to
hear them.

Max's eyebrow shot up, eyes too much like Delilah's studied Seb. Seeming to come to some sort of conclusion, Max leaned back in the chair. "So that's how it is."

Seb cursed himself for letting Max see too much of what he kept buried deep inside, the depth of his feelings for Delilah.

"Yeah, that's how it is." Seb righted his chair and sat back down, feeling deflated and wishing he were alone. *You will be soon enough.* The reminder cut through him like a newly sharpened knife.

"And does she know how you feel?" Something about Max softened ever so subtly. "Does she feel the same way?"

"I don't know......." Seb let the statement linger, he really didn't care how Max took it.

Soon, Delilah and Bobby would be gone with Cody. Lord knew where he would take them, he knew they couldn't go back down south. He had nothing but his love to offer her, and he was terrified of offering so little to someone that deserved so much more.

"What exactly is going on in my kitchen?" His mother's voice pierced through his thoughts.

"Nothing, mom, everything is fine." Seb didn't turn around to look at her, he was afraid that she would see the emotions that he felt raging inside of him.

"Fine, my foot." She came to stand by him at the table, resting her hand on his shoulder. "I heard the distinct sound of chairs hitting the floor and raised male bravado."

"I need some air." Seb got up from the table, took one last look at both his mother and Max, who was still studying him and walked out of the house.

He felt his entire body relax as he made it to the tree line that surrounded his childhood home. Breathing in the fresh mountain air, willing it to wash away all of his hurt and confusion. Seb had enjoyed growing up in the small mountainous town of Weaverville, California. It would probably do him some good to come back and get his head right, become one with nature and all that.

Seb had just started picking his way through the trees when her voice called to him. The setting, plus the music of her soft voice carried to him on the wind, if he closed his eyes, it could be a dream. A dream that he would be having for a long time to come, one where he walks away from what he really wants. How would he live with himself, if he never even took a chance, never told her how he felt about her? *You won't be able to!*

Turning to head back to the house, the reality rushed through Seb, he had to tell her. Even if she shot him down, he could not live the rest of his life never having told her.

He had only made it a couple of feet, before he saw her, walking toward him. Her hair was down, her brick red curls wild and bright against the backdrop of the forest colors. She wore a ridiculously bright yellow dress, with deep blue flowers on it. She looked like the most beautiful forest imp or maybe queen of the fairies. His body reacted to the sight of her, with an overwhelming need. But it wasn't just a physical need, it was his heart that needed her more than anything else.

"Sebastian." They stood only feet apart, she looked unsure as she stared up at him. "I thought you were going to make me chase you through the forest."

"Sorry, I heard you, I just didn't know it was real." Seb knew that his answer sounded crazy, he felt crazy. "Come with me, I want to show you something."

He grabbed her hand, looking down at her shoes, he grimaced. Delilah wore flimsy flip-flops, not exactly forest hiking shoes. "Are you going to be able to walk in those things?"

She put her free hand on her hip, he immediately recognized her classic defiant positioning. "I will have you know that I can walk for miles in these shoes."

"Okay, whatever you say." Seb turned and started to lead her further into the woods.

"We aren't going to be walking for miles, are we?" Delilah was trying to not sound worried, failing horribly, making him laugh. "Seriously, how far are we going?"

"Not that far." Seb laughed at her annoyed questions because he could hear the smile in her voice.

Every story Delilah had ever read where someone got led into the woods ended badly, yet here she was being dragged into the forest. Well, she had always said that anyone dumb enough to walk off into unknown territory deserved what they got; she was no exception. Her gaze raked over the man holding her hand, her small fingers were lost in his strong warm grasp. He made his way through the trees, being guided by something that she could not see. Seb was so sure of every step, like he knew exactly where he was going.

"Here we are." Seb stopped and looked back at her, his eyes were expectant, so she looked around to try and figure out what made "here" so special.

It looked just like all the trees that they had walked through so far; she could not tell a difference. He laughed at her obvious confusion.

"Look up." Seb took a finger and lightly tilted her face upward, her breath caught when she saw it.

"Wow." It was a very impressive tree house, it was not only one house, but there was also a rope bridge with wood platforms that connected two of the trees together. With the two structures linked together, it was more like a community in the trees. She thought back to her own childhood, they had barely had a yard. What she wouldn't have given to have something like this. "This is amazing."

"Thanks, we worked hard on it." Seb spoke with pride as he pointed out the specifics of his tree world. "It started as one ordinary tree house, then my mom got tired of Melanie and I fighting over who could have their friends over. It was a constant "boy's only" versus "girl's only" scenario. So, she came up with the plan to make another tree house that connected to the first one. Much to my mother's chagrin, it did not stop the fighting, but it did result in some exciting treehouse wars."

Delilah was laughing at picturing Seb as a little boy wooden sword in hand, defending his treehouse to his last breath.

"Bobby, would love this." Delilah didn't mean to sound wistful, at the idea that this wasn't their world, it was Seb's. The reality of it was that he hadn't even hinted that he wanted them to be part of it.

"I could take him up." The excitement faded from his eyes; he became hesitant. "If that is okay with you."

"Is it still safe." Delilah had her doubts about how trustworthy the impressive treehouse was, something told her it had been a while since anyone had been up there.

"There is only one way to find out." Seb led her toward the ladder that she hadn't noticed, it was well camouflaged against the trunk of the tree. "Ladies first."

He looked down at her, with a blatant dare twinkling in his green eyes. She grinned at him; she was a sucker for a dare. Delilah started ascending the ladder, her right arm was not happy with ladder climbing, but the pain was lessening every day. She could feel Seb follow her up, he stayed a couple rungs below her.

"Is this how you snuck a peak up girl's skirts when you were younger?" Her cheeks reddened as she quickened her pace, knowing that the only way to end her embarrassment was to get to the top.

Seb laughed. "No, even though that is a good idea. I'm currently noticing what a very good idea it is, in fact." There was a heat in his voice that made her wish they were on even ground.

Delilah got to the top. It was in surprisingly good shape, no visible holes. The inside of the treehouse was clean. There was a small desk against one wall, posters of sports stars hung from the wall, weathered, and torn with age. A pile of what looked like blankets sat in the corner, there was a piney smell that hung in the air, she noticed a handmade incense holder hanging from the ceiling.

"It looks good. I think mom lets the neighbor kids play up here once in a while, she must keep it clean for them." With Seb in the small space, the available room in the treehouse seemed to shrink. He couldn't stand up completely straight, but he only had to slouch a little.

"So, we didn't need to come up here to see if it was safe for Bobby?" Delilah put her hands on her hips, glaring at him, but not being able to help the smile on her face.

"Busted." Seb shrugged, it made him look bashful and handsome. She liked having him have to slouch, she reached up and stroked a hand on his face that was covered in the starts of a beard. It matched the hair on his head, she wondered what he would look like with a beard, probably sexy as sin.

"What am I going to do with you?" She had thought it, but she hadn't meant to say it out loud. *Why did I say that? Dammit!*

Chapter 28

"What do you want to do with me?" Delilah looked into his eyes, not surprised to see the desire that lit them, it was the same desire that raged inside of her.

"Stop it, this is hardly the place for that, plus I'm...." What was she going to say, scared, worried, heartbroken at the thought of leaving you?

Seb's face hardened and his eyes took on a sad gleam, she wanted to fix whatever made him hurt. "I know your leaving, but I need to tell you something before you go." He hesitated, looking both physically uncomfortable and emotionally, only one of those things she could fix.

"Why don't we sit down and talk, that way you don't get a permanent crook in your neck." She tried to sound lighthearted, but she was worried about what he was going to say.

"Good idea, who would want me with a crooked neck, right?" She could tell it was meant as a joke, but he also fell just short of selling the light mood.

I would still want you; I would want you no matter what.

She kept the words in, not wanting to say them, not brave enough to say them.

Once they were seated, both leaning against a different wall of the treehouse, their feet were almost touching as they sat close to a corner.

"What did you want to tell me?" Delilah asked, so afraid that all he wanted was to apologize for their love making or give her some sort of brush off.

Seb ran his fingers through his hair, he started speaking before bringing his head out of his hands. "I was deployed to Iraq three times, not as much as some, but more than others. During my last deployment I had to patrol through a small village, there was a small boy there. He would follow our Humvee as we drove through, when we would get out, he would be the first to run to us. Mo had a huge smile, missing teeth, and big dark brown eyes. He was always so filled with joy. His joy was so out of place. You would look around at the hovel that he lived in, and you couldn't understand what in the world he had to be so happy about. I sure as hell didn't find any joy in the sand ridden place, he couldn't read very well, especially not in English. So, when I saw him for the fourth time, he called me Rock."

"That's why you reacted that way to Bobby calling you that." Delilah didn't want to interrupt whatever it was that he needed to tell her, so she was relieved when he continued.

"Right. I know it is weird, but at the beginning Bobby reminded me so much of Mo, I was having trouble with flashbacks. Usually I can push them away, but sometimes they are too strong." Seb looked at her, his eyes were a window straight into his soul, his wounded soul. She couldn't stand to be apart from him any longer. Delilah crawled over to his side, putting her hand on his arm.

"What happened to Mo?" It was not going to be a happy ending she could tell that much by the hurt in his emerald eyes.

Seb intertwined his fingers with hers. "For the most part it was a peaceful village, well as peaceful as a village in Iraq can get at least. We had never seen any signs of aggression by any of the locals, none of the things that we are trained to look for. I had started bringing Mo the candy from my MRE and was looking forward to seeing his excitement, because that day I had his favorite. I jumped down, my boots barely touching the ground, when I heard the first shot crack in the air. I froze as I saw Mo, standing in the middle of the road, in the middle of the gun fire. All of my training flew out the window, I didn't wait for cover fire, I didn't do anything to protect myself. I ran toward him I was steps from reaching him, from saving him.... the bullet hit him with enough force that it knocked him off from his feet. His small limp body landed almost at my boots, I bent to pick him up, still hoping that I could get him to safety. As I ran back towards the Humvee, I heard my brothers yelling to me, I spotted them and ran in their direction. They had abandoned the vehicle and had taken cover around one of the buildings. Seconds after I reached them, the explosion shot up in the air as an RPG hit the Humvee. I had run towards certain death twice that day, but somehow made it out mostly unscathed."

Delilah sat in silence rubbing her hand over his back, remembering the scars she had seen there and on his chest. Wondering if in Seb's book those wounds constituted unscathed. She sent a silent selfish prayer of thanks to heaven that he had made it back from such an ordeal.

"I'm so sorry Sebastian." It wasn't enough, nothing she could say would be enough. "You didn't have to tell me that, not if it hurt too much."

Seb looked at her, she could see that he desperately needed her to understand something. "Yes, I did, and yeah it hurts like hell to talk about it. I don't talk about it."

"Not even with your friends, the ones that were there with you?" Delilah wanted to believe he had someone to talk to.

"My brothers in arms, that's what we call ourselves. No, I don't talk to them about it, they know that I would rather write my feelings. That's what I do, I write down everything that I'm either too scared or ashamed to say out loud. My failures, my hopes and everything that it is too hard to vocalize." Seb looked at her with emotion filled eyes that took her breath away. "I wrote about you."

Delilah winced at the thought of what Seb could have written about her, about his crazy protection detail that wouldn't keep her hands to herself. Is that how he saw her?

Seb brought his hand not entwined with hers to her face, at first, he tried to put one of her unruly curls behind her ear, she winced as it popped free almost immediately. He smiled a smile that made her feel like she was the center of his universe, at least for that moment in time.

"Thank you for telling me about Mo, I know that can't be easy." Delilah meant every word, no matter what happened between them in the future, he had allowed her to see more than he let most people see. It wasn't much, but if she had to, she could cling to the knowledge that at least he cared for enough to share a part of himself.

"I needed to tell you. You need to understand more about me, before......" Seb got a faraway look in his eyes as he stared out the miniature window of the treehouse.

"Before I leave." Delilah hated each word as it slipped past her lips, each one filled her with the dread that this was his way of saying goodbye. She wasn't the type of woman to sit back and let what she wanted slip through her fingers, not without a fight at least. *Fight Dammit!* "That is not what I want."

She heard his breath catch in surprise. "Well, that wasn't what I was going to say, because it isn't what I want either. I brought you to this treehouse, to my hometown, heck it might even be why I brought you to Weaverville in the first place. I thought maybe surrounded by where I was raised, I could better explain to you who I am."

"Isn't this who you were?" Delilah couldn't let him give himself so little credit for all the years that had shaped him into the strong, capable, trustworthy man that she had fallen in love with.

"In a way yes, but it never really left me." He sighed and ran his fingers over her neck, sending quivers of need pulsating through her. It was like his fingers were a paint brush and he was coloring parts of her as his, the idea thrilled her. "I changed and I have seen bad things, done bad things. Then I went into the private protection business, it felt like a way to atone for Mo. Maybe I convinced myself that if I protected all these other people, I could fill the void that losing him left in my heart."

His hand had ventured to the swells of her breasts, his touch was in no way aggressive or even suggestive. Like he was trying to memorize every inch of her, *for when he left her?*

"But that didn't work, nothing worked. Not until I met you, everything changed when you walked into your apartment all fiery defiance." Seb took his hand away from its exploration, she felt the ghost trails of where his fingers had been, wishing she could have them back. "I don't have much to offer you Delilah, I have no idea what I'm going to do for work, I do own a home here in the mountains. One I purchased when I was deployed, but it isn't anything extravagant. When Cody buys me out, I will have a nest egg that I could take care of you and Bobby with." He looked at her desperate for her to say something, but she didn't know what to say. She stared at him, shocked, *did he want her to stay? With him here in this picturesque place?*

"I don't need your money, and I know that we can't go home again. Maybe after everything we have been through, maybe you can't truly go home from that. We would never feel safe there again, and I don't want that life anymore. I want a life with you, Bobby loves you……. I love you." It took all of Delilah's bravery to look him straight in his forest eyes, they were ripe with emotion.

In one swift movement he picked her up and placed her on his lap, it had felt like a lifetime ago when she had last tasted his kiss. There was an eagerness to his movement as he stroked her back with his hands, with his tongue he played and teased her own. Angling his mouth slightly to deepen the kiss, she was lost in the world he created. A euphoric state where only the two of them existed.

She reached under his shirt, needing to feel his skin, hating every boundary that stood between them. He let out a small hiss as one of her nails grazed his nipple.

"Did I hurt you?" She tore her mouth from his to ask.

He let out a low passion filled chuckle, Seb had begun to nibble her ear lobe, doing things with his tongue on her neck that made her moan with pleasure.

"No, you didn't hurt me, I liked it." Seb's voice was heavy with his need, she could feel his need press against her thighs as she sat across his lap. "I need to see you."

She nodded even though he could probably tell how much she wanted him. He tugged her dress from beneath her bottom, she put her arms up as he lifted it from her body. Ignoring the twinge of pain from her wounded arm. She had not bothered with a bra, so the movement left her sitting on his lap in only her black lace panties. He seemed to devour her with his eyes, she felt it like a physical touch.

"You are beautiful, too beautiful." Seb's words seemed awed as he trailed his fingers down her. Started at her neck slowly gliding over her aching breasts, she desperately wanted him to stay there and pleasure her, but he kept going. He dipped a finger into her belly button, then finally made it to her single covering, her panties. "I like these, a lot." Almost as evidence of his enjoyment she felt him move beneath her, where he strained against his jeans.

He was stroking her through her panties, and she was starting to develop a serious dislike for them, wanting them gone. She decided to take charge, maybe his need could wait but hers couldn't. Delilah moved her legs so that she straddled him, not asking permission before lifting his shirt. He complied with a devilish grin on his face, *is this what he wanted? Had he been seeing how far he could push me before I couldn't take anymore?*

"Pants." Delilah got off from his lap just long enough for him to follow her order, by the time she wrapped her legs around him again, there were no barriers between them. It felt so wondrous to be almost as close as they could get to each other, but it wasn't enough, it would never be enough.

Seb's tongue flicked over her nipple that he was gently sucking, being driven past the point of being able to wait. She quickly positioned herself over him, his eyes flicked to her, uncertain.

"I want to make sure you are ready." Seb's concern spoke straight to her heart, the man she loved, she had hope that someday he would speak the words to her. "I enjoy making you ready."

The confession was enough to make her wet with need, she wanted this man like she had never wanted before in her life. The intensity should have shocked her, but it didn't. Instead, it made her feel more complete than she had ever felt.

"I more than enjoy it, but right now, I need you inside of me." Delilah would not normally speak about such things, she would normally be too shy, but the groan that came from deep inside of his throat told her that he liked it.

She eased him inside of her, loving watching his face as she sheathed him with her body. His eyes were such a dark green now that they were the color of the forest itself. Seb guided her with his hands on her hips, he raised his own hips to meet every movement. They danced with each other to their own rhythm, their own self-made music. A symphony that their love created.

Delilah had closed her eyes, concentrating on the pleasure that was humming through her. Seb took one hand from her hip, her eyes shot open in surprise. She smiled as her sly sexy fox of a man smiled at her, he slipped his finger into the folds of where they were joined and started to imitate their rhythm. Rubbing at the sensitive nub, while quickening their pace. It was too good, she cried out his name. "Sebastian, I love you, Sebastian."

He gripped her hips tightly as she watched his own climax rip through him. She felt him pour into her, she stroked her hands over his sweat slicked body. Mesmerized by the look of satisfaction that was so plain to read on his face, it felt empowering that she was the one that had satisfied this intense man.

She didn't make any move to break their connections, knowing that they shouldn't stay gone much longer, but not wanting the moment to end.

"How long do we have to wait to get married? I mean how long for Bobby to be okay with it?" Seb's questions froze her heart mid-beat.

Married?! Who said anything about getting married?!

"I can't marry you." Delilah felt the warmth leave his eyes, like a chill sweeping through her bones. She unwrapped herself from him and started quickly to dress.

"The hell you can't." Seb grabbed her wrists to stop her movement.

Chapter 29

"I'm sorry Sebastian." Delilah's sapphire eyes that were so filled with passion moments before looked up at him with heart wrenching sadness.

"Don't be sorry, be my wife." Seb didn't even care if he sounded desperate, he was desperate. After what they had just shared, the connection that was between them, how could she refuse to marry him? She had said she loved him for God's sake!

She let out a little laugh that was anything but humorous. "You would be sorry if I was your wife."

"No, I wouldn't, Delilah what is this about? You said that you love me, you don't want to leave me. I bared my soul to you, and I had thought you accepted me. Why won't you honor me by becoming my wife?" He felt like yelling, she wouldn't look him straight in the eye.

"Those things are all true, but I am not good at being a wife." Delilah looked down at their joined hands. "We could live together and be a family and then when you got tired of the arrangement or wanted something else. Maybe we could part on good terms, without the mess of being legally bound."

Two things suddenly became very clear to him. One, that she had no idea how much he loved her and two, that whatever made her unwilling to marry again stemmed from her first marriage. He knew that you shouldn't speak ill of the dead, but he cursed Nate for what he had done to the woman that he loved.

"No, Delilah, I don't want that. Call me traditional or old fashioned, but I want a real family. I want you to be my wife, I want Bobby to be my son, maybe never legally but at least in every other way. I want to walk proudly down the streets of my hometown and with my family. I want to be legally, morally, hell maybe even physically bound to you for the rest of the time I walk on this earth. My love for you could revile the greatest loves ever felt." Seb was breathing heavy by the time he was done, emotion raging inside of him, finally being given a voice to pour out of him with.

"You don't understand. I don't know how to be a good wife." Delilah was still fighting him, but he could almost see her defenses coming down. She wanted to believe him; he would not leave this treehouse without her understanding the depth of his feelings.

"Then be a bad wife, even though I honestly don't think that you could ever be bad at anything. All I want is for you to be my wife." Seb got down on one knee, which in the treehouse was more comfortable than trying to stand. "Delilah Reyes, will you take me as I am, flaws and all? Will you allow me to take you as you are, perfection not required? I promise to love and cherish you above all others, except Bobby of course, for the rest of our lives."

He saw the tears streak down her cheeks, he held his breath, not knowing what they meant. Delilah's deep red curls started to bob when she started to nod her head yes, his heart clenched, he was on the precipice of happiness...waiting.

"Yes, Sebastian Rockmiller, I will marry you." Delilah looked at him, the love that filled her oceanic eyes, made him fill with joy.

Seb leapt to his feet to take her into his arms, forgetting exactly how low the ceiling was. "Ouch!" His head made solid contact with the ceiling of the treehouse, Seb was impressed that it held and was thankful that his head hadn't gone right through it.

"Are you okay?" Delilah was biting her lip, though her question indicated that she was concerned, he could clearly see that she was holding back laughter.

"You little imp, are you laughing at my pain?" Seb smiled, what he was sure was the goofiest smile to ever grace his lips, he didn't care, he was delirious with happiness.

"Not at all." She had barely etched out the denial when she started laughing. He grabbed her possessively running his hands over her body, feeling the euphoria of belonging to each other, no more holding back. He started nibbling on her neck, reaching down to the heart of her, wanting to show her how much he loved her.

Delilah pulled away from his embrace, even though the movement was abrupt, he didn't feel any fear. They belonged together, there was no denying that.

"I think that we should head back." He refused to let doubt creep in while she paused. "I know someone who is going to be over the moon with excitement at our big news."

Her face lit up with happiness, making him swell with pride, pride that he would soon be able to call this amazing woman his wife. "Are you talking about Maxie?"

She laughed as she slipped on her dress, his hands itched to hold her again, but he knew she was right. Bobby needed something solid and reliable in his life, something to hold on to, and he planned on being that, along with Delilah.

"I think you know that I'm not." Delilah smiled at him.

They were dressed and ready to climb down from his childhood treehouse, he would never be in the place again without looking at in a whole different light.

"I will go down first, you can follow." Seb wanted to make sure that if she slipped, he could catch her. Knowing that her arm was perfectly usable but worrying that it still caused her pain.

"Trying to look up my skirt again?" Delilah stood with her hands on her hips, he ignored the ever-present urge to put his hands on her.

"Delilah, love, you can just assume that for the rest of your life, I will be constantly trying to sneak a peek." Seb winked at her; his reward was a rosy blush that colored her cheeks.

"Only a peek?" Delilah stared at him with a dare in her eyes.

Seb laughed and started to descend from the treehouse, knowing that if he didn't, he would not be able to keep himself from making love to her again. As much as the thought spurred his need, he forced himself to think about all of the things that they needed to clear up before they could truly be together. It was a mess that he looked forward to putting behind them, but he knew that would be easier said than done.

He could feel the heat from Max's gaze while he spoke, in the room sat his mother and Meema, Bobby, Max and Colt-who had arrived when he and Delilah had been on their walk. The memory of the time spent in the woods with his future wife, made a blissfully happy smile play on his face.

"I don't know what you are thinking about to put that smile on your smug foxy face, but it better not be my sister." Max shot his usual daggers at Seb; he could only hope that Delilah's brother would warm up to him before the wedding.

"Considering that we are going to be married, I rather think that his smile better be about me." Delilah's eyes danced with laughter as she defended him.

Meema laughed and winked at Delilah, they had become fast friends. "Very well said my girl."

"What is your plan from here, I mean besides abandoning me and our company." There was only a small amount of animosity in his business partners voice, but it was smothered by a vein of understanding. One that Seb would like to dig into and find the route of, but that was for another time. "I will handle the Hawthornes for you, consider it an early wedding present."

Seb nodded his thanks to Cody, he had not been looking forward to talking with Hawthorne again. He would gladly let Cody take care of it for him, he had happier things to concentrate on.

"Our plan is to settle down here for now, coast on the money I will get from selling my half of a very lucrative business to some sucker with a pension for adrenaline rushes." He laughed at Cody's response. "As far as Delilah and the danger, what do you think Max, is this far enough away for her and Bobby to be safe?"

He loved catching Max off guard and by his reaction, his question had done just that.

"I wouldn't risk my family's life on it, but I think the heat on Delilah and Bobby is going to cool significantly." Max was being evasive with his answer, a natural trait in a spook.

"Why?" Delilah asked before Seb had a chance.

"Well, the body of our prime suspect was found lying in a Napa ditch. Word on the street is that the leader of the gang was none too happy when he found out that he had allowed there to be a witness to the drive-by. But then when he let that witness escape, well I guess it was one too many screw-ups." Max looked relieved by the information that he was sharing, Seb shared in his feelings one hundred percent.

"I can't believe that we are free." Delilah seemed awed, Seb's arm was around her and he pulled her closer and kissed her lightly on the forehead. The smell of honey and freesia filled his nose, he felt like he was in a dream, being able to soon call this woman his wife. "Bobby what are you drawing, sweetheart?"

Bobby had been pretty quiet. He was happy when Delilah had told him that they were going to be married, but since then he had withdrawn and started coloring while everyone spoke. Seb was worried that everything was happening too quickly for the little guy, he would slow down if it was what Bobby needed, he loved the little boy with all his heart.

"Our family." Bobby announced, getting up from the floor and bringing his mom the picture he had made.

Delilah sucked in a breath, put her hand to her mouth and started to cry. On full alert, Seb reached for the picture. There were trees and a house, in front of the house stood three figures. From the fiery red hair, it was clear that one was Delilah, then there was a small boy, and lastly a tall man with silver for hair, which he assumed was him. The picture made his heart soar, until he looked at the cloud in the sky. Standing in the cloud was a man that had the same hair color as the little boy, dread shot through Seb as he recognized Nate. Was this Bobby's way of telling them that it was too soon?

"Is that daddy in the cloud?" Delilah voice was weak with emotion.

Bobby nodded his head, clearly uncomfortable with his picture making his mother cry.

"Mommy, I know you miss him, I do too." He placed his small hand on her leg. "But Meema said that he is in heaven now and for the rest of my life I will have my own guard angel." The deep brown eyes turned to Seb, his heart swelled with pride and love. "So, now I have Rock here to protect me and daddy watching from heaven. We will be safe now, mommy, I just know it."

Seb could not express in words the feeling in his heart as he embraced his family. He was overwhelmed with gratitude that his path in life had brought him to this moment, so filled with love. He felt a tear trickle down his cheek as he thought about what Bobby had said. Maybe, just maybe, there was a little boy with chocolate brown eyes watching out for him from heaven.

The End

About the author

I have been in love with books for as long as I can remember. It is a love that has rarely let me down and has never abandoned me. Being born and raised in a small town, surrounded by the picturesque Northern California, my imagination and books were the only entertainment to be found. It didn't take long to find that romance was the genre of book that I most often turned to. I am, and will always be, a sucker for a happy ending.

After marrying the love of my life and having my two amazing sons, I was searching for more than just a fun read. I wanted to be the orchestrater of my own symphony. To write books that sing to people. To the very heart of what makes us human, our ability to love and the gift of being loved.